Night Watch

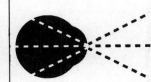This Large Print Book carries the
Seal of Approval of N.A.V.H.

Night Watch

Suzanne Brockmann

LARGE
PRINT
PRESS

Waterville, Maine

Published in 2005 by arrangement with
Harlequin Books S.A.

The text of this Large Print edition is unabridged.
Other aspects of the book may vary from the original edition.

Set in 16 pt. Plantin by Elena Picard.

Printed in the United States on permanent paper.

The Library of Congress has cataloged the Wheeler edition® as follows:

Brockmann, Suzanne.
    Night watch / Suzanne Brockmann.
        p. cm.
    ISBN 1-58724-786-0 (lg. print : hc : alk. paper)
    ISBN 1-59413-101-5 (lg. print : sc : alk. paper)
    1. United States. Navy. SEALs — Fiction.   2. Los Angeles (Calif.) — Fiction.   3. Single mothers — Fiction.   4. Blind dates — Fiction.   5. Large type books.   I. Title.
PS3552.R61455N54 2004
813´.54—dc22   2004053576

For Ed and Eric,
who understand what friendship means.
I love you guys.

My heartfelt thanks to the real teams of SEALs, and to all of the courageous men and women in the U.S. military who sacrifice so much to keep America the land of the free and the home of the brave. And an even bigger thanks (if possible) to the wives, husbands, mothers, fathers and children who are waiting for our military heroes and heroines to do their jobs and then come safely home. God bless — my thoughts and prayers are with you!

Chapter 1

Brittany Evans hated to be late. But parking had been a pain in the butt, and she'd spent way too much time trying to decide what to wear — as if it really mattered.

She surveyed the scattering of people standing around the college baseball stadium's hot dog stand as she came out the door that led from the locker rooms.

And there he was.

Standing under the overhang, out of the gently falling rain, watching the players on the ball field. Leaning against the wall with his back to her.

At least she thought it was him. They'd never really met — at least not for more than two and a half seconds. Brittany, this is whatever-his-naval-rank-was Wes Skelly. Wes, this is Melody Jones's sister, Britt.

Hey, how are you, nice to meet you, gotta go.

The man who might or might not be Wes Skelly glanced at his watch, glanced toward the main entrance of the stadium. His hair was longer and lighter than she remembered — of course, it was hard to remember much from only two and a half seconds of face time.

She could see his face better as he turned slightly. It was . . . a face. Not stunningly handsome like Mel's husband, Harlan "Cowboy" Jones. But not exactly Frankenstein's monster, either.

Wes wasn't smiling. In fact, he looked a little tense, a little angry. Hopefully not at her for being late. No, probably just for being. She'd heard a lot about Wes Skelly over the past few years. That is, assuming this was really Wes Skelly.

But he had to be. No one else in the place looked even remotely like a Navy SEAL.

This guy wasn't big, though — not like her brother-in-law or his good friend Senior Chief Harvard-the-Incredible-Hulk Becker — but there was something about him that seemed capable of anything and maybe a little dangerous.

He was dressed in civilian clothes — khaki pants with a dark jacket over a button-down shirt and tie. Poor man. From what Mel had told her about Wes, he would rather swim in shark-infested waters than get dressed up.

Of course, look at her. Wearing these stupid sandals with heels instead of her usual comfortable flats. She'd put on more than her usual amount of makeup, too.

But the plan was to meet at the ball game, and then go out to dinner someplace nicer than the local pizza joint.

Neither of them had counted on rain screwing up the first part of the plan.

Wes looked at his watch again and sighed.

And Brittany realized that his leaning against the wall was only feigned casualness. He was standing still, yet somehow he remained in motion — tapping his fingers or his foot, slightly shifting his weight, searching his pockets for something, checking his watch. He wasn't letting himself pace, but he wanted to.

Gee whiz, she wasn't *that* late.

Of course maybe her five-minute delay wasn't the problem. Maybe this man just never stood still. And wasn't that just what she needed — a date with a guy with Attention Deficit Disorder.

Silently cursing her sister, Brittany approached him, arranging her face into a smile. "You have that same 'Heavenly Father, save me from doing favors for friends and relatives' look in your eyes that I've got," she said. "Therefore you must be Wes Skelly."

He laughed, and it completely transformed his face, softening all the hard lines and making his blue eyes seem to twinkle.

Irish. Darnit, he was definitely at least part Irish.

"That makes you Brittany Evans," he said,

holding out his hand. It was warm, his hand-shake firm. "Nice to finally meet you."

Nice hands. Nice smile. Nice steady, direct gaze. Nice guy — good liar, too. She liked him instantly, despite the potential ADD.

"Sorry I'm a few minutes late," she said. "I had to drive almost all the way to Arizona to find a parking space."

"Yeah, I've noticed that traffic really sucks here," he said as he studied her face, prob-ably trying to figure out how she could pos-sibly be related to gorgeous, delicately angelic-looking Melody Jones.

"We don't look very much alike," she told him. "My sister and I."

She'd surprised him with her directness, but he recovered quickly. "What, are you nuts? Your eyes are a little different — a dif-ferent shade of blue. But other than that, you're a . . . a variation on the same lovely theme."

Oh, for crying out loud. What had her sis-ter's husband told this guy? That she was a sure thing? Just liberally sling the woo, Skelly, and she'll be putty in your hands because she's lonely and pathetic and hasn't had a man in her bed — let alone a date — in close to a decade?

It was her own stupid fault for giving in to Melody's pressure. A blind date. What was she thinking?

Okay, she knew what she was thinking. Mel

had asked her to go out with Wes Skelly as a favor. It was, she'd said in that baby sister manipulative manner of hers — the one that came with the big blue eyes, the one that had enabled her to twist Britt around her little finger for the past several decades — the only thing she wanted for her upcoming birthday. Pretty please with sugar on top . . . ?

Britt should have cried foul and gotten her a Dave Matthews CD instead.

"Let's set some ground rules," Brittany told Wes now. "Rule number one — no crap, okay? No hyperbole, no B.S. Only pure honesty. My sister and your so-called friend Harlan Jones manipulated us to this particular level of hell, but now that we're here we're going to play by our own rules. Agreed?"

"Yeah," he said. "Sure, but —"

"I have no intention of sleeping with you," she informed him briskly. "I'm neither lonely nor pathetic. I know exactly what I look like, exactly who I am and I happen to be quite happy with myself, thank you very much. I'm here because I love my little sister, although right now I'm trying to imagine the most painfully horrific way to torture her for doing this to me — and to you."

He opened his mouth, but she wasn't done and she didn't let him speak.

"Now. I know my sister, and I know she was hoping we'd gaze into each other's eyes,

11

fall hopelessly in love and get married before the year's end." She paused for a fraction of a second to look searchingly into his eyes. They were very pretty blue eyes, but her friend Julia had a Alaskan husky with pretty blue eyes, too. "Nope," she said. "Didn't happen for me. How about you?"

He laughed. "Sorry," he said. "But —"

"No need for excuses," she cut him off again. "People think alone means lonely. Have you noticed that?"

He didn't answer right away. Not until it was good and clear that she was finally finished and it was his turn to talk.

"Yeah," he said then. "And people who are together — people who are a couple — they're always trying to pair up all of their single friends. It's definitely obnoxious."

"Well meant," Britt agreed, "but completely annoying. I am sorry that you got roped into this."

"It's not that big a deal," he said. "I mean, I was coming to Los Angeles anyway. And how many times has Lieutenant Jones asked me to do him a favor? Maybe twice. How many times has he bailed out my butt? Too many to count. He's an excellent officer and a good friend, and if he wants me to have dinner with you, hey, I'm having dinner with you. He was right, by the way."

Britt wasn't sure she liked either the gleam in his eye or that grin. She narrowed her own eyes. "About what?"

"I *was* having a little trouble there for a while, getting in a word edgewise."

She opened her mouth, and then closed it. Then opened it. "Well, heck, it's not exactly as if you're known throughout the SEAL teams as Mr. Taciturn."

Wes's grin widened. "That's what makes it all the more amazing. So what's rule number three?"

She blinked. "Rule three?" She didn't have three rules. There was just the one.

"One is no bull — Um. No bull," he said. "Two is no sex. That's fine 'cause that's not why I'm here. I'm not in a place where I'm ready to get involved with anyone on that permanent of a level, and besides, although you're very pretty — and that's not crap. I'm being honest here as per rule one — you're not my type."

"Your type." Oh, this was going to be good. "What or who exactly is your type?"

He opened his mouth, but she thumped him on the chest as the action on the field caught her eye. It was a very solid chest despite the fact that in her heels she was nearly as tall as he was.

"Hold that thought," she ordered. "Andy's at bat."

Wes fell obediently silent. She knew that he didn't have children, but he apparently understood the unspoken parental agreement about paying complete and total attention when one's kid was in the batter's box.

Of course, her kid was nineteen years old and a college freshman on a full baseball scholarship. Her kid was six feet three inches tall and two hundred and twenty pounds. Her kid had a batting average of .430, and a propensity for knocking the ball clear over the fence, and quite possibly into the next county.

But it had just started to rain harder.

Andy let the first ball go past him — a strike.

"How can he see in this?" Britt muttered. "He can't possibly see in this. Besides it's not supposed to rain in Southern California." That had been one of the perks of moving out here from Massachusetts.

The pitcher wound up, let go of the ball, and . . . *tock*. The sound of Andy's bat connecting with the ball was sharp and sweet and so much more vibrant than the little anemic click heard when watching baseball on TV. Brittany had never known anything like it until after she'd adopted Andy, until he'd started playing baseball with the same ferocity that he approached everything else in life.

"Yes!" The ball sailed over the fence and Andy jogged around the bases. Brittany alternately clapped and whistled piercingly, fingers between her teeth.

"Jones said your kid was pretty good."

"Pretty good my eye," Britt countered. "Andy's college baseball's Barry Bonds. That's his thirty-first homerun this year, I'll have you know."

"He being scouted?" Wes asked.

"Actually, he is," she told him. "Mostly because there's another kid on the team — Dustin Melero — who's been getting lots of attention. He's a pitcher — a real hotshot, you know? Scouts come to see him, but he's still pretty inconsistent. Kind of lacking in the maturity department, too. The scouts end up sticking around to take a look at Andy."

"You gonna let him play pro ball before he finishes college?"

"He's nineteen," Brittany replied. "I don't let him do anything. It's his life and his choice. He knows I'll support him whatever he decides to do."

"I wish you were my mom."

"I think you're a little too old even for me to adopt," she told him. Although Wes was definitely younger than she was, by at least five years. And maybe even more. What was her sister thinking?

"Andy was what? Twelve when you adopted him?" he asked.

"Thirteen." Irish. Melody was thinking that Wes was Irish, and that Brittany had a definite thing for a man with a twinkle in his eyes and a smile that could light his entire

15

being. Mel was thinking about her own intense happiness with Harlan Jones, and about the fact that one night, years ago, Britt had had a little too much to drink and admitted to her sister that her biggest regret about her failed marriage to That-Jerk-Quentin was that she would have liked to have had a child — a biological child — of her own.

That would teach her to be too heavy-handed when making strawberry daiquiris.

"That definitely qualifies you for sainthood," Wes said. "Adopting a thirteen-year-old juvie? Man."

"All he really needed was a stable home environment —"

"You're either crazy or Mother Teresa's sister."

"Oh, I'm not a saint. Believe me. I just . . . I fell in love with the kid. He's great." She tried to explain. "He grew up with no one. I mean, completely abandoned — physically by his father and emotionally by his mother. And then there he was, about to be shipped away again, to another foster home, and there I was, and . . . I wanted him to stay with me. We've had our tough moments, sure, but . . ."

The look in Wes's blue eyes — a kind of a thoughtful intensity, as best she could read it — was making her nervous. This man wasn't the happy-go-lucky second cousin to a leprechaun with ADD that she'd first thought him to be. He wasn't jittery, as she'd first thought, although standing still was clearly a challenge for him. No, he was more like a lightning bolt — crackling with barely harnessed excess energy. And while it was true he had a good sense of humor and a killer smile, there was a definite darkness to him. An edge. It made her like him even more.

Oh, danger! Danger, Will Robinson!

"You were going to tell me about your type," she reminded him. "And please don't tell me you go for the sweet young thing, or I'll have to hit you. Although, according to some of my patients, I'm both sweet and young. Of course they're pushing 95."

That got his smile back. "My type tends to go to a party and ends up dancing on tables. Preferably nearly naked."

Brittany snorted with laughter. "You win, I'm not your type. And I should have known that. Melody has mentioned in the past that you were into the, uh, higher arts."

"I think she must've meant martial arts," he countered. The rain continued to pour from the sky, spraying them lightly with a fine mist whenever the wind blew. He didn't seem to notice or care. "Lt. Jones told me that you came to Los Angeles to go to school. To become a nurse."

"I *am* a nurse," she told him. "I'm taking classes to become a nurse practitioner."

"That's great," he said.

She smiled back at him. "Yes, it is, thank you."

"You know, maybe they set us up," he suggested, "because they know how often I *need* a nurse. Save me the emergency room fees when I need stitches."

"A fighter, huh?" Brittany shook her head. "I should have guessed. It's always the little guys who . . ." She stopped herself. Oh, dear. Men generally didn't like to hear themselves referred to as the little guy. "I'm sorry. I didn't mean —"

"It's okay," he said easily, no evidence of the famous Skelly temper apparent. "Although I prefer short. Little implies . . . certain other things."

She had to laugh. "A, I wasn't thinking — not even for a fraction of a second — about your . . . certain other things, and B, even if I were, why should it matter when we've already established that our friendship isn't going to have anything to do with sex?"

"I was going with Rule One," he countered. "No crap, just pure honesty."

"Yeah, right. Men are idiots. Have you noticed?"

"Absolutely," he said, obviously as at ease with her as she was with him. It was remarkable, really, the way she felt as if she'd known him for years, as if she were completely in tune with his sense of humor. "And as long as it's established that we're

18

well-hung idiots, we're okay with that." He peered toward the field. "I think they're calling the game."

They were. The rain wasn't letting up and the players were leaving the field.

"Is it temporary? Because I don't mind waiting," Wes added. "If Andy were my kid, I'd try to be at every home game. I mean, even if he wasn't Babe Ruth reborn, I'd want to, you know? You must be beyond proud of him."

How incredibly sweet. "I am."

"You want to wait inside?" he asked.

"I think there's some other event scheduled for the field for later this afternoon," Britt told him. "They don't have time for a rain delay — they'll have to reschedule the game, or call it or whatever they do in baseball. So, no. It's over. We don't have to wait."

"You hungry?" Wes asked. "We could have an early dinner."

"I'd like that," Britt said, and amazingly it was true. On her way over, she'd made a list of about twenty-five different plausible-sounding reasons why they should skip dinner, but now she mentally deleted them. "Do you mind if we go down to the locker room first? I want to give my car keys to Andy."

"Aha," Wes said. "I pass the you'll-get-into-my-car-with-me test. Good for me."

She led the way toward the building. "Even

better, you passed the okay-I-will-go-out-to-dinner-with-you test."

He actually held the door for her. "Was that in jeopardy?"

"Blind dates and I are mortal enemies from way back," Britt told him. "You should consider the fact that I even agreed to meet you to be a huge testament to sisterly love."

"You passed my test, too," Wes said. "I only go to dinner with women who absolutely do not want to have sex with me. Oh, wait. Damn. Maybe that's been my problem all these years. . . ."

She laughed, letting herself enjoy the twinkle in his eyes as he opened yet another door — the one to the stairwell — for her. "Sweetie, I knew I passed your test when you asked me to adopt you."

"And yet you turned me down," he countered. "What does that tell me?"

"That I'm too young to be your mother." Brittany led the way down the stairs, enjoying herself immensely. Who knew she'd like Wes Skelly this much? After Melody had called, setting up this date, she and Andy had jokingly referred to him as *the load*. He was her burden to bear for her sister's birthday. "You can be the kid brother I always wanted, though."

"Yeah, I don't know about that."

The hallway outside the locker rooms wasn't filled to capacity as it usually was after a game, with girlfriends and dorm-mates of the players crowded together. Today, only a very few bedraggled diehards were there. Brittany looked, but Andy's girlfriend, Danielle, wasn't among them. Which was just as well, since Andy had told her Dani hadn't been feeling well today. If she were coming down with something, standing in the rain would only make her worse.

"My track record with sisters isn't that good," Wes continued. "I tend to piss them off, after which they run off and marry my best friend."

"I heard about that." Britt stopped outside the home team's locker room door. It was slightly ajar. "Mel told me that Bobby Taylor just married your sister . . . Colleen, wasn't it?"

Wes leaned against the wall. "She tell you about the shouting that went down first?"

She glanced at him.

He swore softly. "Of course she did. I'm surprised the Associated Press didn't pick up the story."

"I'm sure it wasn't as bad as she —"

"No," he said. "It was. I was a jerk. I can't believe you agreed to meet me."

"Whatever you did, it wasn't a capital of-fense. My sister apparently forgives you."

Wes snorted. "Yeah, Melody, right. She's really harsh and unforgiving. She forgave me before Colleen did."

"It must be nice to know you have such good friends."

He nodded. "Yeah, you know, it really is."

He met her gaze, and there it was again. That darkness or sadness or whatever it was, lurking back there in his eyes. And Brittany knew. The outwardly upbeat Irishman would be fun to hang around with and was even adorable in his own loudly funny way. But it was this hidden part of him, this edge, that would, if she let it, make him irresistible.

He was, without a doubt, her type. But she wasn't his, thank you, God.

Eddie Sunamura, the third baseman, popped his head out of the locker room. His wife — June — was one of the soaking wet diehards. She lit up when she saw him, and he grinned back at her. They were only two years older than Andy, a thought that never failed to give Britt a jolt.

"Give me ten more minutes, Mrs. S.," he called to June, and Brittany couldn't keep from groaning.

"Eddie, you're unbelievably hokey," she said.

"Hey, Britt."

"Have you seen Andy?" she asked him.

He pointed down the hall before he vanished back into the locker room.

And there was Andy. At the end of the hallway. In the middle of what looked to be a very intense discussion with the team's star pitcher, Dustin Melero.

Andy was tall, but Dustin had an inch on him.

"Man, he grew," Wes said as he looked at Andy. "I met him about four years ago, and he was only . . ." He held his hand up to about his shoulder.

It was then, as they were gazing down the hallway at the two young men, that Andy dropped his mitt and shoved Dustin with a resounding crash against the wall of lockers.

Brittany had already taken three steps toward them, when Wes caught her arm. "Don't," he said. "Let me. If you can, just turn around and don't look."

Yeah, like hell . . .

Still, she managed not to follow as Wes hustled down the hall to where Andy and Dustin were nose to nose, ready to break both the school rules and each others' faces.

As she watched, Wes put himself directly between them. They were too far away for her to hear his words, but she could imagine them. "What's up, guys?" The two younger men towered over him, but Wes somehow seemed bigger.

Andy was glowering — the expression on his face a direct flashback to the street-smart thirteen-year-old he'd once been.

He just kept shaking his head as Wes talked. Finally, Dustin — who was laughing — spoke. Wes turned and gave the taller boy his full attention.

And then, all of a sudden, Wes had Dustin up against the lockers, and was talking to him with a great deal of intensity.

The new expression on Andy's face would have been humorous if Brittany hadn't been quite so worried at the amount of damage a full-grown Navy SEAL could inflict on a twenty-year-old idiot.

Dustin's sly smile had vanished, replaced with a drained-of-blood look of near panic.

Finally, unable to stand it another second, Brittany started toward them.

". . . so much as look at her funny, I will come and find you, do you understand?" Wes was saying as she approached.

Dustin looked at her. Andy looked at her. But Wes didn't look away from Dustin. All that intensity aimed in one direction was alarming.

She wasn't sure what to do, what to say. "Everything okay?" she said brightly.

"Do you understand?" Wes said again, to Dustin.

"Yes," he managed to squeak out.

"Good," Wes said and stepped back.

And Dustin was out of there.

"So," Brittany said to Andy. "This is Wes Skelly."

"Yeah," Andy said. "I think we're kind of past the introduction stage."

Chapter 2

Remarkably, Brittany Evans didn't jump down his throat.

Remarkably, she didn't immediately demand to know what on earth would possess him to physically threaten a kid more than a dozen years his junior. Forget about the fact that he did it in front of her impressionable teenaged son.

In fact, she didn't say anything about it at all.

Wes took that as a strong hint that he'd surely hear about it later.

But she'd merely talked about her sister's current pregnancy and friends they had in common as they drove to a Santa Monica café, not too far from the house Brittany shared with her kid.

The questions didn't come until they'd sat down to dinner, until they'd ordered and had started to eat.

"You surprised me back at the fieldhouse," Brittany introduced the topic. The table was lit by candlelight, and it made her seem warmly, lushly exotic in a way that her little sister would never look. Not in a million years.

Wes used to think that Melody was the prettier of the Evans sisters, and maybe according to conventional standards she was. Britt's face was slightly angular, her chin too pointed, her nose a little sharp. But catch her at the right moment, from the right angle, and she was breathtakingly beautiful.

Sex was not an option, he reminded himself. Yes, this woman was very attractive, but he wasn't interested. Remember? He definitely had to deal with all the emotional crap rattling around inside of his own head before he went and got naked with someone who would want a real relationship rather than a happy night or two of the horizontal cha-cha.

The odds of her wanting a night of casual sex with him were pretty low to start with. She so didn't seem to be the type. But even if he was wrong, those odds would slip down to slim-to-none after he told her the truth — that he couldn't give her more than a night or two because he was in love with someone else. No, not just someone else. Lana Quinn. The wife of one of his best friends — U.S. Navy SEAL and Chief Petty Officer Matthew Quinn, aka Wizard, aka the Mighty Quinn, aka that lying, cheating, unfaithful sack of dog crap.

Brittany Evans was sitting across the table

from Wes, gazing at him with the kind of eyes he loved best on women. Warm eyes. Intelligent eyes. Eyes that told him she liked and respected him — and expected the same respect in return.

Lana had looked at him — at all of the SEALs — like that.

"Yeah," Wes said, since Brittany seemed to be waiting for some kind of response. "I kind of surprised myself back at the fieldhouse." He laughed, but she didn't join in.

She just watched him as she took a sip directly from her bottle of beer and he tried not to look at or even think about her mouth. The bottom line was that he liked her too much as a person to mess around with her as a woman, as hot as he found her. But if she were some random babe that he caught a glimpse of in a bar, he'd make a point to get closer, to see if maybe she might want some mutually superficial sex.

So, okay. He was man enough to admit it. If all things were equal, he'd throw Brittany Evans a bang. No doubt about it. Forget about Lana — because, face it, he had to. She was married, off-limits, verboten, taboo. He couldn't have her, so he took pleasure and comfort wherever he could find it. And he kept his heart well out of it.

But things here were definitely not equal. Not even close. Brittany was Lt. Jones's sister-in-law, which was probably even worse than if she were his sister. A sister wouldn't tell a brother about a night of hot sex with a near stranger. Well, probably not. But a sister just might tell a sister. Provided the two sisters were close. Which Brittany and Melody certainly were.

And word would definitely get back to Jones, which wouldn't be good.

No, this was not going to happen, not tonight, not ever. Which, on that very superficial and completely physical level, was a crying shame. He would have liked, very much, to see Brittany Evans naked.

"What did he say to you?" she asked, looking at him in that way she had — as if she was trying to see inside of his skull and read his mind. Good thing she couldn't. "Melero, I mean."

"That kid is a total . . ." Wes chose a more polite word. "Idiot."

Brittany smiled at him. "That's not what you were going to say."

"I'm working hard to keep it clean."

"I appreciate that."

God her smile was a killer. Wes forced himself to stop cataloging everything he wasn't going to do to her tonight. Enough self-torture already. He brought the conversation back on track. "Melero was just being a jerk. That's another good word for him — jerk."

"I've met him plenty of times before," she

28

countered, narrowing her eyes slightly. "I'm well aware that he's capable of extreme jerkdom. But Andy knows that, too. What exactly did this guy say to Andy to piss him off like that?"

"It was about a girl," Wes said, unsure just how much to tell her.

"Dani?"

"Yeah, that's the one."

"She's Andy's girlfriend."

"I gathered that," he said.

"What did he say?" she persisted.

Wes paraphrased and summarized. He'd heard quite a bit this afternoon that he didn't want to repeat. It really was none of his business. "Melero told Andy that he'd, uh, you know, slept with her. Only, he put it a lot less delicately."

"I'm sure." Britt let out an exasperated laugh. "And Andy didn't just walk away? What a lunkhead. That girl is devoted to him — she thinks he makes the sun rise. She's a nice kid. A little low in the self-esteem department in my opinion, but, okay, she's still young. Maybe it'll come. I just hope . . ." She shook her head. "I'm not sure she's right for Andy and I'd really hate for her to get pregnant. I preach safe sex pretty much nonstop. He just rolls his eyes."

"Yeah, well, you can cross that off your list of things to worry about, at least for right now." Wes finished his beer before remembering he'd planned to make it last all through dinner. Crap. "Apparently Dani is all about taking it really slow." Ah, hell, why not just tell Brittany all of it? It wasn't his business, but clearly this wasn't something Andy would bring up in a conversation with his mother. "She's a public virgin."

Brittany put down her fork. "Excuse me?"

"She's a virgin, and apparently she's not afraid to tell people — you know, make it public knowledge that she has no intention of messing around before she's good and ready."

"Well, you go girl! Good for her. I had no idea she had that much backbone."

"But now Melero's telling everyone he popped her cherry and —" Holy God, what was he saying? And to Lt. Jones's sister-in-law, no less. "Look, he was beyond crude, okay? When I heard what he'd said, I wanted to throw him up against the wall myself."

"You did."

She was looking at him so pointedly, so like the way Mrs. Bartlett, his third grade teacher had looked at him, he had to laugh. Man, he hadn't thought about Mrs. B. in years, God bless her. "Yeah," he said, "no. I didn't do that until he said the other thing."

"Which was . . . ?"

She wasn't going to like this. "I went into caveman mode," he apologized first. "I'm sorry I did that in front of your kid. That was the wrong message to send, but when

30

that little cow turd started laughing and saying you were hot, and that you were next on his list . . ."

Brittany looked surprised for about half a second. Then she laughed. Her eyes actually sparkled. "Sweetie, that was just a schoolyard taunt. And your mother, too . . . You know? This boy is a total jerk and a bully, but he's not any kind of a real threat. And even if he was, I could take care of myself. Believe me."

"Yeah, I picked that up from you right away," Wes said. "And I told him that."

"After which you told him you were a Navy SEAL and if he so much as breathed in my direction, you were going to . . . what?"

Wes scratched his chin. "I may have mentioned something about my diving knife and his never having offspring."

She laughed again. Thank God. "That must've been when he looked like he was going to faint."

"How is everything?" The waiter was back, but the place was crowded and he didn't wait for an answer. He deftly removed the empty beer bottles from the table. "Another?"

"Yes, please." Brittany smiled up at the guy, and Wes said another short prayer of thanks that his knee-jerk treatment of Melero hadn't made her decide not to like him.

"Sir?"

"Yeah. Wait! Make it a cola."

"Very good, sir." The waiter vanished.

"I'm trying to cut back," Wes felt the need to explain as the warmth of her gaze was focused back on him. "One beer a night. Two becomes six a little too easily these days, you know?"

"I appreciate it," Brittany said. "Especially since you're driving."

"Yeah, well, I'm a sloppy drunk. It's not pretty. It's definitely not a good way to make new friends." Why the hell was he telling her this? He didn't even talk with Bobby about his fears of becoming an alcoholic, and Bobby Taylor was his friend and swim buddy from way back. "This is a very interesting first date. We talk about your son's sex life and my potential drinking problem. Shouldn't we be talking about the weather? Or movies we just saw?"

"It finally stopped raining, thank goodness," Brittany said. "I just rented *Ocean's Eleven* and loved it. When did you quit smoking?"

Damn. "Two days ago. What'd I do? Pat my pocket, searching for my nonexistent pack?"

"Yup."

Crap. He resisted another urge to reach into his pocket. Not that he could've had a cigarette until later. This restaurant was smoke free.

"It must be driving you crazy," Brittany

observed. "To stop smoking and cut back on your drinking all at the same time."

"Yeah, well, I've tried to quit before, I don't have a whole hell of a lot of faith in myself. I mean, the longest I've gone without a cigarette is six weeks."

"Have you tried the patch?"

"No," he admitted. "I know I probably should. I don't know, maybe the idea would appeal to me more if I could get Julia Roberts to glue it to my ass."

Brittany laughed. "Maybe not smoking would appeal to you more if you had a girlfriend who told you that kissing you after you smoked was similar to licking an ashtray."

He forced a smile. "Yeah, well . . ." The woman he wanted to be his girlfriend was married. He didn't want to think about the one time he did kiss her. As easy as it was to talk to Brittany, he couldn't talk about Lana. This was a date, after all, not therapy.

Not that he'd managed to talk to the team shrink about Lana, either, though. The only talking he'd done was when he was completely skunked.

The waiter brought their drinks to the table and vanished again. Wes took a sip of his soda and tried to like it, tried not to wish it was another bottle of beer.

"My ex used to smoke," Brittany told him. "I tried everything to get him to quit, and finally drew a line. I told him that if he was going to smoke, he couldn't kiss me. And he said okay, if that's what I wanted."

Wes knew what was coming from the rueful edge to her smile.

"So he stopped kissing me," she told him.

The adjectives he used to describe the bastard were blistering — far worse than anything that had come out of Dustin Melero's mouth that afternoon, but she just laughed as he winced and apologized.

"It's all right," she said. "But cut him some slack. He wasn't entirely to blame. You know, he smoked when I married him, so it was pretty unfair of me to make those kinds of demands. Bottom line, sweetie, is that you've got to quit smoking because you want to quit smoking."

"Or at the very least, I've got to want Julia Roberts to glue the patch onto my —"

"Yes," she said, laughing. "That might do it."

"He was a fool," Wes told her, reaching across the table to take her hand. "Your ex."

The smile she gave him was stunning as she squeezed his fingers. "Thank you. I've always thought so, too."

Brittany took a sip of her coffee. "Melody told me you had leave for a week —"

"Two," Wes interjected.

"And that you were spending that time here in L.A. as a favor to a friend?"

"Yeah." Wes Skelly had a nervous tell. Even sitting at the table, he was constantly in motion, kind of like a living pinball. He was always fiddling with something on the table. His spoon. The saltshaker. The tablecloth. His soda straw. But when he got nervous — at least Britt thought it was nerves he was feeling — he stopped. Stopped moving. Stopped fiddling. He got very, very still.

He was doing it right now, but as he started to talk, he started stirring the ice in his soda. "I'm actually here as a favor to the wife of a good friend. Wizard." He glanced up at her, and she knew it was an act. He was working overtime to pretend to be casual.

"I don't know if your sister ever talked about him," he continued. "She may not know him. I don't know. He's with SEAL Team Six, and he's always out of the country, so . . . Very hard to find. So he's gone again, and his wife, Lana, she's, you know, very nice, very . . . We've been friends for years, too, and . . . Well, she was worried about her sister. Half sister, actually. Her father's second marriage, and . . . Anyway, Lana's half sister is Amber Tierney and —"

"Whoa." Britt held up her hand. "Wait a sec. Information overload. Your friend Wizard's wife Lana's —" Lana, who was *very nice,* "— half sister is Amber Tierney from *High Tide?*"

"Yeah."

"Holy moly." With her heavy schedule at school and exhausting rotations in the hospital, Brittany didn't have time to keep up with the various TV and movie stars who made headlines in L.A. But Amber Tierney had been impossible to miss. She'd been TV's current It Girl ever since her sitcom, *High Tide*, had first aired last September. "Her sister's worried . . . that she's making too much money . . . ? That Tom Cruise wants to date her . . . ? That —"

"She's being stalked," Wes finished for her.

Britt cringed. "Sorry. That is a problem. I shouldn't have tried to make it into a joke."

"I'm not sure how real the threat is," Wes told her. "Lana says Amber's shrugging it off, says the guy's harmless, he wouldn't really hurt her. But see, Lana's a shrink, and some of this guy's patterns of behavior are freaking her out. It's a little too obsessive for her comfort level. So she called me, and . . . Well, here I am."

Lana, who was, *you know, very nice* calls and Wes jumps all the way to L.A.? Oh, Wes, please don't be having an affair with the wife of a friend. That was just too snarky and sleazy and downright unforgivable. You're a far better man than that.

Brittany chose her words carefully. "I know Navy SEALs are very good at what they do, but . . . isn't this a job for the L.A.P.D.?"

Wes finished his cheesecake, and he wiped

his mouth on his napkin before answering. "Amber doesn't want to involve the police. It would be instantly all over the news — especially the tabloids. Like I said, she thinks this guy's harmless. So Lana asked me to come to L.A. and quietly check out Amber's security system, make sure it's good enough, make sure she's really safe."

"And the reason that what's-his-name — Wizard — can't do this is . . . ?"

"He's out of the country. He's been gone for — I don't know — ten of the past twelve months."

"So Lana called you."

"Yeah." He wouldn't meet her eyes.

"You must be really good friends," Britt said. "I know you don't get a lot of vacation time, and to spend some of it here, doing this kind of favor . . ."

"Yeah, well . . ." Again, no eye contact.

"Although, of course, Amber Tierney . . . Sheesh. She's gorgeous. And currently single, according to the *National Star.* If you play your cards right . . ."

Wes laughed. "Yeah, right. No, thank you. That's the dead last thing I need. And Amber — I'm sure she doesn't need another idiot drooling over her."

"You don't think your friend Lana sent you here to set you up with her little sister?"

He looked up at her then, seriously taken aback. "God, what a thought."

"Sisters do those kinds of things," Britt said. "They know a single guy who's really nice, they really like him a lot, they have a sister who's single, too . . ."

He was shaking his head. "I don't know . . ."

Are you sleeping with her? Brittany didn't ask. That was definitely a question that required a friendship that was more than a few hours old. And even if she had known Wes for years, it was none of her business. She kept her mouth tightly shut.

Although, what better way to spend a few weeks with a lover? Husband is conveniently out of town ten out of twelve months a year, but the neighbors might notice if one of his best friends starts coming over for slumber parties. Little sister needs a brave Navy SEAL to check out her security system, so Wes toddles off to L.A. Whoops, there's some kind of a problem, Lana comes to town to "help . . ." And gee, there they are. Wes and Lana in L.A., away from everyone who knows that she's married to someone else, for two blissful weeks.

Ick. Britt hoped she was wrong.

The waiter brought the check, saving her from asking nosy questions.

As Wes looked it over, he took out his wallet.

Brittany opened her purse, too. "Let's just split it right down the middle."

"Nope," he said, taking out a credit card, sliding it into the leather folder that held the bill and holding it up so the waiter could grab it on his way past. "This one's mine."

"Nuh-uh," she disagreed. "This wasn't a date."

"Yes, it was," he countered. "And actually, I think it was the nicest date I've ever been on."

What a sweet thing to say. "Wow, you don't get out much, huh?"

He laughed.

"Seriously, Wes," she said. "It's not fair that you should have to pay for my dinner just because my brother-in-law —"

"How about I let you pick up the tab next time?"

The waiter was back. "I'm sorry, sir. Your credit card's expired. Would you like to use a different card?"

Wes swore as he looked at the credit card. "I only have this one." Brittany opened her mouth, but he cut her off. "No, you're not going to pay. I have cash." He looked at the waiter. "You do take cash?"

"Yes, sir."

He opened his wallet and just about emptied it. "Keep the change."

"Thank you, sir." The waiter vanished.

"Well, that was embarrassing." He looked at the credit card again. "I thought they were supposed to send me a new card before the expiration date runs out."

"What do you do with junk mail?" Britt asked.

He looked at her as if she'd lost her mind. "I throw it away. What do you do with it?"

"Do you throw it away without opening it? Mailings from mortgage companies and insurance companies and . . ." She paused dramatically. ". . . credit card companies?"

"Ha. You think they sent me a new card but I threw it away without even opening it," he concluded correctly. "Well, hell, aren't I just too efficient for my own damn good?" He forced a smile as he put the expired card back into his wallet. "Oh well."

Brittany suspected his expired card created a bigger snafu than he was letting on. "Where are you staying tonight?"

"I don't know. I guess I'll drive back to San Diego. I was going to stay at a motel, but . . ." He shook his head and laughed in exasperation. "I'm supposed to meet Amber pretty early in the morning over at the studio, so if I go home, I won't have time for much more than a short nap before I have to turn around and come back to L.A."

"If you want, you could sleep on my couch," Britt offered.

He looked at her, and his blue eyes were somber. "You may want to learn to be a little less generous with men you just met."

She laughed. "Oh, come on. I've been

hearing about you for years. I seriously doubt you're a serial killer. I mean, the word probably would've trickled down to me by now. Besides, what are your other options? Are you going to, like, sleep in your car?"

That's exactly what he'd been planning to do. She could see it in his eyes, in his smile. "Seriously, Brittany. You really don't know me."

"I know enough," she said quietly.

Wes sat there looking at her for many long seconds. She couldn't read the expression on his face, in his eyes. If she were young and foolish and prone to thinking that life was like a romance novel, she would dare to dream that this was the moment when Wes Skelly fell in love with her.

Except they'd agreed that there wasn't going to be anything romantic between them, she wasn't his type, he was definitely connected in some way to the wife of his good friend Wizard, and Brittany didn't really want anyone to be in love with her. She had too much going on with school and Andy's college and getting used to living on the west coast and . . .

Maybe the man just had gas.

"Okay," he finally said. "Your couch sounds great. Thank you. I appreciate it very much."

Brittany stood up, briskly collecting her purse and her sweater. "You can't smoke inside the house," she told him as he followed her to the door.

"I told you, I quit."

She gave him a pointed look, and he laughed. "Really," he said. "This time is going to be different."

Chapter 3

"Hey, Andy," Brittany called as she opened the door to her apartment.

"Hey, Britt," her adopted son called back. "How'd it go with the load?"

Brittany looked at Wes, laughter in her eyes. "Um, sweetie?" she called to Andy. "The, uh, load came home with me."

Wes had to laugh, especially when she added, "And he ain't heavy, he's my brother."

Her place was extremely small, but it was decorated with comfortable-looking furniture and bright colors. A living room, an eat-in kitchen, a hallway off the kitchen that led to the back where there were two bedrooms.

Britt had told him on his way over that even though the place was significantly tinier than their house in Appleton, Massachusetts, it had the essential ingredient to shared housing — the bedrooms were large, and she and Andy each had their own bathroom.

Andy emerged from the hallway, dressed down in shorts and a T-shirt, his feet bare, and his dark hair a mess. He was trying to play it cool, but the kid practically throbbed with curiosity.

"Hey," he said to Wes. He looked at Wes's overnight bag, and then at Brittany. "Isn't this outrageously unusual."

"He's sleeping on the couch," Brittany told him in her refreshingly point-blank manner. "Don't get any ideas, devil child."

"Did I say anything?" Andy countered. "I didn't say anything." He reached out to shake Wes's hand. "Nice to see you again, sir. Sorry about the load comment."

"It's not sir, it's chief," Wes corrected him. "But why don't you just call me Wes?"

Andy nodded, looking from Wes to Brittany with unconcealed mischief in his eyes.

"Don't say it," Brittany warned him, as she went to a living room trunk and removed sheets and a blanket for the couch.

"What?" Andy played an angel, giving her big, innocent eyes. But beneath the play-acting was an honestly sweet kid, who genuinely cared for his mother.

Jeez, that was who Andy reminded him of. Ethan. Wes's little brother. Ah, Christ.

"There was a credit card mishap," Brittany told Andy, putting the linens on the coffee table. "And Wes needed a place to sleep. Since we have a couch, it all seemed to line up quite nicely. I have an extra pillow on my bed that you can use," she told Wes, before

44

turning back to Andy. "Wes is not a candidate."

Wes couldn't keep from asking. "A candidate for what?"

Andy was watching Britt, too, waiting to see what she was going to say.

She laughed as she led the way into the kitchen, turning on the light and taking a kettle from the stove and filling it at the sink.

"This proves it," she said to Andy. "I'm going to tell him the truth, which I wouldn't do if he were any kind of real candidate — not that there are any real candidates." She turned to Wes. "Ever since I adopted Andy, he's been bugging me to 'get him a father.' It's really just a silly joke. I mean, gosh, who's on the candidate list right now?" she asked the kid as she put the kettle on the stove and turned on the gas.

"Well, Bill the mailman just came out of the closet, so we're down to the guy who works the nightshift at the convenience store. . . ."

"Alfonse." Brittany crossed her arms as she leaned against the kitchen counter. "He's about twenty-two years old and doesn't speak more than ten words of English."

"But you said he was cute," Andy interjected.

"Yeah. The way Mrs. Feinstein's new kitten is cute!"

"Well, there's also Dr. Jurrik from the hospital."

"Oh, he's perfect," Britt countered. "Except for the fact that I would rather stick needles into my eyes than get involved with another doctor."

"That leaves Mr. Spoons."

"The neighborhood bagman," Brittany told Wes. "Be still my heart."

Wes laughed as he leaned against the counter at the other end of the kitchen.

"The reason the list is so lame," Andy told Wes, "is because she won't go out and meet anyone for real. I mean, once every few years someone sets her up with the friend of a friend and she grits her teeth and goes, but other than that . . ." He shook his head in mock disgust.

"The truth is, most men my age *are* loads," Brittany said.

"The truth is," Andy told Wes, "she was married to a real load. I never met the guy myself, but apparently he was a piece of work. And now she's gun-shy. So to speak."

"I'm sure Melody and Jones completely filled in Wes as far as my tragic romantic past goes," Britt said to Andy as she rolled her eyes at Wes. "Don't you have studying to do?"

"Actually Dani just called," Andy said. "She's coming over."

"Oh, is she feeling better?"

"I don't know," he said. "She sounded . . . I don't know. Weird. Oh, by the way, the landlord called and said he was replacing the broken glass in your bathroom window with Plexiglas." He grinned at Wes. "There's a group of kids down the street really into stickball and they've managed to break that same window three times since we've moved in — which is pretty impressive." He looked back at Britt. "The Plexiglas isn't going to look too good, but the ball should bounce off."

Brittany snorted. "Ten to one says that my bedroom window breaks next."

The doorbell rang.

"Excuse me," Andy said as he went into the living room.

"He's a good kid," Wes said quietly. "You should be very proud."

"I am." She opened one of the kitchen cabinets and took out a pair of mugs. "Want tea?"

He laughed. "SEALs aren't allowed to drink tea. It's written in the BUD/S manual."

"BUD/S," she repeated. "That's the training you go through to become a SEAL, right?"

"Yeah."

"Jones had a few pretty wild stories about something called Hell Week."

Hell Week was the diabolically difficult segment of Phase One training, where the SEAL candidates were pushed to extremes, physically, emotionally and psychologically.

"Yeah, you know, I don't remember much of Hell Week," he told her. "I think I've blocked most of it out. It was hard."

"Now, there's an understatement." Brittany smiled at him, and Wes wished — not for the last time this evening, he was sure — that he wasn't sleeping on that couch tonight. Her smile was like pure sunshine — God, it was trite, but true.

"Yeah, I guess," he said. "Like I said, I don't remember much of it. Although, Hell Week was where Bobby Taylor and I finally stopped hating each other. The guy's been my closest friend for years, but when we were first assigned as swim buddies — you know, we had to stick together no matter what during BUD/S — we hated each other's guts."

Brittany laughed. "I had no idea. Your friendship with Bobby is legendary. I mean, Bobby and Wes. Wes and Bobby. I keep expecting him to show up."

"He's on his honeymoon," Wes told her.

"With your sister." Her eyes softened. "That must feel really strange. It must be hard for you — your best friend and your sister. Suddenly it's not Bobby and Wes, it's Bobby and Colleen."

It was amazing. Everyone who'd heard about Bobby's marriage to Colleen had made noise like, how great was that? Your best friend gets to join your family. Wasn't that terrific?

And yes, it was terrific. But at the same time it was weirder than hell. And Brittany had hit it right on the head. Wes's entire friendship with Bobby had been based on the fact that they were two unattached guys. They shared an apartment, they shared a similar lifestyle, they shared a hell of a lot.

And now, while Wes didn't quite want to call what he was feeling jealousy, everything had changed. Bobby now spent every minute he wasn't on duty with Colleen instead of hanging out with Wes watching old, badly dubbed Jackie Chan movies.

Bobby and Wes had definitely turned into Bobby and Colleen — with Wes trailing pathetically along, a third wheel.

"Yeah," he said to Brittany. "It's a little weird."

From out in the living room, Andy's voice got loud enough for them to hear. "You can't be serious!"

The kid didn't sound happy, and Wes took a quick glance in his direction.

Andy was standing at the open door. His girlfriend hadn't even made it into the living room. She was a pretty girl, with short dark hair, but right now her face was pinched and pale, and she had dark circles beneath her eyes.

"Will you please come in so we can talk about this?" Andy asked, but she shook her head. Her reply was spoken too softly for Wes to hear.

"What, so you're just *leaving?*" Andy, on the other hand, was getting louder.

Wes stepped farther into the kitchen, attempting to give them privacy. Clearly this was not a happy conversation. It sounded, from his experience, as if Andy was getting the old dumparooney.

He looked at Britt who winced when Andy said, loudly enough for them to hear, "You're just going home to San Diego — you're not even going to finish up the term!?"

Again, the girl's reply was too soft for Wes to hear.

"The biggest problem with having a small apartment," Brittany said, as she poured hot water over the tea bag in her mug, "is that there's no such thing as a private conversation."

"We could go for a walk," Wes suggested. "You up for a walk?"

She put the kettle back on the stove, giving him another of those killer smiles, this one loaded with appreciation. "Absolutely. What I really wanted was iced tea, anyway. Let me get a warmer jacket."

But as she went down the hall to her bedroom, the conversation from the living room got even louder.

"Why are you doing this?" Andy asked. He was really upset. "What happened? What'd I do? Dani, you've got to talk to me, because, God, I don't want you to leave! I love you!"

Dani burst into noisy tears. "I'm sorry," she said, finally loud enough for them all to hear. "I don't love you!"

The door slammed behind her.

Oh, cripes, that had to have hurt. Wes met Britt's worried eyes as she came back out into the kitchen. She'd obviously heard that news bulletin, too.

Andy was silent in the living room. He'd have to come past them to get to the sanctuary and privacy of his room.

And even if they were going to go for a walk, they'd have to go out right past him. If Wes were in Andy's shoes, having to face his mother and her friend was the last thing he'd want after getting an *I don't love you* response to his declaration of love.

"How about a tour of your bedroom instead?" Wes asked Brittany. If they went into her room and shut the door, that would give Andy an escape route.

"Yes," she said. "Come on."

She grabbed his hand and pulled him down the hall.

Her room was as brightly colored and cheerful as the rest of the place, with a big mirror over an antique dresser and a bed that actually had a canopy. As she closed the door behind them, Wes had to smile.

"Gee, I wish it was always this easy to gain entry to a beautiful woman's bedroom," he said.

"How could she break up with him like that?" Brittany asked. "No explanation, just *I don't love you!* What a horrible girl! I never really liked her."

They heard a click as Andy quietly went into his room and locked the door. The kid turned music on, no doubt to hide the noise he was going to make when he started to cry.

Brittany looked as if she was going to cry, too.

"Maybe I should go," Wes said.

"Don't be ridiculous." She opened her door and marched back into the kitchen and out into the living room where she started putting the sheets on the couch.

"I can do that," Wes said.

She sat down on the sofa, clearly upset. "From now on, I'm going to screen his girlfriends."

Wes sat down next to her. "Now who's being ridiculous?"

Brittany laughed, but it was rueful and sad. "He was so damaged when I first met him, when he was twelve. He'd been so badly hurt, so many times — shuffled from one foster family to the next. No one wanted him. And now this . . . Rejection really sucks, you know?"

"Yeah," he said. "Actually, I do. I mean, not on the scale that Andy's faced it, but . . . So now you want to protect him from everything — including girls who might break his heart." He shook his head. "You can't do it, Britt. Life doesn't work that way."

She nodded. "I know."

"He's a terrific kid. For all the bad crap that happened to him in his life, he's got his relationship with you to balance it all out. He's going to deal with this. It's going to hurt for a while, but eventually he's going to be okay. He's not going to come unglued."

She sighed. "I know that, too. I just . . . I can't help but want everything to be perfect for him."

"There's no such thing as perfect," Wes said.

Except there was. Brittany's eyes were a perfect shade of blue. Her smile was pretty damn perfect, too.

If she were any other woman on the planet, he would have given her a friendly, comforting hug. But he didn't trust himself to get that close.

She exhaled loudly — a supersigh. "Well. I have to get up early in the morning."

"I do, too," he told her. "Amber Tierney awaits."

Her smile was more genuine now. "Poor baby." She stood up. "Towels are in the closet in the bathroom. Help yourself. I'll get you that pillow."

"Thanks again for letting me crash here," he told her.

"You're welcome to stay as long as you like."

Chapter 4

Wes's car was in the driveway in the late afternoon, when Brittany got home from her last class.

When she'd gotten up in the very early morning to go in to the hospital, she'd left a key on the kitchen table, along with a note telling Wes to help himself to breakfast and to feel free to come back when his meeting with Amber was over.

As she juggled her keys with the grocery bags she was carrying in from her car, he opened the door and took one of the bags from her.

He had his cell phone tucked under his chin, but he greeted her with a smile and a twinkle of his eyes as he carried the bag into the kitchen.

"Is there more?" he mouthed. He was wearing jeans, and he had a barbed wire tattoo encircling his left biceps, peeking out from the sleeve of his snugly-fitting T-shirt.

Dressed up in a sports jacket and nice pants, he looked like an average guy — with a thick head of pretty-colored hair and those dancing blue eyes working to cancel out his lack of height. But with some of his natural scruffiness showing, in jeans that hugged a world-class set of glutes and a T-shirt that clung to his shoulders and pecs, with his hair not so carefully combed, and that tattoo . . . He was eye-catching, to say the least.

"I can get it," she said, but he shook his head and went out the door and down the wooden steps to the driveway. Wasn't that nice?

She started unloading the groceries, and he returned with the last two bags.

He was still on the phone. "I know," he said to whomever he was talking to. "I understand." He paused. "No, I don't think you're crazy, although, you're the shrink — you should know." Another pause. "Look, I'm on the case. I'm going out to her place tonight — there's some kind of party and . . ."

Even though he was talking to someone — and Brittany would've bet big money that it was his very nice "friend," Lana — he helped by putting the milk and yogurt in the refrigerator, the frozen vegetables in the freezer.

"No, I only spoke to her for about fifteen minutes — while she was getting her hair done in her trailer," Wes reported. "She said this guy's just a fan who's gone a little bit overboard. He's no big deal." Pause. "No, those were her words, not mine. I haven't met the guy." Pause. "Yeah, she mentioned that she came home last week and he was in her garage. She seems to think the only way he could have got in there was if he wandered in while she was leaving in the morning and hung out there all day, which is — yes, you're absolutely right — it's pretty freaky. I'm with you totally on that, and yeah, she seemed to talk about him as if he was some kind of stray animal — *he wandered in*. It's more likely he snuck in. But she also said that he left immediately, as soon as she asked. And she didn't get out of her car until he was out of there and the garage door was closed, so at least we know that your sister's not a total brainless idiot."

With all the groceries put in the various cabinets, he sat down at the kitchen table.

"Definitely," he said. "I'm going out there tonight. I'll look over her security system, and I'll talk to her again. And I'll call you soon, okay?" Another pause, then he added, "Yeah, you know, Lana, about Wizard . . ." Wes rubbed the bridge of his nose, right between his eyes. "Yeah. No, I haven't heard from him. I was, you know, wondering if you had?" He laughed. "Yeah, right. Yeah, okay babe, talk to you soon."

He closed his cell phone with a snap and very salty curse. "Sorry," he said as he realized Brittany was still standing there. "God, I would sell my left . . . shoe for a cigarette."

This time, Brittany couldn't keep her mouth shut. "Are you sleeping with her?"

Wes met her gaze and there was something in his eyes that looked an awful lot like guilt. "Who, Amber? Of course not," he said, but she knew he knew exactly what she was talking about.

Was he sleeping with Lana — who was *very nice.*

Britt just waited, watching him, and he finally swore and laughed, although there wasn't any humor in it.

"No," he said. "No, I'm not. It's not . . . It's never gone that far. It's not going to, you know? I wouldn't do that to Wizard."

But he wanted to. He was in love with the woman. It had dripped from every word he spoke while on the phone with her.

Brittany's heart broke for him. "Has it occurred to you that she might be taking advantage of you? I mean, asking you to come out to L.A. to do something she should be paying a private investigator to do . . . ?"

"I had to take leave," Wes told her. "The senior chief insisted. And believe me, coming down here was better than staying in San Diego with all that time on my hands. It's not easy to be there — especially when Wizard's away." He laughed again, rubbing his forehead as if he had a terrible headache. "Yeah, like it's easy to be there when he's home. It sucks, okay? Wherever I am, 24/7, it really sucks. But it sucks even more when she's a five-minute ride from my house."

Brittany sat down across from him at the table. "I'm so sorry."

"Yeah, well . . ." He forced a smile.

"You said . . . She's a psychiatrist?"

"Psychologist," he corrected her.

"Does she know you're in love with her?" How could Lana not know? How could a trained psychologist not take one look at Wes and know without a shadow of a doubt that he was head over heels in love with her?

But, "No," Wes said. "I mean, yeah, she knows I run hot for her, sure. I've done a few stupid things to give that away, but . . . She also knows that I'm not going to act on it. You know, my attraction to her. It's not going to happen. She knows that."

Brittany kept her mouth closed over the harsh words she wanted to say. Like, how could Lana use Wes as her errand boy like this, knowing that he'd do darn near anything for her? What kind of woman would take advantage of this kind of devotion from a man who wasn't her husband?

Lana didn't sound very nice to her. In fact, she sounded an awful lot like a snake.

"You know what the real bitch of it all is?" Wes asked. "I found out something today — from Amber — that's really making my head spin. It's . . ." He shook his head. "I'm sorry.

59

You probably don't want to hear this."

Brittany sighed. "Do I look like I'm in a hurry to go someplace?"

He sat there, just looking at her, somber and weary of life's burdens. This was a Wes Skelly that most people never got a chance to see. Britt realized that he hid this part of himself behind both laughter and anger.

"I've been caught in the middle for years," Wes said quietly. "Between Lana and Wizard, I mean. Wizard — the Mighty Quinn — he doesn't exactly include fidelity as part of his working vocabulary, you know what I mean?"

Britt did know.

"He's been stepping out on Lana for years," he continued, "and when I've called him on it, he's got this 'What she doesn't know won't hurt her' kind of ha-ha-ha attitude about it. So there I am. Do I tell her? Do I not tell her? I was Wizard's friend first, so I've kept my mouth shut, but it's been driving me freaking crazy. Because if I tell her, it's going to seem as if I'm doing it for selfish reasons, right? But today . . ."

He started fidgeting, straightening the napkin holder and the salt and pepper shakers.

"I was talking to Amber, you know, about this guy who's been following her," Wes told her, "and how Lana's worried about him, and Amber, she says that Lana worries about everything." He stopped fidgeting and looked

60

up at her. "She said, that's what happens when you have a lying, cheating dog for a husband. You worry about everything."

He laughed. "I was, like, floored. I was, like, 'How do you know about Wizard?' And she looked at me like I was from Mars and said, 'Lana told me.' " There was still shock and disbelief in his eyes. "All this time, I'm protecting Lana from the truth, protecting Wizard, too, and it turns out she knew."

"My ex-husband was like Wizard," Brittany told him. "He couldn't keep his pants zipped. You learn to recognize the signs."

"Just now, when I was talking to her on the phone, I wanted to ask her about it. I mean, why is she still with him? But what was I supposed to say? 'Hey, Lana, so when'd you find out you've been sharing the Wiz with dozens of other women and why the hell do you put up with that?' "

"Maybe she hopes he'll change," Britt suggested. "Of course, if she does hope that, then she's a fool. Men like that don't change."

Britt understood Wes's confusion. Lana had to know that Wes could be hers with a snap of her fingers and a short trip to a surgical specialist — a divorce attorney who could remove her malingering growth of a husband from her otherwise healthy life.

It was so obvious that Wes would be like a pit bull when it came to a relationship. He would never be unfaithful. Boy, he couldn't even be unfaithful to Wizard, in terms of their friendship.

Brittany had no doubt that Wes was going to love Lana until the end of time.

She was envious. If Lana got her head on straight and ditched Wizard for Wes, she was going to have that same, rare happily ever after that Melody and Jones had found.

"So now you know way more about me than you wanted to, huh?" Wes said with a rueful laugh. He stood up. "Well, at least I didn't smoke for three days."

"Oh, no you don't." Britt stood up, too, and blocked his way into the living room. "You are not going out to buy cigarettes. You are quitting. Even if I have to go buy a nicotine patch and stick it on you myself."

That got a smile and a trace of sparkle back into his eyes. "That might be fun."

"It goes on your arm," she told him as he kept moving toward her. She kept backing up, too, all the way through the living room, until she bumped into the door. As she hit it, she spread her arms, as if sealing it closed. As if that would keep him from leaving. "I'm a nurse, remember? I know these things."

"I'm dying for a cigarette," he admitted.

"So what?" Brittany said. "There're lots of other things in this world that you can't have, either." Including Lana. "Suck it up, Skelly."

62

The door opened behind her with no small amount of force, whacking her hard on the derriere and pushing her forward. It was like being hit by a linebacker. She tripped on the throw rug and would have landed on her face if Wes hadn't moved to catch her.

Brittany was nearly Wes's height and she would've bet big money that his jeans had a smaller waist size than hers. But despite that, despite his being slight of stature and seemingly slender, the man was solid muscle. She didn't even come close to knocking him over. But as a result of his catching her, she couldn't have stood any closer to him if she'd tried.

At least not with their clothes on.

While Wes had caught her, she'd caught herself by grabbing him, too, and as Andy stood looking at them now from the front door, she had to unwrap her arms from around Wes's neck.

"Oops. Sorry." Andy started to leave, closing the door behind him.

"Wait!" Brittany untangled herself from Wes and pulled the door open. "I was just keeping Wes from buying cigarettes."

Andy laughed. "Well, that's one effective way to do it."

Wes laughed, too. "I wish. But she was actually standing right in front of the door. You almost knocked her over, kid."

"Sorry." Andy didn't sound sorry at all. In

fact, he sounded entirely too cheerful. But it was definitely forced.

Brittany searched his face, wondering if he and Dani had patched things up.

"You're staying here again tonight, right?" he asked Wes. "I mean, I hope you'll stay again tonight. I was hoping we could maybe, I don't know. Shoot some baskets or something."

In guy-speak, or at least in Andy-speak, *shoot some baskets* meant *talk*.

And talking — man to man — was something Brittany couldn't give to Andy. She turned to Wes. "Please stay."

"Actually," Wes said, "I spoke to my credit card company. They're overnighting a new card to me care of a Mailboxes Plus office here in L.A. But I won't get it until tomorrow. So I was hoping —"

"Terrific," Brittany told him. "And actually, you can stay for as long as you like. Save the money you'd spend on a hotel, as long as you don't mind sleeping on the couch. Just chip in a little for groceries." She looked at Andy, unable to keep herself from asking. "Is everything all right? Did you see Dani?"

"Nah, she's gone." He was almost too flip, too unconcerned. Which meant he was terribly hurt. "She packed up all her stuff and cleared out of her dorm room." He laughed, but it sounded a little too harsh. "Apparently, after spending the past six months talking me into taking things slowly, she really did sleep with Dustin Melero."

And what could Brittany possibly say to that?

Wes swore softly.

Andy went into the kitchen, apparently determined to move on. "What's for dinner?"

He didn't want to talk about Dani. Not now. Maybe not ever — not with Britt. But maybe it was part of the guy stuff he wanted to discuss with Wes.

She hoped so. "You tell me. It's your turn to cook." She followed Andy, pushing Wes ahead of her. "No cigarettes," she told Wes sternly. "You can get through one more day."

Andy put his backpack down on the kitchen table and opened the refrigerator. "Tonight we dine on . . . pasta."

"Wow! What a surprise. You know, I just got some chicken. We could light the grill and —"

"You guys want to go out for dinner?" Wes interrupted. "Like in about an hour? Because I've been invited to this party where there's going to be a buffet. The downside is we'll have to get dressed up. But I've got to go check out Amber's security system and I kind of promised I'd do it tonight."

"Amber?" Andy asked. If he were a dog, his ears would have pricked up.

"Amber Tierney," Wes told him. "Want to come to a party at her house tonight?"

Andy laughed, his enthusiasm a little more genuine. "Yeah. She's only the hottest woman in America. You actually know her?"

"Amber's sister — half sister, really — is a pretty good friend of mine."

"Don't you have homework?" Brittany asked Andy.

He looked at her. "Don't you?"

"Of course." She smiled. "Race ya to see how much of it we can get done in the next forty-five minutes."

Andy grabbed his bag and bolted for his bedroom. "I don't have a lot — the baseball team's going to Phoenix tomorrow, remember?"

Brittany wasn't too far behind him. "Race ya anyway."

"I guess that's a yes," she heard Wes say as she closed her door.

Chapter 5

There was no doubt about it. Wes was certain that a picture of Amber Tierney's house was going into the next edition of *Webster's* dictionary — right next to the definition for pretentious.

How much house — it was a castle, really — did one little twenty-two-year-old need?

"Are you sure she's not going to mind you bringing two mere mortals to her fancy party?" Brittany asked him as they approached the front gate — also pretentious. The gate itself was iron, but it connected to a high stone wall that had ornate iron pikes sticking out the top, like some kind of fortified medieval keep. The only thing missing were the severed heads of the enemy.

Except the stones in the wall could give even a seven-year-old the toeholds necessary to scale the damn thing. And those pikes, although dramatic looking, wouldn't even keep Wes's grandmother out.

"I'm positive," he told Brittany as they

waited for the goon at the gate to find his name on a guest list. "I told her I'd stayed with you last night — I thought maybe she might know Lt. Jones and Melody, but she didn't. When she gave me the invite, she said, bring your friends. And that's a direct quote."

And indeed, they were all waved past the gate and into the yard.

As far as mere mortals went, Brittany really couldn't be counted among them — not dressed the way she was. She had definitely transcended earthly limitations. She was wearing a black evening gown that accentuated her curves in a way that was entirely too distracting. The dress wasn't low-cut or see-through the way some women's were, but every time he glanced at her, it was like, *hello.*

With her hair piled atop her head, and only slightly more makeup than she usually wore, she looked glamorous and elegant — as if she'd stepped out of a movie. Her smile was so damn genuine and relaxed. Everyone else looked tense, as if they had an agenda.

And indeed, everyone was looking at them, no doubt wondering who the heck she was.

"Everyone's looking at you," she whispered to Wes. "Nothing like a handsome man in uniform to create a stir."

He laughed. She needed to visit San Diego and reacquaint herself with the rest of Team

Ten so she could get a clearer picture of what handsome was. "I hate to break it to you, but they're looking at you, babycakes."

"Actually," Andy joked, "they're looking at me."

Brittany laughed and even more people looked in their direction.

And Wes, idiot that he was, couldn't stop thinking about how perfectly she'd fit in his arms. True, she'd only been there for a few short seconds, but she'd hit him with a full-body slam — chest to thighs. It was almost enough to make him regret telling her about Lana.

God, he couldn't believe he'd finally told someone the truth. He'd never told anyone about his feelings for Lana before — at least not when he was sober.

But somehow, telling Brittany felt right. It felt good in a very strange way — knowing that someone else finally knew.

Except here he was now, lusting after that same someone else.

Of course, he'd trained himself to do that. To act on his attraction to women besides Lana. If he hadn't, he'd be in a five-year dry spell instead of one that had lasted only ten months.

Ten months without sex. Something was seriously wrong with him. But he honestly hadn't wanted it.

Correction. He *had* wanted it, but never

when it was blatantly available. Although it had been close to forever since he'd wanted it this much.

And right now, God help him, he was finding it hard to think about anything else.

"Did I tell you that that dress makes you look like a goddess?" he murmured to Brittany now.

She laughed, but her cheeks got a little pink. Wasn't that interesting?

He put his hand at her waist, pretending it was to steer her around a series of lounge chairs as they approached a huge swimming pool, but really just because he wanted to put his hand at her waist. She was warm and her dress was soft beneath his fingers, but not as soft as her skin would be, and . . .

And he had to stop trying to figure out the best way to get her naked. He liked this woman too much to do anything that could hurt her.

And telling Brittany all about how much he loved Lana and then trying to take her to bed would definitely hurt her.

Or royally piss her off.

Unless maybe he was honest about it . . .

Yeah, that would be nice. *Hey, Britt, of course you know I'm in love with Lana, but she's not here and you are, and you're really hot. . . .*

Christ, he needed a cigarette. He needed to take his hands off of Brittany and find a beer for one and a cigarette for the other.

But she turned toward him, moving even closer, lowering her voice to say, "Oh, my God! The entire cast of *High Tide* is here. And isn't that Mark Wahlberg? And what's his name, from *Band of Brothers?* And that girl who used to be on *Buffy* . . ."

"Oh, yeah," Andy said. "That's her."

Britt's body brushed against Wes's and he forced himself to take a step back, made himself let go of her.

She didn't seem to notice, one way or the other. "Whoa, there's that actress who plays that nurse on *E.R.* She is *so* good. Her mother must be a nurse, or maybe she just spent a lot of time doing research. Let's go schmooze in her direction, can we?"

"Why don't you guys schmooze without me for a bit," Wes said. "I should go inside, see if I can't find Amber, maybe take a quick look at the security system. I'll catch up with you later, okay?"

Andy was already drifting off in the direction of the actress from *Buffy.*

"Do you want me to come with you?" Britt asked.

Yes, he most definitely did, in a completely *Beavis and Butthead* kind of way. Heh-heh.

"Nah," he said. "Go talk to your nurse. I'll be back before you know it."

"This is fun," she told him, her eyes sparkling and her smile warm. "Thank you so much for inviting us."

"My pleasure," he said. He let himself watch her walk away, then headed for Amber's castle.

Wes's big mistake was wearing the uniform.

Without it on, in street clothes, he would be easy to overlook in a crowd, especially a crowd like this one, filled with the brightest stars in the firmament. But with all those colorful ribbons adorning his chest, in that white jacket that had been tailored to fit his trim body, his eyes seemed an even darker shade of blue, and his jaw seemed more square.

Or maybe it had always been that square and Brittany just hadn't noticed.

Everyone wanted to talk to him — and not just the twenty-something young women, either. He was surrounded pretty constantly by men, too. And not necessarily gay men.

Brittany had overheard two of Amber's friends talking. "He's a Navy SEAL," one reported to the other.

"A real one?" the other asked. "You mean, that's not just a costume?"

They hurried over to join the crowd around Wes.

Amber wasn't among them, however.

She was holding court herself, on the other side of the swimming pool, and the few times she'd glanced in Wes's direction, she'd seemed a little peeved. Or maybe Brittany was just imagining that, expecting her to act like the spoiled starlet that she was.

Britt leaned back against the cabana and sipped a glass of wine. She couldn't hear what Wes was saying, or what any of the crowd were saying to him, but he was starting to eye a strikingly pretty young woman in a midriff-baring dress who was standing close to him.

No, strike that. He was eyeing her cigarette.

Just at that moment, Wes looked up and caught Britt's eye.

She put two fingers to her lips as if she were smoking, and shook her head, making a stern face at him. Don't do it.

He made a face back at her. And then he said something to his groupies — a fairly long story filled with gestures and big facial expressions. When he was done, he pointed directly at Brittany. And they all turned to look at her, almost as one.

And wasn't *that* disconcerting. Weakly, she raised her wineglass in a salute.

Wes was grinning at her. What had he told them about her?

He gestured to her and although she couldn't hear him, she could read his lips. *Come here, baby.*

Baby?

Those Irish eyes were positively dancing

with mischief. *Come on, honey. Don't be shy.*

Honey, huh?

What was it Han Solo always said to Chewbacca? *I have a bad feeling about this.*

But *shy* wasn't a word she'd ever used to describe herself. Curious, however, was.

Britt pushed herself up off the wall. As she approached, the crowd parted for her, as if she were some kind of queen.

"Hey, babe," Wes said when she got closer. "I was just telling everyone — everyone this is Brittany, Britt this is everyone."

"Hello, everyone," she said, trying not to be overwhelmed by the famous faces she spotted among them. Was that George Clooney standing at the edge of the crowd? If it wasn't, it was his even better-looking clone. He nodded to her, his dark eyes nearly as warm as his smile.

"I was telling the old story of how you nursed me back to health after I was injured, you know, when my squad was ambushed by *al Qaeda* forces." Wes managed to capture her complete attention.

"Oh, you were, were you? And when was this?"

"Not the first time," he said. He looked at the crowd and closed his eyes briefly, shaking his head in mock exasperation. "There were actually two times and she always gets them confused —"

"Where will you be honeymooning?" the

woman with the belly button and the cigarette interrupted to ask.

What an . . . interesting question. Brittany looked at Wes, eyebrows raised. Apparently there were parts of that "old" story that she needed to be filled in on with just a little more detail.

"I told them about the second time we were ambushed," he told her. "You know, when the doctors were so sure I was going to die, only I opened my eyes and I saw you, and since the choice was between going to you or going to the light, I of course picked you."

"Of course," she echoed. She had to bite the insides of her cheeks to keep from laughing aloud. And Wes knew it, the devil. "Where will we be honeymooning, Lambikins? Last time we discussed it, it was a toss-up between Algeria and Bosnia." As Wes choked back a laugh, she turned to the crowd. "I'm afraid poor Wesley needs that little extra rush of adrenaline that comes from vacationing in countries with a high incidence of terrorism — to keep him revved up. You know how some men are. And so unwilling to ask the doctor for a simple Viagra prescription. I'd be happy with Hawaii, but, no."

Wes put his arm around her, pulling her so that she was pressed up against him. He kissed her, right next to her ear. "Thanks *so* much," he murmured.

She gave him a big smile. "Any time. Sweetie honey pumpkin pie."

"How do you handle it when he goes off to fight?" a woman with dark glasses asked. Brittany wasn't positive, but she thought she'd seen her a time or two on daytime TV, while on break at the hospital.

"Faith," Britt said. She'd asked the same question of her sister, and Melody had given that exact answer.

"Aren't you afraid he's going to, like, attack you in the night?"

What? "Since I'm not a terrorist," Brittany said, "no."

Wes apparently liked her answer. He gave her a squeeze.

He still had his arm around her, and her entire left side was pressed against him. She could feel the muscles in his thigh, the solidness of his chest. That-Jerk-Quentin, her ex-husband, had been both taller and wider, but nowhere near as well endowed. Muscularly, that was, of course.

"Is it true that in order to marry a SEAL — which stands for Sea, Air and Land, right? — you have to get it on in all of those places?"

Good God. Brittany doubted it, but she honestly didn't know. Was there some secret club she didn't know about? Her sister had managed to get pregnant at thirty thousand feet, but at the time Melody had had no intention of getting married. As for sea and land, well, land was easy enough, and most SEALs had access to a boat. Unless . . .

"By sea do you mean underwater or on top of the water?" she asked. It was such a ridiculous question, she started to laugh. She turned to Wes. "Because, honey, we've done underwater a few times, haven't we? Once when we were scuba diving off the coast of Thailand, and once in the Bering Strait?"

Wes was making that odd, choking sound again.

"I'm so sorry," Britt said. "But my dearest darling needs some air. War wounds, you know, acting up. Excuse us."

The crowd parted like magic, and she was able to lead Wes into Amber's house, through a kitchen that was twice the size of Brittany's entire apartment, and down a long marble-tiled hallway.

Most of the guests were outside, and once they were alone, Wes leaned back against the wall and laughed until his eyes watered. "The Bering Strait?" he gasped. "Do you know the average water temperature in the Bering Strait?"

Well, considering it was up by Alaska . . . "Cold?"

"Very cold, my dearest darling. No one's doing anything raunchier than Eskimo kisses underwater up there. Believe me. You go into that water, and you're in a dry suit. Which is even more cumbersome than a wet suit. And then, even within the dry suit, there's the small matter of the effect of freezing temperatures on male anatomy. Pun intended."

Brittany grinned at him. "Men are such fragile, delicate creatures."

"Tell me about it." He grinned back at her. "Look, I'm sorry I didn't ask you to marry me before introducing you as my fiancée, but some of those women were starting to circle like sharks. It was just a matter of time before they attacked."

"And you really don't want that?" Brittany had to ask him, suddenly serious. "I would never say this in front of Andy, and if you repeat it to him, I'll deny having said it, but it's not as if these women are looking for a lifetime commitment right from the start. And you . . . You can't exactly have Lana, right? I certainly won't think less of you if you —"

"Thanks, but no thanks," he said. "Unless you decide to join the circling sharks." He was only teasing. He wiggled his eyebrows at her as he leaned closer. "I'll be your bait any day, babydoll. Have I mentioned how much I love that dress?"

"Repeatedly," she told him. "Wes, come on. Seriously. Who knows? Maybe one of these girls actually has a soul. Maybe you'll meet her and forget all about Lana. You'll never know if it's even possible if you don't let yourself get close to anyone else."

He sighed. "Britt, these women don't want to discuss philosophy with me. They want to jump me in their car."

"Gee, what's that enormous blob blocking out the sun? Oh, my God, is it your ego?"

Wes laughed. "Yeah, no, I said it wrong. They don't want to jump *me,* they want to jump a SEAL. Any SEAL. It has nothing to do with me. They just want to be able to tell their friends that they got it on with a SEAL. You know, add that to their sexual resume."

Ew. "Really?"

"Yeah. SEALs get laid simply by being SEALs. Anywhere, any time. It doesn't matter what we look like, doesn't matter who we are. And yeah, I've taken advantage of that more than I like to admit and . . . I don't know. Right now I'm tired of it. I'm going through this phase, I guess, where I want the woman I'm in bed with to like me for me — at least a little bit."

"Well, all they have to do is talk to you for a few minutes," Brittany told him. "I mean, I liked you right away. You're very likable. That can't be too hard to —"

"How many times have you had sex with a stranger, just for the sake of having sex?" he asked.

She didn't have to think about it. "Never."

"And how many times have you had casual sex?"

"Once," she admitted. "It was awful, and I cried for four days afterwards, and I never did it again."

"There," he said, as if it proved his point. "You've obviously got a different agenda when it comes to meeting men. You think in terms of friends or potential lifemates, rather than tonight's quick screw. Walk with me, okay? I want to go check out Amber's garage. I think it's over this way."

They retraced their steps back toward the kitchen and down a different corridor.

"Just for the record," he added, "I like you a lot, too."

The garage was protected by the same high-quality security system that was wired throughout the rest of Amber's castle. There were no windows, so Amber's overly enthusiastic fan either had to have wandered in from the street, or come in through the house.

Wes pushed the button for one of the automatic door openers to verify that, yes, the garage doors were built right into the stone wall that surrounded the place. Although there was a gate and a driveway in the front of the house, he suspected that was mostly used for limousines.

He pushed the button again, and the door slid back down.

Like everything else in the house, the garage was spacious, with three bays. Each was filled, and filled very nicely, with a Mazaradi, a Porsche and a vintage 1966 Triumph Spitfire — be still his heart.

Two regular doors led into the house — one was the door Wes and Britt had come through, from the kitchen, and the other . . . He opened it.

"Jeez, this place is freaking huge."

Britt looked over his shoulder. "Ah," she said. "It's the laundry-slash-ballroom. Of course."

The laundry room had stairs leading down into the basement — an enormous, cool concrete area, complete with a wine cellar.

It took a while, but Wes checked the windows, making sure the security system was hooked into them all, as Brittany trailed after him.

Everything was kosher. All the windows were secure.

"Do you really think a grown man could fit through those tiny windows?" Brittany asked.

"I could fit," he told her.

"Yeah, but you're . . . in really good shape. Anyone with a tummy is going to get stuck."

He looked at her. "You were going to say *little*, weren't you? Don't worry, it doesn't bother me."

"I don't think you're little," she told him.

"I think you're just . . . more compact than most men."

Wes laughed at that. "My father's a real giant," he told her. "He's six foot four. My little sister Colleen is big, too. She's actually taller than me. So's my brother Frank. As luck would have it, I took after my mother's side of the family. The elfin side. We're short, but we're fast and we're tough."

"It bothers you, doesn't it?"

Yes. "Of course not. I mean, sure, it took me a few years to recover from the shock when I stopped growing but Colleen didn't. And I've gotten into more than my share of fights through the years, you know, proving what a tough guy I am despite my lack of height and . . ."

Brittany was just looking at him. He'd told her the truth about Lana, for crying out loud.

"Yeah," he admitted. "It sometimes bothers me — it was just a genetic crapshoot, that I should be short and Colleen should be tall, you know?"

"Yeah, I do. I used to hate the fact that Melody was so much prettier than me," Brittany told him. "I love her dearly, of course, but even now I sometimes get envious. It's all part of being human — the envy. I don't pay it too much attention, because I'm at the point in my life where I really do happen to like myself just the way I am. But it's like a holdover from when I was a teenager, when I hadn't accepted yet that there were things out of my control. I mean, yeah, I could get a nose job, but why? I'm really glad now that I didn't."

"You have a great nose," he told her.

"Thank you." She smiled at him. "It's pointy, but thank you."

"I happen to like pointy," he said.

Her smile got wider. "And I happen to like compact."

Bare bulbs lit the basement, but they didn't light it very well. Shadows loomed in the dimness. Shadows and intriguing possibilities.

But the last time this woman had had casual sex, she'd told him that she'd cried afterwards — for days.

"God, I want a cigarette," Wes blurted. No, what he really wanted was to close the distance between himself and Britt, take her into his arms and kiss the hell out of her.

"Well, you can't have one." She started for the stairs. "What's the next step in this investigation, Mr. Holmes?"

"I have to talk to Amber, find out if her alarm system was completely on, on the day that guy got into her garage. It's possible she shunted the system — you know, had it only partly on, bypassing, say, the patio door," Wes said as he followed Brittany back into the kitchen. "It'd be a piece of cake for someone to climb the wall, get into the yard

83

and hang out and watch to see if a door or window is left open so they can sneak in when Amber goes out."

She stopped just short of the doors that led outside. "You know, Sherlock, if you're right about people being able to hop over the wall — and I'm not convinced you are because I sure couldn't do it — this place is big enough that your guy could have sneaked in while Amber was home. She never would've known."

"Yeah, you're right."

"Which is kind of scary, huh?"

"Kind of."

"You better go talk to her," Brittany told him. "I think it would be a good idea for her to make sure her alarm system is on all the time. No shunting. Even when her house-keeper's here."

"Aye-aye, Captain Evans," Wes said. "But you better come with me, because once I step out that door, I'm sharkbait."

Brittany laughed. "Shall I try to look enormously satisfied — like we just had a quickie in the closet?"

Wes laughed, too, as he put his arm around her waist, pulling her so that their hips were touching. "Just stay close and, you know, run your fingers through my hair every now and then as you gaze at me adoringly."

She reached up to push his hair back from his face, her fingers gentle and her eyes suddenly so soft. "How's that?" she whispered.

As he looked down at her, his heart was actually in his throat. When was the last time that had happened?

She was standing close enough to kiss and for about a half a second he was toast. He was going to kiss her. He had to kiss her — forget about all of his reservations.

But then the corner of her mouth quirked up, as if she were trying to hide a smile, and failing.

And he knew she was just pretending. This was just a game she was playing. They were playing. He was playing it, too.

"That's pretty damn perfect," he managed to say instead of kissing her. "Let's go find Amber."

Chapter 6

Amber Tierney didn't take her sister's — and Wes's — concerns very seriously.

She was even prettier up close and in person then she was on TV, all cascading red curls and bright green eyes and a face that was nearly a perfect oval. As Britt watched Amber talk to Wes, she found herself wondering about Lana. If she looked anything like Amber, was it any surprise Wes was ga-ga over her?

Lana-the-Bitch. That was how Britt had started thinking of her. Lana-the-Bitch had a husband who was nicknamed Wizard. Wizard-the-Loser. Lana-the-Bitch knew Wizard-the-Loser was unfaithful, but instead of dumping the chump, she instead boosted her self-esteem by telling another man — Wes — to jump through hoops for her.

Well, okay, maybe she should cut Lana a little slack. Brittany knew how awful it had been to find out that That-Jerk-Quentin was cheating on her. There had definitely been a time of uncertainty, when she'd been paralyzed and unable to take action. True, with Britt it had only lasted about twenty minutes, but some women spent weeks or even months going through all the different phases of a dying relationship.

Denial. Anger. Grief. Acceptance. More anger.

Although it sure seemed as if Lana-the-Bitch had settled on acceptance a little too early in the process — like, she'd accepted her husband's philandering. And instead of the relationship dying, her own self-respect had gone belly-up.

"I remember that the door from the garage to the kitchen was locked," Amber said, her attention flitting to some new guests who'd just arrived. She stood on her tiptoes and waved. "Carrie! Bill! I'll be right with you." She turned back to Wes. "I really don't have time to talk about this right now."

"I think you might want to consider adding some kind of security team to your staff," Wes suggested. "Maybe just as a temporary thing."

"You mean bodyguards?" Amber widened her eyes and laughed. "Look, I'm at the studio, I'm on set or I'm here at home. I don't have time to go anywhere, and I really don't think I need a bodyguard to go from my bedroom to my kitchen."

"You may not need a bodyguard," Brittany said, "but you probably could use a Sherpa."

Amber didn't hear her because she'd already scurried off to air kiss Carrie and Bill, but Wes did.

He laughed, but it turned rueful very quickly as he watched Amber head for the bar, arm in arm with her latest guests.

"I'm going to have to make another appointment to talk to her," he said. "Maybe with her manager or her agent. Someplace we can sit down and she can attempt to pay attention to me for, jeez, maybe a whole half an hour." He shook his head in exasperation. "She doesn't think anyone can climb over this wall, either."

"That's a very high wall," Brittany told him. "Once you're up there, how the heck do you get down?"

"You jump."

"And sprain your ankle," she said. "Which would put a crimp in your stalking plans. Hard to stalk when you can't walk."

Wes sighed. "I'm going to have to set up a demonstration, I guess. Maybe that's the thing to do. Set up an appointment to meet with Amber and her manager and agent, here in her house. Tell her to turn on her security system, tell her to wait in her kitchen. And then I'll just blow right past the entire setup — come in over the wall, get into the house without a single bell going off. Did you know her third-floor windows aren't even protected?" He shook his head in disgust.

Brittany shaded her eyes from the spotlights that lit the house as she looked up at the third story. "Can I watch?" she asked. "Because I've never seen a man fly before. That *is* how you're going to get up there, right?"

That got the response she was hoping for. He grinned and his eyes actually twinkled. Oh, dear, he was just too adorable when he did that. White teeth, tan skin, laughing blue eyes, those slightly reddish highlights in his hair.

"Last time I tried to fly, it didn't end so well," he told her. "In fact, I managed to break both my nose and my wrist."

She narrowed her eyes as she looked at him. "Let me guess. You were ten and it involved climbing up onto the roof of your house with a cape with a big *S* on it."

"I was seven," he said, "and it wasn't a cape. It was a sheet from my parents' bed. I tied a corner to each of my ankles and wrists and jumped. I didn't quite get the results I'd hoped for."

Britt laughed. "What, did you think you'd float down to the ground?"

"Well, yeah," he said. "It always worked when Bugs Bunny did it."

One of the belly button women — there were so many of them in dresses designed to show off their perfect abs — was approaching, eyeing Wes like he was one of those incredibly delicious crab pastries Britt had taken from the buffet table for her dinner.

Brittany closed the gap between them, slipping her arm around his waist. She reached up with her other hand to play with the hair at the nape of his neck. He had lovely hair, so soft and thick. "How long was it after that before you were back on the roof?" Her voice sounded a little breathless — no doubt a result of the sudden heat in his eyes. Wes was really good at looking at her as if no other woman in the world interested him in the slightest when she was standing so close.

"Three days," he admitted. He used one finger to push a stray strand of hair back from her face, hooking it behind her ear. Anyone looking at them would think they were entirely, completely wrapped up in each other.

"God bless your poor mother," she said.

He played with her earring, still with only one finger. "I figured if I couldn't fly, I better get really good at keeping my balance."

She sank her own fingers more deeply into his hair. "And it never occurred to you that if you broke your wrist once —"

"And my nose," he added, closing his eyes and sighing.

"And your nose, that you could maybe slip and fall and break something else?"

"Well, that was the idea," he said. "To get so good that I'd never fall again."

"And did you?" she asked.

He laughed. "Well, let's just say I never fell unintentionally. Or without being shoved."

She pulled back from him. "Shoved. Off the roof?"

Wes put his arm around her and reeled her back in. "I got into a lot of fights as a kid — people thought they could push me around because I was short, you know? So I had to fight to prove I was a tough guy. Sometimes all I proved was that a five foot ten inch, hundred and thirty pound kid can do a lot of damage to a four foot eleven, eighty-five pound shrimp. But still, I usually won because I was like the Energizer Bunny. They'd knock me down, and I'd get back up and come at 'em again." He touched her necklace lightly, lifting the pendant with one finger. "This is very pretty."

She refused to be distracted. "Please don't tell me you really had fights up on roofs."

"I was a fight magnet," he admitted, letting the necklace drop and lightly tracing her collarbone, which was harder to ignore. "I managed to get into fights even in church."

"Oh, God, you were probably just like Andy back when he was thirteen. If someone so much as looked at him funny, he'd be down in the dust, fighting with them in a matter of seconds. Your mother must've gone prematurely gray." Her voice came out sounding breathless again. She hoped he'd think it was merely part of the act.

He nestled her even closer to him, and there was no longer any doubt about it. No one at this party would have even the slightest doubt that they were deeply involved. It seemed kind of ironic, because out of all the people here, Wes and Britt weren't the actors.

"Yeah, but you see, my older brother became a priest," he told her. "He got all As in school, too, so that kind of canceled out all the trouble I caused."

"I would've thought it would make it much harder for you," she said. "That's a tough act for a kid to follow. A perfect older brother . . . ? Of course it can be just as difficult when the younger sibling is the perfect one."

"No one's perfect," he told her. "Not even Frank."

"Melody was," she countered. "She really was. Is. She really is that sweet — it's not just an act, you know."

"You're sweet, too," he told her. "You pretend you're not, you try to hide it, but I think you're even sweeter than she is."

She tried to turn it into a joke. "Is that a compliment or an insult, bub?"

Wes just smiled. "You can take it however you want. I happen to think you're one of the sweetest, smartest, funniest and, yeah, prettiest women I've ever met."

Talk about sweet. He was standing so close, his face inches away from hers. Brittany really didn't think before she did it — it just seemed like such a natural thing to do after he said something that nice.

She kissed him.

It was just a tiny little kiss, the softest press of her lips against his.

But when she pulled back, he looked stunned. He tightened his grip on her as he opened his mouth and took a deep breath, no doubt to tell her she'd crossed the line in this charade they were playing, when a scream erupted from the other side of the swimming pool.

It wasn't an "isn't this fun?" scream. It was a frightened scream. And it was taken up by even more voices.

People were moving back, fast, from a bedraggled-looking man who stood near the deep end.

Wes swore sharply. "This guy's got a knife."

Sure enough, the wind blew and the light from the bouncing Chinese lanterns strung across the yard glinted off of a dangerous-looking blade.

"Someone's hurt," Brittany said, pointing across the pool, to where a man was on the ground, cradling his arm or his chest — she couldn't tell which. His white shirt was bright red from blood.

"Someone call 9-1-1," Amber shouted.

"Stay here," Wes ordered Brittany. "Don't go over there, don't move until this guy is under control. Do you understand?"

"What are you doing?" Britt asked, but he was already gone. Heading around the pool, toward the man with the knife. Of course. "Be careful," she called after Wes, but he didn't turn around, all of his attention focused on that knife.

Oh, God.

About fifteen feet away from the man with the knife, Amber was inching closer to the wounded man.

Britt started around the other side of the pool from Wes. If he could distract the guy with the knife, she and Amber could pull the injured man back, and start giving him medical attention. She had surgical gloves in her evening bag. Like most medical personnel in this day and age of disease, she carried them wherever she went. She opened her bag now and slipped them on.

"Put it down," Amber said, her voice ringing clearly. "Just put it down and then we'll talk. Okay?"

"No," he said. "No!"

Was the guy with the knife someone Amber knew? He was wearing a suit, but it was wrinkled and dirty and even torn — as if he'd been sleeping in it for about a week. His hair was a mess and he had several days' growth of beard on his face. He looked as if he'd been on some kind of binge. Having worked in hospital emergency rooms for years, Brittany had seen that plenty of times before — seemingly average guys looking like homeless bagmen after spending even just a few days living on the street, drinking or doing God knows what kind of drugs.

"Steven, how badly are you hurt?" Amber called to the man on the ground, but if he answered, it wasn't more than a whisper.

From the sounds he was making . . . "He may have a punctured lung," Brittany said. She spoke directly to the man with the knife. "I'm a nurse. This man is injured, possibly quite seriously. Please let me help him."

"No!"

Andy pushed his way out of the crowd and met her over near Amber.

"Don't go near him," she said to him in a low voice.

"Don't you, either," he countered softly. "What is Wes doing?"

Wes was still moving, slowly and calmly, as if he were just taking a stroll, toward the man — who had just noticed him.

"Stay back!" the man said, his attention now split between Amber, Britt, and Andy — and Wes.

Wes held out both of his hands, keeping

them low, at his waist. It was more of a gesture of reassurance than surrender, especially since he kept moving toward the guy. "If you don't put the knife down, someone else is going to get hurt, and I'm afraid it's going to be you."

"Let's try to distract him," Britt said in a low voice to Amber and Andy. "If he's paying attention to us, it might be easier for Wes to get the knife away from him."

Amber pulled off her shirt. "Hey!"

"Well, okay," Britt said. "That's one way to do it."

It was going to work. Wes was forgotten as the man stared at Amber's perfect body.

As Britt watched, Wes dropped his relaxed posture. He was ready to spring, as soon as he got close enough. . . .

But two of the bouncers who'd been working the gate chose that exact moment to come running up.

One of them reached inside of his jacket and drew a gun. "Drop your weapon!"

The man with the knife barely even glanced at them. He took a step toward Amber.

"Freeze!" the guy's voice went up about an octave. "Move again, and you're a dead man!"

God, if this bozo with the gun shot at the bozo with the knife and missed, he could very well hit Wes.

The bozo with the knife took another step toward Amber, and Wes moved.

Fast.

"Hold your fire!" he shouted.

He was a blur of motion as he came at the knife, doing some kind of fancy kung fu type move that, oh God, definitely broke the guy's arm.

The knife clattered to the ground, and Wes deftly kicked it away.

Britt, Amber and Andy ran for the injured man — Steven, Amber had called him.

But the guy with the knife had to be on some kind of mind-altering substance. The pain from his arm should have taken the fight out of him. But it didn't.

Brittany had seen that in the E.R., too. Men with bullet wounds that should have made them pass out from the pain, having to be strapped down to keep them from attacking the doctors and nurses who were trying to save their lives.

He charged Wes, knocking him down and crashing them both into some lounge chairs.

Britt made herself focus on Steven. Yes, he'd been stabbed in the chest as well as the arm.

"I don't want to die," he gasped. "I was just standing there. I didn't even see the knife."

"You're going to be okay," she told him as she worked to stop the flow of blood. "I promise. You've got one lung that's still working fine. I know it feels like you can't get enough air, like someone's sitting on your chest, but you're not going to die." She could hear the sirens as an ambulance approached. "Andy, go out to the gate and tell the paramedics it's a chest wound."

He ran.

She could hear the sound of more lounge chairs crashing as behind her the fight kept going. Please God, don't let Wes get hurt, too. She had to battle her desire to look away from Steven, to make sure Wes was still all right. Trust him — she had to trust him.

But then she heard a splash as Wes and the crazy man went into the swimming pool, and she knew — just from the conversations she'd had with her brother-in-law — that that was intentional.

Wes had brought the man into a Navy SEAL's natural habitat, so to speak. Most people panicked underwater, but Wes would be right at home.

The paramedics ran up, and Brittany moved back to give them the space they needed. The police were finally here, too, thank God.

She could see Wes in the pool, still underwater. How long had they been down there?

Andy came to stand beside her. "You need to take off those gloves and wash your hands."

She nodded, letting Andy lead her back toward the cabana, where there were changing rooms and bathrooms. She needed to do more than wash her hands — she needed to get out of this bloodied dress. But her full attention was still on that swimming pool — at least until Wes broke the surface with another splash and a huge gasp of air.

Thank God.

The crazy knife man was more than half-drowned, and the police helped Wes get him out of the pool, where he lay coughing and sputtering as they handcuffed him.

Wes pushed himself out of the pool in one athletic motion. He was dripping wet and his uniform clung to him.

As Brittany watched him, he looked around and registered the fact that Steven was being taken out on a stretcher. He saw Amber, who came toward him, her shirt back on. But he kept looking, scanning the crowd until . . .

Bingo. He relaxed visibly as he found her and Andy.

She held up her gloved hands, and pointed to the cabana.

He nodded, then turned to listen to whatever it was Amber was saying.

"Do me a favor?" Britt asked Andy. "Go see if Amber has any clothes in my size. I doubt it because she's much smaller than me, but I'd love it if I didn't have to wear this dress home."

Andy nodded. "You were great, Mom. And Wes . . . Man, he's, um, he's pretty impressive." He cleared his throat. "I couldn't help but notice that you and he have, uh . . . Well, I just want you to know that I think it's great. Honest. I know I've teased you a lot about, you know, when are you going to get me a dad and all that, but I wasn't serious. I just . . . I want you to be happy, and it sure seems like this guy makes you smile, so . . ."

Oh, dear. "Andy, we were just pretending. He gets hit on when he wears his uniform, and believe it or not, he's not interested in mindless sex."

"He is interested in you," Andy told her. "If you want to call it pretending, that's fine. If that's how you want to deal with it, but . . . he's not pretending. You should see him look at you, Britt. That's not make-believe."

She sighed. "Andy . . ."

"Get washed up," Andy told her. "I'll check with Amber about some clothes."

Oh, dear.

Brittany took off her gloves with a snap and washed her hands and arms with lots of soap.

Andy was going to be disappointed when Wes went back to San Diego.

He wasn't the only one.

"Brittany, you still in here?" Wes called as

he went into the cabana, pulling off his soggy jacket.

Amber's bathhouse was the size of a small country, and it was set up like a locker room in a really tony health club. There were big mirrors on walls that were painted in the colors of the southwest. The toilets were in individual rooms, and there were separate areas for changing, as well as a room-size closet that held bathrobes and bathing suits of all shapes and sizes.

There was a row of sinks, and inside of one, soaking in water, was Brittany's dress.

God, what a shame. It was a great dress, but in his experience, blood didn't wash out very easily.

However, if her dress was here, that meant she was wearing . . . ?

Hmmm.

Wes could hear the sound of water running, and he unbuttoned his wet shirt as he headed toward it on shoes that squished.

This was definitely going to be interesting.

She'd kissed him. It wasn't a very big kiss, sure, but she *had* kissed him. Unfortunately — or maybe fortunately — he hadn't gotten a chance to kiss her back. He'd been about to, though. He'd been that close to covering her mouth with his and kissing the hell out of her.

There was one central shower room in this cabana, with lots of stalls. They were separated from the main part of the room by shower curtains. He stopped in the open archway. "Britt?"

"I'm in the shower," she called out. "There were bathrobes a-plenty, and my dress was worse than I thought, so . . ."

"Are you okay?" he asked.

"Yes, I am, thanks."

Can I come in to make absolutely sure? He clenched his teeth over the words.

"I'm a little off balance, though, and very, very grateful that Andy wasn't standing over where Steven was when this guy pulled out that knife. Can you imagine, just standing there at a party and suddenly . . . whammo. Stabbed in the chest." Brittany poked her head out from behind the curtain, giving him just a flash of her bare shoulder. "Are you okay?"

He must've been staring at her stupidly, because she added, "Are you hurt?"

"Uh, no," he said. "No, I'm . . . a little off balance, too, I guess."

"That was some fancy move you did, Jackie Chan, getting him to drop that knife," she told him with one of those million-watt smiles.

He laughed. "Yeah, well, it was actually pretty sloppy. Jackie would have been appalled. But it got the job done."

"Are you really all right?" Her eyes skimmed his body, lingering on the open front of his shirt and his bare chest beneath. She frowned. "God, you're going to get some bruise."

He looked down, and sure enough, there was a purple mark forming right beneath his ribs on his right side. And here he'd thought she'd been ogling his ripped physique.

"You didn't even know that was there, did you?" she accused him.

"It doesn't hurt."

"It's going to."

"Nah. I've had worse."

"Take off your shirt," she ordered him.

Wes laughed. "What are you going to do, give me a physical right here?"

"I want to make sure you're okay," she said. "I *am* a nurse."

"You're a naked nurse," he pointed out. He peeled his shirt off his arms. "You want to check me out? I'll come in there and you can check me out. That way I can check you out, too, make sure you're really all right."

"I'm not the one who was wrestling with a lunatic." There was a flush of pink on her cheeks. "Besides, after Amber did her little show-and-tell, I've pretty much decided that no one's ever going to see me naked again. Wait a sec," she ordered him and snapped the curtain shut.

The water ran for a few more seconds and then went off. The towel that was hanging over the curtain rod disappeared as Britt said, "Seriously though, I thought she was very brave. I've decided it's okay if you marry her."

Wes laughed as the curtain opened with a screech.

"Follow me," Brittany commanded, as if she were wearing an admiral's uniform instead of a towel that just barely managed to cover her.

"I don't want to marry her."

"Well, that's your loss, then. She's beautiful and she's courageous."

"Not to mention rich."

"There you go. And she's definitely your type. I bet we could get her to dance on a table with very little effort. She obviously has no trouble with the naked part."

"I still think I'll pass, thanks."

Wes trailed her back to the room with the bathing suits and bathrobes hanging in it, watching water drip from her hair onto her shoulders as they went. She had incredible shoulders and gorgeous legs and . . . .

She took a terrycloth bathrobe from one of the hooks and put it on. With her back to him, she slipped out of her towel, and fastened the front of the robe. It went all the way down to her calves and completely covered her shoulders. What a shame. Although he still could get quite a bit of mileage out of the fact that she was naked beneath that robe.

As he watched, she rummaged through the drawers and pulled out a bathing suit, tossing it to him. "Put this on, hero-man. Andy checked with Amber's housekeeper and all these suits are up for grabs. There are T-shirts in one of the drawers, too."

Wes draped his wet jacket and shirt over a bench and started to unfasten his pants. "So the good news is that I won't be needing to make any additional demonstrations about the ineffectiveness of that wall in keeping anyone out," he told her.

Obviously, she hadn't expected Wes to drop trou right there. "Oh?" she asked as she turned her back to him, looking through the women's bathing suits as if they were tremendously interesting.

"This guy got into the party by hopping the wall," he told her as he kicked off his shoes and peeled off his socks. "The police already found part of his jacket — it caught on one of the spikes and tore on his way over. Amber is now convinced that she needs additional security."

"But at least this guy is in custody now," Brittany said. "Right? I mean, I know there's still a threat from all the other crazies out there, but —"

"This isn't the guy we were worried about," Wes told her as he stepped out of his pants.

"It's not?" In her surprise, she turned to face

him, but then quickly turned around again.

Wes caught sight of himself in one of the mirrors on the wall. His boxers were white — they had to be under his uniform's white pants — and when they were wet they became pretty damn transparent. He quickly skimmed them off and pulled on the bathing suit she'd given him.

"Are you saying that this guy isn't the guy who was in Amber's garage that day?" Brittany asked.

"Apparently not. She says she's never seen tonight's guy before in her life. You can turn around now," he said. "I mean, you could've turned around before. You're a nurse, right? What haven't you seen before?"

Brittany came toward him, her eyes narrowing as she caught sight of another bruise that was forming on his left thigh. He'd hit one of those lounge chairs and was pretty sure he broke it. The chair, that is. Not his leg. It took a lot more than that to break a Skelly's leg.

But, "This one hurts," he admitted.

"Turn around."

He obeyed. "My shoulders feel a little rug burned. I landed on my back on the concrete a few times and skidded, you know? That guy was a effin' maniac, and he had a few pounds on me, so . . ."

He felt her hands, cool on his shoulders. "You're a little red, but it doesn't look too bad. We can put some lotion on it when we get home."

God, he liked the sound of that *we*.

"You're sure you didn't hit your head when that happened?" she asked. She came around in front of him, exploring the back of his head with the tips of her fingers, checking for any lumps or bumps.

Jesus, that felt good. It would feel even better if she was kissing him when she did that.

He took a deep breath. "Look, Britt. About before —"

"I know," she said, stepping away from him. "I'm sorry. I shouldn't have kissed you. I just got caught up in the make-believe. It wasn't real — I know it's not real. You don't have to worry about that, and you don't have to say anything else."

Well, jeez, he sure as hell wasn't going to say anything now, especially not, *I'm dying to kiss you again.*

It wasn't real, that kiss. Okay. That made sense. It didn't make him happy, but it made sense.

"Do you think Ethan'll mind much if we leave pretty soon?" he asked her instead.

"Ethan?" she asked.

He swore. "Did I really call him Ethan? Andy. I meant Andy. God, I'm losing it."

"Who's Ethan?"

"He was my little brother," Wes told her.

"There's something about Andy that reminds me of him a little, you know?"

Was. He saw from her face that she caught his use of the past tense. Of course she had. He had a feeling that Brittany caught everything.

"I'm going to go see if I can set up something with Amber for tomorrow," he told her before she could say anything or ask any more questions. "If Andy doesn't want to leave now — if *you* don't want to leave now, I could always call a cab."

"I'd like to leave, too," she said. She held up a tank suit. "I'm going to borrow a swimsuit from Amber. I feel a little funny going home in just a bathrobe. I'll be out in a sec, okay?"

She went into one of the changing rooms, and he brought his wet clothes out to the sinks and attempted to wring them out.

"Did you find everything you need?"

Wes turned to see Amber watching him. "Oh," he said. "Yeah. Although, Britt said something about T-shirts." He forced a smile as he gestured to his bare chest. "I feel a little underdressed."

"Men who are built like you shouldn't be allowed to wear shirts," she said. And damn, wasn't *that* weird. Lana's little sister was giving him a definite "Come on, baby" look. She hadn't given him a second glance before this.

She led the way back to the room with the bathing suits. "Steven's going to be all right. I just called the hospital."

"That's great." Of course, maybe he was just imagining her interest. He decided to experiment. "You know, women who look like you shouldn't be allowed to wear shirts, either," he countered.

Okay, now was she going to hit him or was she going to give him a flirtatious smile?

Ding, ding, ding. The flirtatious smile won. She gave it to him along with a T-shirt that advertised her TV series.

Well, hell. Okay, he could use her sudden interest to his advantage. "So we need to get together and talk more about your security system," he told her as he pulled on the shirt.

"You could stick around," she suggested meaningfully. "The party's already breaking up."

Yikes. There was no way he was going to stick around and get cozy with Lana's sister. No flipping way. Now, if it had been Britt suggesting that . . .

Wes shook his head. "Can't do it. I'm sorry. What's tomorrow like for you?"

"I'm busy all day," she said. "But I could do dinner."

"Okay."

"Here," she said. "Seven o'clock."

"Great," Wes said. "I'm glad — and Lana

will be, too — that you're taking this seriously."

"Oh, I am," she said. "I'm taking it very seriously. See you tomorrow."

And with that, she was out the door.

"Did she ever thank you for saving her life and the lives of her guests?" Brittany asked, startling him. She came into the room.

"How much of that did you hear?" he asked.

" 'You could stick around,' " she imitated Amber. "I can't believe you said no. What's wrong with you? Every heterosexual man in the free world wants to stick around Amber Tierney, and you said no."

"I'm hung up on her sister," Wes said.

Brittany had no snappy comeback for that. She just smiled at him, but it was a very sad smile. "Yeah," she said quietly. "I guess you really are, huh?"

Chapter 7

When they got back to the apartment, Brittany made a point of obviously and definitely saying good-night to both Andy and Wes, and going into her bedroom — alone.

Andy rolled his eyes at Wes as they both rummaged in the kitchen, looking for a late-night snack.

"The baseball team's going to Phoenix tomorrow," Andy told him as he poured milk over a bowl of corn pops. "We'll be gone . . . I think it's four days."

Wes nodded as he put two slices of bread into the toaster. In other words, he and Britt would have the place to themselves. Not that that was really going to matter. He wasn't going to act on his attraction to Brittany.

Unless she came to him and told him that she knew he wasn't looking for anything serious, and that *she* wasn't looking for anything serious either and . . .

Yeah, like that was going to happen. And even if it did, man, that would make an already confusing situation even more complicated. If she approached him, he'd do his damnedest to keep her at arm's length.

"I'd like to see you play some time," he said to Andy, trying to change the subject. The kid was sitting at the kitchen table, already packing away his second bowl of cereal. He was a good-looking young man, with dark hair and eyes and a face that reminded Wes a little of James Dean.

When Wes was nineteen, he'd still looked about twelve. He'd chugged powershakes and practically mainlined doughnuts in an attempt to leave his ninety-pound-weakling stage behind. God, he'd worked his butt off to get some muscles. Andy didn't have that problem. No one could ever call him *scrawny.* Lucky kid.

"Do you have any home games in the next week or so?" Wes asked.

"Yeah, I'm pretty sure we do." Andy laughed. "You know, that's one way to get on Britt's good side."

"That's not why I want to see you play."

"Well . . . okay. I'm just saying —"

"Your mother wants us to be just friends, so quit it with the innuendo," Wes told him as he opened the refrigerator, got out the butter and put it on the table.

Andy stopped eating his corn pops. "What about what *you* want?"

"Sometimes you just don't get what you want," Wes said evenly.

"Yeah," Andy said darkly. "Tell me about it."

Wes's toast popped, and he put the slices on a plate and carried it to the table. He sat down across from Andy. "Did you get that girl's phone number tonight? She seemed nice."

"Yeah." The kid morosely stirred his cereal. "Did I really want her phone number? No. Am I going to call her? Probably not." He sighed. "I can't stop thinking about Dani and that son of a bitch Melero." He looked up at Wes, real pain in his dark eyes. "She slept with him. She really did. I mean, I was so sure it was just Melero's crap, you know? But I talked to her roommate this afternoon. Sharon's a friend of mine, too, she wouldn't lie to me. Not about something like this. And she said Dani told her she spent the whole night with Melero. This is after nearly six months of her telling me that she wasn't ready for that kind of a relationship." He laughed, but it wasn't because he thought it was funny. "I guess she was finally ready, huh?"

"What is it about guys who are assholes?" Wes asked as he brushed crumbs from his fingers. He was thinking about Wizard-the-Mighty-Quinn. Wherever the Wiz went, women fell into his lap, too. "Women just flock to them. I don't get it."

"I don't either." Andy pushed his cereal

bowl forward, his appetite apparently vanished. "I just keep picturing her, with him, in his bed. God, it's killing me."

"I know what you mean." And Wes certainly did. He didn't have to work very hard at all to imagine Lana with Quinn. He shook his head to get rid of the image. "You've got to stop thinking about it. It doesn't do you any good."

"Yeah, I know, but —"

"No buts. You've got to let it go. Move on. You know, just grieve and let go of her and . . . just move on."

Jesus, listen to him, giving this kid advice that he himself should have paid attention to years ago.

And for the first time, his own words really seemed to resonate. What the hell was he doing, wasting his life, pining away after Lana when the world was filled with beautiful, smart, sexy women who wanted to be with him?

Brittany, for example.

Well, okay, maybe not Brittany. She'd made it more than clear that he wasn't her type, that she didn't want to be more than friends. That was a crying shame, but he refused to let himself get hung up on yet another woman who was unattainable. Wouldn't that be the ultimate irony? To push himself to get over Lana and instantly fall for a woman who didn't want him?

But Amber Tierney — damn, she was sure interested in exchanging bodily fluids with him, and that was sure a nice place to start. And Britt had been right. The woman was courageous and smart — and in possession of the most perfect pair of breasts he'd ever seen in his life. Not that he'd had time for more than a glance, but maybe, tomorrow night, he could remedy that.

So what if she was Lana's sister? Maybe that was a good thing. What better way to completely blast Lana out of his system, right?

"Give yourself a couple of days," he advised Andy. "And then, you know, when you come back from Phoenix, call that girl you met tonight. Put her phone number somewhere where you won't lose it and take her out to the movies when you get back into town."

"Yeah, I don't know," Andy said. "I just . . . I thought I knew her. Dani. You know?"

"Yeah," Wes said. "But sometimes people do things that don't seem to make any sense. But it makes sense to them for their own reasons. I mean, why would a woman stay with a man who was — for example — cheating on her? I mean, after she knows about it. The best I can come up with is there's something else going on that I don't know about."

Andy stood up and poured his bowl of cereal down into the garbage disposal. "Britt didn't. She kicked her husband's butt out of the house once she found out."

Wes had to smile. "Brittany wouldn't put up with anyone's crap for a second longer than she absolutely had to." Including his own. Which was why she was adamant about keeping her distance.

Andy loaded his bowl and spoon into the dishwasher and held out his hand for Wes's plate.

"Look, Andy, for what it's worth, chalk this thing with Dani up to a learning experience," Wes told him. "But don't let it turn you into one of the dickheads, all right? Women are drawn to jerks, it might be true, but the women you want to get involved with — they're the ones like your mom, who are looking for a good man, a man who'll treat 'em with the respect they deserve. Do you hear what I'm saying?"

"Yeah." Andy closed the dishwasher. "If I don't see you in the morning, have a nice weekend."

"You, too."

"And whatever happens between you and my mom —"

"Nothing's going to happen," Wes said again.

"Just make sure you treat her nicely, all right? She doesn't go out very often. Take

116

her out. To dinner or a movie. You want to win huge points? Take her dancing."

Wes opened his mouth to speak, but Andy talked right over him. "Even if it's just as friends," he added.

"It is," Wes said.

"Yeah, right," Andy said as he headed down the hallway to his bedroom. Or maybe he said, "Good night."

Wes's car pulled into the driveway the next evening at about a quarter to ten.

Brittany sat at the kitchen table, finishing up her homework, her reading glasses perched on the end of her nose.

This was the test. This was the real, honest-to-goodness test. If Wes came in that door and she kept her glasses on, then she really, honestly didn't want to be anything more than friends with him.

And if she took the glasses off . . .

She could hear him whistling as he came up the stairs.

He sounded happy and relaxed. As if he'd had a good time with Amber. A good, happy, relaxing time. Except if he'd had a really good, happy, relaxing time, he'd still be there now, wouldn't he?

The screen door opened and he came into the house and then into the kitchen. "Hello, hello!"

She looked down to see her glasses in her

hands. Darnit. It was impossible to tell if she took them off on purpose or if it was merely reflex and force of habit kicking in. She could put them back on, of course, but what would be the point? She set them down on the table instead.

"How was dinner?" she asked.

Wes laughed and opened the refrigerator. "I've come to the conclusion that Hollywood stars don't eat real food." He was wearing his sports jacket again, only this time over jeans and a white button-down shirt. He'd already loosened his tie, probably on the drive home.

"The spread at the party last night was lovely," she protested.

"Yeah," he scoffed. "If you like food that's ninety percent air. What was that stuff they were serving?"

"They're called pastries," she told him. "They're supposed to be light."

"Chick food," he dismissed it. "There should have been another table with cold cuts and bulky rolls."

"And pretzels and beer?" She raised her eyebrows.

"You got it, babe." He grinned at her over the top of the refrigerator door. "Tonight we had a wide array of salads. Salads. I was ready to eat my shoe."

"Well, help yourself," she said, even though he already was, taking Andy's loaf of white bread, the peanut butter and the jelly out of the fridge. "We've got plenty of other kinds of manly food here, too. You know, Twinkies and Froot Loops and Cocoa Krispies and Pop-Tarts. And currently our manly man index has dropped by one, so you can have it all for yourself. Twinkies are just too manly for lil' ol' me."

"Ha, ha," Wes said as he slathered peanut butter onto a slice of bread. "You're so funny. But that's right — Ethan's in Phoenix. Andy. Andy." He swore. "I have to stop doing that."

"He really reminds you of your brother, huh?" Brittany rested her chin in her hand as she watched him tackle the jelly. "It's funny, Andy's coloring is nothing like yours or your sister's. You've got that Irish thing going and . . . Colleen's got red hair and freckles, right? While Andy's biological mother was at least part Italian."

"It's not a physical thing. It's more of a spiritual resemblance." Wes slapped his forehead with the palm of his hand. "God, I can't believe I said that. I've been living in California for way too long." He put the slice of bread with the peanut butter on top of the slice with the jelly and took a bite. "Mmmm. Finally, food I can chew," he added with his mouth quite full.

"Where are you from originally?" she asked. "Not California, I guess."

He came and sat down across the table

from her, waiting until he swallowed to answer. "Everywhere. Nowhere. I'm a Navy brat. You name it, we lived there. My father was regular Navy — a master chief. But right after I enlisted, the old man retired, and he moved the family to Oklahoma — that's where my mom's parents lived. These days if I go home, that's where I go, but it's weird because I never lived there with them, you know?"

"I can imagine."

"My dad did a tour in Hawaii that absolutely rocked. I loved it there. I learned how to surf and spent, you know, my formative years there, if you want to call 'em that. When I think of home, I think of Oahu. Unfortunately, I haven't been back there in years."

Brittany had to laugh. "When I was little, I loved all those old Gidget movies. I wanted to move to California or Hawaii and find my own Moondoggie."

"Oh yeah?" Wes said. "Well, here I am, babe." He wiggled his eyebrows at her. "Live and in person. Like, your own personal surfer dude."

"Do you still surf?"

"Yeah," he said. "Every now and then. I don't have a lot of extra time these days to hit the beach, but when I do, well, I can still keep up with the youngsters."

Keep up. She would bet big money that

Wes would leave them in the dust. She smiled at him. "That's so cool."

He smiled back. "Jeez, I didn't realize it would take such little effort to impress you. I also know how to ride a bike. And I can stand on my hands and —"

"Hush," she said. "Don't tell me about little effort. I've tried to surf. I know how hard it is to do."

"Nah, it's all about balance," he said.

"Yeah, and I was the kid in gym class who didn't travel more than four inches on the balance beam before falling on her head."

"I don't believe that," Wes said. "You're very graceful."

"I think I've got some kind of weird inner ear thing."

He grinned at her. "That's always a good excuse. Trip over your own feet and fall on your face — whoops, my inner ears are acting up again."

She smiled back at him. *Tell me about Ethan, who was your brother, past tense.* "Tell me about Amber," she said instead. "Have you convinced her to get a bodyguard?"

He rolled his eyes as he finished the last bite of his sandwich, and he grabbed a napkin from the holder to wipe his mouth before he spoke. "She says she'll get a bodyguard — but only if I agree to take the job."

"I-ee-eye will always love you-whoo-whoo," Brittany sang.

He snorted. "Yeah, I guess she's trying to turn this situation into a three hanky movie — which, incidentally, means something completely different for a guy."

Brittany hooted with laughter. "I never thought of it that way — and I'd rather not have to think of it that way ever again, thank you *so* very much." But she couldn't stop giggling.

"Sorry." He wasn't sorry at all, and she'd opened the door for more gross-out jokes by laughing like that. He'd discovered her shameful secret, and now she was doomed. Thank God Andy wasn't home.

"Frankly, she seems up for making either or maybe even both versions of this particular movie," Wes told her. "You know, wacka-chicka, wacka-chicka, 'Hello, I am your bodyguard. In order to protect you more completely I must go into the bathroom with you while you shower. . . .' " He rolled his eyes. "She was definitely all over me, all night long."

"Oh, poor baby. How you must have suffered."

Wes brought his plate to the sink and rinsed it before putting it into the dishwasher. Holy cow — a man who cleaned up after himself.

He turned to face her. "You know, I actually went there thinking, Why the hell not? Like, it occurred to me last night, you know, that I've been waiting for Lana to discover the truth about Wizard for all these years, and Christ, now it turns out she's known for a while and . . . So what am I waiting for? Hell's apparently not going to freeze over, is it? I can either spend the rest of my lousy life whining and miserable or snap out of it and go for the gusto. I figured it was gusto time. I mean, Amber Tierney — why the hell not, right? So I got to Amber's tonight, you know, after stopping at the drugstore to pick up . . . you know, a little, you know. But, Britt . . ." He shook his head. "Amber leaves me cold. She's beautiful, she's sexy, she's smart, and all throughout dinner I'm sneaking looks at my watch because I'm dying to get out of there. I don't know. Maybe something's wrong with me."

Lana was what was wrong with him. Brittany's heart broke for him even as she tried desperately not to be jealous. God, she was really starting to hate Lana Quinn.

She didn't want to think what that meant in terms of her feelings for Wes Skelly.

She stood up and opened the door to the refrigerator, pulling out two bottles of beer.

"Here's a news flash, genius. You can't just decide to stop loving someone." She twisted off the cap and handed one of the bottles to him, opened the other for herself. "Love doesn't work that way."

"Thanks," he said, lifting the bottle in a

toast. "The perfect complement to PB and J. Besides a cigarette, that is. I don't suppose you have one of them lying around?"

"Not a chance."

"Yeah, I didn't think so."

Brittany brought the conversation back on track. "Don't get me wrong — I think it's really great that on one level you've recognized that the chance of a relationship with Lana might be something of a dead end, but you need to give yourself a little time to absorb that. To let it sink in. Allow yourself to spend some time acknowledging your loss."

Then go searching for the gusto. And try looking someplace other than Lana's sister's house. Although she'd practically pushed Amber at him last night, after thinking it through, she'd changed her mind. Amber was not the right woman for Wes Skelly. Not right now, anyway. Talk about making things complicated. . . .

He'd drained practically half the bottle in one slug, and now he laughed. "Yeah, you know that's roughly what I told Andy last night when we talked about Dani."

"You did?" It was all Brittany could do not to grab him by the lapels and grill him. What did Andy say? What really happened with Dani? Instead, she asked, "Is Andy okay? He seemed all right last night at the party, and then again this morning, but . . ."

"Yeah, it's just an act," Wes said as he took

off his tie and slipped it into his jacket pocket. "He's doing a good job hiding how hurt he really is. Apparently, Dani really did get busy with that other kid, what's-his-name. The jerk from the baseball team."

"She did? The little bitch!" Brittany couldn't help herself. "Andy must be devastated." She closed her eyes and pressed the cold of the bottle against her forehead. "Oh, my God. And he had to sit on the same bus as Dustin Melero for seven hours today."

"You know that expression, what doesn't kill you makes you stronger?"

She looked at Wes. "I'm not really that worried about Andy. Dustin's the one who might get killed."

"Oh, come on. That sounds like something I might've done when I was nineteen, but not Andy." Wes took off his jacket and hung it on the back of the chair before he sat down at the table and started rolling up his sleeves. "He's smart enough to know that fighting with Melero isn't going to make the situation any better."

"He may know that intellectually, but emotionally . . . ?" Brittany sat down across from him. "Andy still carries a lot of anger inside of him from when he was little. I'm pretty sure his biological mother used to beat the hell out of him. Whatever the case, he learned pretty early on to try to solve his problems by using his fists. You and I both know that doesn't solve anything."

Wes rolled his eyes. "Yeah, I'm still working on learning that one, myself. And my parents didn't even hit me. Well, I mean, my dad sometimes smacked us, but it was meant to startle, you know, not injure."

"I don't think kids should *ever* be hit," Britt said. "I've seen enough kids in the E.R. whose parents only meant to startle them."

"Yeah, I'm with you there, completely. But my dad was old school, so . . . Still, I'm sorry Andy had to deal with that."

"He's still dealing with it. He works very, very hard to control himself, but the potential for violence is always back there. I guess it is in a lot of people, but Andy — because of his past — really struggles. He'd never hit a woman, I know that for a fact, but in his mind any man who pisses him off is fair game. I know he reminds you of your brother, Wes, but he's not Ethan. He's not even close."

"Yeah." Wes drew circles on the table with the condensation from his beer bottle. "I know he's not Ethan." He looked up at Brittany, his eyes somber. "I do know that."

She wanted to reach for his hand, but she didn't dare. "When did he die?" she asked softly.

He turned his attention to his beer bottle, his fingers fidgeting with the label, peeling it off in strips. He was silent for such a long time, she thought he simply wasn't going to answer.

"It was right after I went through the first phase of BUD/S," he finally said. "You know, SEAL training." He forced himself to look at her, forced a smile. "So I guess it's been . . . damn — more than ten years. God." He drained the last of his beer and pushed himself out of his chair. "You probably have more homework to do, so I'll —"

"I'm done." She held up her beer. "This signifies the official end of the night's homework."

"Well, you probably have to get up early," he said as he rinsed his empty bottle in the sink.

"No earlier than usual." She stood up, too. "How did he die?"

"Car accident." He stood there, with his back to her. "He was coming home from work and apparently, there was a patch of ice. He hit a telephone pole. It was, um, pretty bad."

"I'm so sorry."

He glanced at her before putting his bottle in with the other recyclables. "Yeah, that was a lousy night. Colleen called to tell me he was, you know, dead. Jesus, it's been ten effin' years, but when I say it aloud, I still get hit with this wave of disbelief. Like, you know, it can't be true. He was just sixteen. There was nobody who met him who didn't love him. He was . . . He was a great kid."

"You don't get a chance to talk about him very often, do you?" she asked quietly.

He rinsed out the sponge, squeezed it out and started wiping off the kitchen counters, unable to stand still, especially talking about this.

"I never talk about him," he admitted. "I mean, I flew home for his funeral. It was, like, unreal. I flew in and flew out right away because I was in the middle of training. I was in Oklahoma for about four hours total. Bobby Taylor came with me, which was a good thing because I was numb. He pretty much moved me around — made sure I was in the right place at the right time. He got me back on the flight to California. He even got me drunk and started a fight with these marines who were hanging at one of the local bars — he knew I needed to pound the crap out of someone, you know, to start coping with . . . everything."

That was how he'd coped? "You did let yourself cry, right?"

Wes looked at her as if she'd suggested he should put on a pink ballet tutu and pirouette around the room. Okay, maybe crying, even over a dead brother was something to which he didn't want to admit. She hoped he had cried. Imagine holding all that grief inside for ten years . . .

"Did you go to grief counseling?" she

asked as he dried his hands on the towel hanging on the handle of the stove door.

He laughed at that. "Yeah, right. What is it with women and group therapy? Colleen found all these counseling groups out in San Diego and tried to get me to join one of them. I think I went to one meeting and stayed for like two minutes. It was so not my style."

"So you just . . . never talk about Ethan. Not with anyone?"

"No. I mean, Bobby knows, of course. He was at the funeral, but . . ." He shook his head. "Most people don't want to hear about my dead kid brother."

"I do," Brittany said.

Wes just stood there, looking at her, with the oddest expression on his face. She would've paid six months rent to know what he was thinking.

But then he turned away, started fiddling with the controls to the toaster. "It's not something I, uh, really know how to do. You know?" He glanced at her. "I mean, do I start by telling you that he bled to death, trapped inside the car, before the rescue team even got to the accident scene?"

Oh, God. "Yes," Britt said.

He shook his head. "I'm sorry. I can't. I . . . It's better if I don't. . . ."

"Was he conscious?" she asked.

Wes sat down at the table and ran his

hands down his face. "Ah, Christ, you're going to make me talk about this, aren't you?" He looked up at her. "Seriously, Britt, I don't think that I can."

She opened the refrigerator and took out the rest of the six-pack of beer. She set it on the table in front of him. "Maybe you need a little more lubrication."

"What, are you going to get me drunk?"

She sat down next to him. "If that's what it takes to get you talking, yeah, maybe I am."

He pushed the beer out of his reach. "I told you before, I'm a sloppy drunk. All kinds of nasty truths come out when I drink too much. Let's just not go there, okay?"

"Maybe that's a good thing. You can say whatever you want, whatever you feel. I swear, it'll never leave this room."

He looked her in the eye, his gaze unwavering. "I'm afraid I'm an alcoholic," he said. "I have this one beer a day limit that I've imposed on myself, but I start anticipating it and planning for it by about noon. Where'm I going to go to get it? What kind of beer is it going to be? If I get a draft, the glasses are sixteen ounces, compared to a bottle which is only twelve — but both only count as one beer, so I usually always have a draft." He smiled ruefully. "See, I'm not afraid to tell you personal things. I'm just not ready to talk about Ethan."

"Fair enough," she said, putting the beer back into the fridge. "But if you ever change your mind . . . I'm a nurse. I've seen more than my share of accident victims. I know what a telephone pole can do to a car and the person driving it. And I've seen plenty of DOAs. Most of the time they have massive head injuries. They hit and they're unconscious and —"

"He was conscious," Wes told her. "His legs were crushed though — he had to be in godawful pain."

"Oh, God." She put her arms around him, hugging him from behind as he sat at the table, resting her cheek on the top of his head. "Oh, sweetie, I'm so sorry."

"It wouldn't have made any difference if I was living at home, you know? I've thought about it enough. He had the accident a solid twenty-minute drive from my parents' house. By the time I could have gotten there . . . Unless, I was in the car with him . . ."

"And then maybe you would have been killed, too."

"Yeah, I know," Wes said. He actually sounded disappointed that he hadn't been.

Brittany straightened up and started rubbing his shoulders and neck.

He sighed, tipping his head to the side to give her better access to his neck. "Oh, my God. Don't ever stop doing that."

His shoulder muscles were impossibly tight.

"You're incredibly tense."

"I'm terrified of what you're going to get me to talk about next."

"Okay. Let's talk about something nice. Tell me something good about Ethan."

Wes laughed. "You don't quit, do you?"

"You told me not to stop."

"That's not what I meant."

"Talking about someone you loved shouldn't be hard, sweetie. Tell me . . . Tell me what he was like when he was a little boy."

He was silent for a moment. But then he said, "He was quiet, always reading — not real good at sports, like me and Frank. He was allergic to everything — I think he had asthma. He had one of those inhaler things. But he was always smiling. Always genuinely happy."

"He sounds great."

"He was. And he was smart, too. And very sweet. You know, when he was six he saw one of those Save the Children commercials on TV? And he figured out that if we all pooled our allowances, we could afford the $14.95 a month it cost to sponsor a child. This was a six-year-old. When I was six, I could barely count to twenty. But he was relentless about it. Frank was the holdout — that's kind of ironic since he's the one who became the priest — and Ethan and I spent a lot of nights sneaking into his bedroom, trying to brainwash him into giving up his allowance while he slept. You know, 'You will wake up in the morning and give Ethan all of your money.' Frank had his own room because he was the oldest. Ethan and I bunked together even though he was a lot younger than me, and then my sisters shared a room."

"How many brothers and sisters do you have? I had no idea you came from such a large family."

"There were seven of us — four boys, three girls. Frank, Margaret, me, Colleen, Ethan, and then Lizzie and Sean. The twins. They're much younger than the rest of us. They were my father's little retirement surprise — born right about nine months after he did his last tour on a carrier, right about nine months after he started working at the base in Norfolk, and living full-time at home. I was seventeen at the time — which is a really bad age to have a hugely pregnant mother."

Brittany laughed. "I bet."

"Frank caved in eventually, by the way. No one could say no to Ethan for too long. With my parents' help we sponsored a little girl. Marguerita Monteleone, from Mexico. She's a teacher now, in Mexico City. She still sends birthday and Christmas cards to my parents every year."

Brittany couldn't stop the rush of tears to

her eyes. "Oh, my God, are you serious?"

"Yeah."

"Have you ever met her?"

"No, but Frank did. He went down to Mexico about two years after Ethan died, to see her graduate from high school. I thought . . . Well, my parents decided to send her to college with the money they'd saved for Ethan to go to school."

"Okay," Brittany said. "That's it. Now I have to cry."

"Oh, come on." He tipped his head back to look up at her and smile, and she had to move back, away from him. She had to stop touching him because the urge to lean over and kiss him was just too strong.

And if he didn't want Amber Tierney kissing him, he surely wouldn't want Britt to try.

"Ethan sounds like he was an amazing kid," she said, taking a tissue from the box on the counter and wiping her eyes.

"He was." He turned to face her. "Are you okay? I'm sorry —"

"Your parents are pretty cool, too."

"They're all right. They're not perfect, but . . . They're okay."

"You should definitely go to Mexico and meet her," Britt told him with a final blow of her nose.

"I don't know about that."

"Why not?"

He was silent for a moment as if deciding how to answer that. "It seems a little creepy," he finally said. "Like, he was an organ donor, too, but I wouldn't want to meet the person who got his eyes."

Brittany had to ask. "You really don't talk about Ethan with your parents or your brothers and sisters? When you go home and —"

"I don't go home," he admitted. "Not very often."

Oh, Wes. "So you didn't just lose your brother. You lost your whole family. And they lost you, too."

He put his head down on the table. "Okay. I surrender. I think you better get that beer back out of the refrigerator, because I need all of it, right now, immediately."

Britt didn't move. She just leaned back against the counter, a safe four feet from him. "You know, I don't think that's such a good idea anymore."

He lifted his head off the table and turned to look at her. "I was kidding," he said. "I wasn't serious. I was just . . . . Let's not go any further with the psychoanalysis tonight, okay?"

Brittany nodded. "If you want, I won't keep any alcohol in the house while you're staying here."

"No," he said. "Seriously. You don't have to do that. I mean, unless you really want to.

But I'm not going to, like, go crazy on you or something. I won't. I wouldn't. Not here."

"If you really were an alcoholic, you wouldn't be able to have just one beer a night, would you?" she asked.

"Sure," Wes said. "Not all alcoholics drink until they're blind night after night. Although to be honest, I've been thinking lately about quitting altogether. Zero beers a night. See, every now and then I have more than just one. I have a lot. Way more than what you've got in the fridge there. And I get totally out of control. It used to happen one or two times a year, but lately it's been more often. But like I said, it's not going to happen here. It's not like I turn into Mr. Hyde or something at the random drop of a hat. It's something that I let happen. Kind of intentionally. Like, to blow off steam, or something. When I was younger, I called it partying. Lately it feels kind of ugly though — more like bingeing than partying. It's just . . . I'm at a point in my life where I'd rather not feel the need to get totally skunked and wake up lying facedown in someone's front yard, you know?"

She nodded. "That's a pretty mature observation."

"Problem is, I don't like myself very much when I don't have even just a little bit of a buzz on," he admitted. "I don't like myself very much then, too, but at least I don't care so goddamn much."

God, what could she say to that? "I know you don't want to talk about this anymore right now," Britt said, "but whose idea was it to give Ethan's college fund to Marguerita?"

Wes shrugged and rolled his eyes. "Yeah, okay, it was mine. Good guess. But big deal. It was obvious that it was something Ethan would've wanted to do. And it wasn't like it was my money."

Brittany crossed the room and kissed him. But it was the way she kissed Andy these days, on top of the head. "I'm going to bed," she said. "I'll see you tomorrow. And — in case it's worth anything to you, I like you very much, even when I'm stone sober. I wish you could somehow get inside of me and see yourself through my eyes."

She kissed him again, then headed down the hall, for her bedroom, hoping he would follow. Or at least stop her.

But he didn't move, and he didn't speak.

"Good night," she called. "Don't smoke tonight, okay?"

"I won't," he finally answered. "Hey," he said. "It's me, sorry I'm calling so late," and she realized he'd already dialed his cell phone.

Wes was talking to Lana. Had to be.

Brittany closed and locked her bedroom door, and went into her bathroom, terribly glad that she hadn't done something stupid, like throw herself at him. Just like with Amber, he would have turned her down.

Brittany looked into the mirror above the bathroom sink. Don't fall for this guy, she admonished herself.

But as she thought of him out in her kitchen, talking to Lana-the-bitch, her stomach churned and her teeth were most definitely clenched.

Too late.

He had her at "I think I'm an alcoholic."

Why, oh, why did she do this? Even if this guy wasn't in love with the wife of a good friend, he was completely wrong for Brittany.

He was completely perfect.

No, no, no. He was imperfect. Tragically imperfect. Any woman in her right mind would run from him, screaming.

But Britt, of course, was unable to think of anything besides how badly she'd wanted him to follow her down the hall.

Maybe it was just about sex. Maybe her body instinctively recognized that Wes Skelly would make a good temporary plaything.

Or maybe, just like with her ex-husband, That-Jerk-Quentin, she naturally gravitated toward the men who could hurt her the most.

Chapter 8

I wish you could somehow get inside of me and see yourself through my eyes.

Wes sat in his car outside of Amber Tierney's castle, eating doughnuts and drinking coffee and watching for her "enthusiastic fan" or stalker, depending on who he was listening to.

I wish you could get inside of me. . . . Brittany hadn't meant it that way, dirt brain. So stop thinking about that.

But holy God, if only she had. . . .

If she had, he wouldn't be sitting here right now with his teeth on edge and his nerves jangling. He wouldn't have woken up this morning with a relentless ache that made him wish he'd given in to the urge last night to lock himself into the bathroom and . . .

Sex or a cigarette. He wanted one or the other within the next two minutes or he was going to scream.

Of course, all he'd pretty much have to do was knock on Amber Tierney's door and . . .

And he'd instantly go cold.

No, it was Brittany Evans who heated him up.

Man, oh, man it had taken every ounce of willpower he had not to follow her into her bedroom last night — crawling after her on his hands and knees — when she'd said, "I wish you could somehow get inside of me and see yourself through my eyes."

Ow, ow, ow! He'd nearly started bleeding from his ears and eyeballs. For about two minutes, he'd been convinced that his head was going to explode.

And it wasn't just the very innocent, very unintentional sexual innuendo that had him going. Although that was certainly part of it. No, it was the fact that she freaking meant it.

The woman actually liked him.

But how much?

Not enough, apparently.

She'd come over and kissed him on top of the head, like some kind of flipping child. But God, she'd smelled so good.

And when she massaged his shoulders and neck, her strong fingers cool against his skin . . .

He'd kept himself from following her by calling Lana. He'd promised to keep her updated, and he fought the temptation that was Brittany Evans by giving her a report of his dinner with Amber.

It was kind of funny, but the entire time he

140

spoke to Lana, he was thinking about Britt. He was listening to the sounds of the water in the pipes, to the distant sounds of movement as she got ready for bed.

As she took off her clothes and slid beneath the covers.

No, there was no way she slept naked. Not with Andy in the apartment.

But Andy wasn't there last night.

Wes could have knocked on Britt's door. He could have rubbed his eyes to make them a little red, and then knocked on her door, and said, "I can't sleep," implied that he couldn't stop thinking about Ethan and added, "Can I come in and just, you know, hold on to you for a while?"

Yeah, lying scumbag that he was, that would've gotten him into Brittany's bed — where nature would have taken its course, because she liked him. Despite her "not my type" speech, she was attracted to him, too.

He knew she was.

It was starting to be this palpable thing between them. He could practically see it hanging in the air whenever they were together. If he lit a match, the entire room would explode.

Good thing he'd quit smoking.

God, he wanted a cigarette.

But what would Brittany have said if he'd been completely honest about last night's dinner with Amber?

"The entire time I was there, Britt, I was looking at my watch and wishing I was back here, with you. And when I pulled into the driveway and saw that your car was there, that you were already home, I wanted to burst into song."

Down the street, Amber's garage door went up, and Wes tried to focus his attention.

There was no one around, no one on the sidewalks, no one sitting in any of the other cars parked on the street.

But that didn't mean Amber's overly zealous fan wasn't watching.

Amber pulled out of the garage in the Spitfire. God, what a car.

God, he wanted a cigarette.

She signaled to make a left, but then changed her mind, and headed toward him.

Directly toward him.

She even freaking waved.

She pulled up alongside of his car and lowered her window.

It was just beautiful. Way to let the stalker know that, A, Wes was here and, B, she knew him well enough to stop and chat.

"Good morning," she said, giving him a smile that was quite the little invitation.

"It's probably better if you don't draw attention to the fact that I'm sitting out here," he told her.

"Oops," she said. "Sorry. I'll go. But . . . are you free for dinner?"

142

"Not tonight," he said. "Sorry. I'm having dinner with the friend I'm staying with. My fiancée. Brittany. She came with me to your party." It wasn't exactly completely a lie. He *was* having dinner with Brittany tonight. She just didn't know it yet.

"Maybe you could come by later," Amber suggested. "After."

Yeah, he didn't think so. And certainly not if he really did have a fiancée. What was Amber thinking?

"I know we have more to discuss, but maybe we could meet for lunch, maybe on Monday." He changed the subject. "You know, you left your garage door open."

She glanced back at it. "It's automatic. It'll go down by itself in about five minutes. That way I don't have to remember to push the button."

Wes just started to laugh.

Weary to her bones and on the verge of emotional meltdown, Brittany came home from the hospital to a brightly lit house where music was playing and the most incredible smell was coming from the kitchen.

Wes was actually cooking dinner.

She stopped just outside of the kitchen doorway. He'd set the table — sort of — and as she watched, he stood at the stove stirring a pot of . . .

God, it smelled like some kind of exotic

dish with curry. And that was definitely the fragrant aroma of Basmati rice, too.

"Are you coming in?" he asked, "or are you going to stand out in the living room all night? Dinner's ready."

The evening was warm, and he was wearing cargo shorts with a white tank undershirt. With his feet bare, that tattoo encircling his upper arm, and his hair still damp from a shower, he looked closer to Andy's age.

And then he put down the spoon and the muscles in his shoulders and arms rippled — yes, they actually rippled, darnit — and he looked every inch the full-grown man.

Brittany peeked around the corner before stepping into the kitchen. "Are you alone?"

He laughed at her. "Yeah, what do you think I'm doing? Cooking dinner for Amber? Get real. There're too many calories in just the smell of this stew."

"Stew," Britt repeated, still moving slowly, cautiously, setting her bag down on one of the kitchen chairs. "Is that what that is? It smells wonderful."

"Chicken, canned tomatoes, green beans and a handful of curry," he told her. "Throw it all together, let it cook for a couple of hours and it comes out great — even if you're in the middle of . . . nowhere."

He'd been about to say Afghanistan. She was sure of it.

"Did you get my message?" she asked. "I didn't have your cell phone number, so I called the answering machine here and —"

"I got it," he said.

She'd called to say that she'd been asked to put in another four hours at the hospital.

"I figured four hours was just long enough to run to the store, pick up some of the supplies you didn't have," Wes told her. "I used the chicken in the fridge — it was dated today. I didn't think you'd mind."

Brittany had to laugh, but it was a Mary Tyler Moore laugh — somewhat wobbly and sounding suspiciously like a sob. "Do I mind that you cooked dinner? Do I mind that something that smells incredible is ready to eat the moment I walk in the door? Although maybe you can turn down the heat for about five minutes, because I really need to shower." Her voice shook.

Wes turned to look at her, concern in his eyes. "You okay?"

"I will be," she said. "But . . . We had a really bad car accident come into the E.R. A minivan — a family. The five-year-old didn't make it. The mother's in a coma. I think she somehow knows and just won't let herself wake up."

"God, that must have sucked," he said. His eyes were filled with compassion and concern. But he didn't move toward her. He didn't make any attempt at all to pull her into his arms in a comforting hug.

"It still sucks," she told him. God, she wanted him to hug her. "It will still suck on Monday, too, when I'm scheduled to go back in. I really have to shower. Do you mind?"

He shook his head as he lowered the heat on his chicken stew. "Of course not." He swore softly. "Look, Britt, I understand completely if you don't want any dinner at all. I won't be offended if you —"

"Thanks, but I didn't have lunch," she said. Maybe he didn't want to hug her. Maybe he instinctively knew that she really wanted much more than a hug, and that the moment he put his arms around her, she'd melt into an emotional puddle on the floor. Maybe he was mortally afraid of that. "I'm not as hungry as I should be, but if I don't eat something soon, I'm going to keel over."

Wes nodded. "Then you better go shower."

Britt nodded, too, still watching him. If he'd moved toward her at all, even just the smallest shift in her direction, she would have thrown herself at him. But he didn't. And she couldn't, for the life of her, read the look in his eyes.

She turned and picked up her bag, and carried it with her into her bedroom, closing the door behind her.

Wes opened the refrigerator and got out another beer. He twisted off the cap and set it down on the table, in front of Brittany.

"Whoa," she said. "What about your limit?"

"It's my limit," he said. "Not yours."

"You don't mind?" She looked at him searchingly.

"No," he said. "I don't mind." There was a lot he didn't mind tonight. Like the fact that after her shower, Brittany had slipped into a pair of cut-off jeans and a snugly-fitting T-shirt. Her shorts and her shirt didn't quite meet in the middle. Actually, they did, except when she moved her arms, or walked.

At those times, he got glimpses of her skin, of her belly button.

It was enough to drive him mad. Of course it was equally maddening at times like right now, when she was sitting still, at the kitchen table.

Her feet were bare, and she wore pink nail polish on her toes. And he found that, for some crazy reason, outrageously sexy.

Of course Wes thought even Brittany's knees and elbows were outrageously sexy.

She wasn't wearing any makeup, and her hair was down loose around her shoulders. She still looked a little tired, but not quite as emotionally fragile as she'd seemed when she'd first walked in the door.

He'd had to work overtime to keep himself from putting his arms around her. But that would've been a mistake. If he'd so much as touched her, he would've gotten himself into trouble.

He would've kissed her, and jeez, she was vulnerable, so she might've kissed him, too. And instead of sitting across from each other at dinner, they'd be in her bedroom right now, naked in her bed. He would be —

"What are you thinking about?" she asked.

Oh, no. No, no. He stood up, carrying their plates to the sink. "I was thinking how badly I want a cigarette." It wasn't a lie. His desire for a smoke was with him 24/7.

"Well, you can't have one."

Cigarettes weren't the only thing he couldn't have. "I know," he said. "I'm trying real hard to be good, here."

"You're doing great," Britt said. "I know how hard it must be for you."

Little did she realize . . .

"Is it really true that you and Bobby Taylor hated each other when you first met?" she continued.

Wes laughed as he took out plastic containers to hold the leftovers. "Yes, it is."

"Tell me a story, Uncle Wesley," Britt said. "Tell me *that* story. I assume it has a happy ending, right?"

"There's really not that much to tell," Wes admitted, thankful she didn't want to crawl around in the deepest darkest reaches of his head tonight. He didn't think he could stand it, two nights in a row. "Bobby and I were in the same BUD/S class. We were assigned to be swim buddies, and it was instant dislike at first sight. I think they paired us up on purpose, because physically we were so different. He's like twice as tall as me and he weighs twice as much, too.

"Yeah, I've met him," she said.

"For a big guy he can move pretty fast — his father played football for Michigan State and was heading for the NFL when he blew out his knee. Did you know that?"

She shook her head.

"Dan Taylor. He graduated and tooled around for about a year, just kind of going where the wind pushed him, you know? And it would have to be a freaking strong wind, because he was big, like Bobby. He met Bobby's mom working on a construction site in Albuquerque, I think it was. She was his boss, which I really would've liked to have seen. She's Native American and about six feet tall herself and . . .

"Anyway, they hooked up and had Bobby. His dad wanted him to play football, naturally. Bobby was huge as a kid, and like I said, he could really run. He probably could've played pro ball himself, but he joined the Navy, which really blew his old man's mind. But he had heard about the SEALs and he wanted to become one.

"So, okay, there he is. BUD/S day one. No one knows anyone else. All we know is that this is it. We're here. We're going to get a shot at being a SEAL. We all know that most guys don't make it through the program, that most guys ring out. They fail. But I'm there and I'm thinking, not me. I'm not going to quit. But I'm also looking around at all these guys from all over the country, and I'm thinking, *Damn, I'm the smallest, skinniest, shortest guy here.*

"And see, after being in the Navy for a few years, I'd recognized that it doesn't always pay off to be noticeably different from everyone else. So I'm a little worried about that. But I'm not too worried. Because like I said, I know I'm not going to quit.

"I might die," he told Brittany, "but I won't quit.

"So I'm looking around and I'm thinking, 'Look at him. He's going to fail. And Jesus, *he's* outta here before the week is through. And oh, holy God, would you look at *this* guy. He's a monster. He's like twice as tall as me, but he's freaking fat. How the hell did he even get into the program? He's so gone in like two minutes.'

"And I'm standing there, listening to the instructors talk about swim buddies, about how we will work in pairs, how we will not go anywhere or do anything — not even take a leak — without our swim buddies until training is over. If we're swimming, we're only swimming as fast as the slowest of the

150

pair of us can swim. If we're running, like-wise. Whatever we do, we're together.

"So I'm trying to focus on what they're saying, you know, but there's a part of me that's thinking, 'Okay, I may be small, but I'm fast and I'm tough as hell, and as long as they don't weigh me down with one of these monster loads . . .' And of course they pair me up with Fatty."

"Bobby Taylor isn't fat," Brittany scoffed.

"He's not now," Wes said. "But at the time he was . . . well, he wasn't exactly toned. He was huge, he was strong, but he had just a little bit of a sumo wrestler thing going."

She laughed. "I don't believe you. You're so full of —"

"Just ask him," Wes protested. "Next time you see him. He'll tell you. He was a kid — we both were. He still had some baby fat.

"Anyway, I'm looking at this guy — you want the rest of this story or not?"

"Yes," she said. "Definitely."

"Okay," he said. "Because if you don't —"

"I do. You're looking at this guy — Bobby, right?"

"Yeah, and he's looking at me, looking me over, and I know he doesn't like what he sees either. And he says, 'You have no body fat. Water temperature's really low this time of year. Surf torture's gonna kill you, man. You'll be gone by freaking midnight.'

"So I say, 'That's okay, I'll just crawl into

your belly button for warmth, Santa Claus.' "

She laughed. "Oh, my God, you're so mean."

"Well, sh— shucks, his first words to me were *you'll be gone by freaking midnight.*"

"What's surf torture?" she asked.

"It's where the instructors send all the SEAL candidates into the ocean, with our uniforms on. The water's freaking cold, and we're supposed to link arms and just sit there for hours and hours, getting pounded by the surf, freezing our balls off. It's like an endurance test."

Brittany was watching him as he moved from the counter to the refrigerator. Her chin was in her hand, a small smile playing about the corners of her lips. God, he loved it when she smiled at him that way.

"Needless to say, my Santa comment wasn't well received. But we followed the rules. I basically pushed and pulled him over the O Course — the obstacle course — and hauled him behind me whenever we had to run or swim. He can outswim me now — don't tell him that — but at the time he was pathetic. His upper body strength sucked, too.

"He, in turn, did help keep me warm when I was about to chatter my teeth clear out of my head. And he turned out to be a better student than me. He helped me quite a bit with the classroom instruction. And as far as carrying the IBS around — we were in boat teams of about eight men, and wherever we went, we lugged around this thing called an Inflatable Boat, Small. Small, my ass. That thing weighed, like, a million pounds. I kind of stood on my tiptoes and touched it with the very tips of my fingers. I was too short. Everyone else was taller than me, especially Bobby. I'm pretty sure he carried his share and my share, too."

"So you came to respect each other over time," Brittany said.

"Nah," Wes said. "It wasn't as gradual as that. We started looking at each other differently on day three of Hell Week. The instructors were riding us, trying to get us to quit. They targeted the pair of us as losers and were trying to weed us out from the real men who were going to make it to the end. So they're screaming at us, and Bobby's getting angrier and angrier, and I just kind of turn to him and say, 'Are you quitting?' And he says, 'Hell no.' And I say, 'Well, then stop listening to them. They're the losers. Just shut them out. Turn the effin' volume down in your head. Because I'm not quitting either, man. They could hold a gun to my head, and I still won't ring that bell.' There's a bell, you know, that you have to ring when you quit. It's a major deal, like there's a little 'I quit' ceremony. You really have to want to quit to go through with it. But a lot of guys do quit.

"Anyway, Bobby looked at me and I looked at him, and again, I knew he saw the same thing in my eyes that I saw in his. We weren't going to quit. I suddenly recognized that in him — the fact that he was in for the duration. And right then, all of sudden, like whoosh, I was freaking glad — like, thank you Mary mother of God — that he was my swim buddy. Because other guys' buddies were dropping out left and right, and they were suddenly on their own, or getting teamed up with someone else who'd been quit on. And quitting is contagious, you know."

"Yeah," Brittany said, finishing her second beer. "I do know."

He took the bottle from her and rinsed it in the sink. "So we made it through Hell Week and Phase One of training, but we were still kind of tiptoeing around each other when I got the call from Colleen — about Ethan. That's when Bobby and I became real friends. He didn't need to go home with me. I didn't ask him to, but he gave me all this B.S. about how swim buddies had to stick together, yada yada, yada, and he wouldn't let me get on that plane alone.

"I was damn glad he was there. And we've been tight ever since. You want another beer, babe?"

Brittany laughed. "Are you willing to carry me to bed?"

Wes laughed, too. Yes. Yes, he was willing. He looked at her, and she was looking back at him, still smiling. But he couldn't for the life of him figure out if she was actually flirting or just making another completely innocent suggestion. "After only three beers? What kind of wimp are you?"

"The kind of wimp who rarely drinks more than one or two beers in the course of a week." She pointed to his cargo shorts. "You're ringing."

He was, indeed. He took out his cell phone and flipped it open. "Skelly."

"Wes, it's Amber. I'm sorry to bother you so late."

He glanced at the clock above the stove. It was barely even 2200. "It's not late. What's up?"

"I've been getting these really weird phone calls all night," she told him. Her voice sounded very young and small over the phone. She was either seriously frightened. Or a good actress. Hmmm. "It's as if someone's calling and then hanging up. And I heard this scary noise from outside, like a loud thump."

"Call the police," he told her. "Do it right now."

"I did," Amber said. "They came out, but they didn't see anyone or anything and . . . So they left. But then I heard the noise again. I'm not going to call the police again.

They already think I'm a flake."

Brittany was watching him, curiosity in her eyes.

"Will you come over?" Amber begged. "I just . . . I would feel much better if you came and checked out the yard and —"

"All right," he said. "I'm on my way." He'd caved, mostly so he wouldn't be tempted to stay and open that third beer for Brittany — so he wouldn't have to carry her to her bed.

God, he really wanted to carry her to her bed.

Hoo-boy.

"Thank you, thank you," Amber was saying as he shut the phone on her.

"She heard a scary noise," Wes told Brittany.

Who laughed. "Yeah, right. Twenty bucks says when you get there, she answers the door in a negligee, saying 'Save me! Save me!' "

He grinned. "Do women still wear negligees? I thought most women liked wearing big T-shirts to bed."

"I don't know about most women," Britt said. "But I happen to have a few negligees at the bottom of my lingerie drawer."

Oh, my God. "Really?" Crap, his voice actually cracked, like he was seventeen again.

"In the event of an emergency," she said, her smile widening. "That's what my mother said when I was throwing out my entire life after I split up with Quentin. 'Keep a few, Britt — in the event of an emergency.' Like what? Aliens invade, time to go put on a sexy nightgown?"

"Well, as far as I'm concerned, it sure as hell couldn't hurt."

"I should have thrown them away," Brittany said. "I'm not the planned seduction type. It's just . . . it's too weird."

What was she telling him?

"I mean, what does a guy think," she added, "when he comes over and a woman's wearing something like that?"

"He thinks *hooray*," Wes said.

"Yeah, but what if he's not into her? Amber's been giving you signals left and right, and because you're still hung up on Lana, you're certainly not leaping for joy."

"It's not so much that I'm still hung up on Lana," he said, desperately trying to figure out what Britt was really saying to him. "Because, you know, I've been hung up on her for years and I've had, uh . . . relationships with women during that time. It's more that . . . I don't know. I guess Amber's not my type."

Brittany blew out a burst of disbelieving laughter. "Are you kidding? She would dance naked on a table without blinking. She's exactly your type."

His mouth was dry and he had to moisten his lips before he spoke. "You know, I think I was probably wrong about what kind of woman my type really is." *You're my type.* Jesus, he was too chicken to say it.

"You better get going," she told him. "Amber's waiting."

"Come with me," he blurted.

She laughed. "Yeah, she'd like that."

"Seriously." He didn't want his evening with Brittany to end like this. And maybe his lack of interest would finally get through to Amber if she saw him again with Britt. "Every time I talk to Amber I mention my fiancée. I think maybe she needs a visual reminder."

"Or maybe she's been talking to her sister who knows you don't really have a fiancée."

That stopped him short. God, he hadn't thought that far ahead, but sure, if Amber talked to Lana, she might mention Wes's "fiancée." Would Lana even care? Maybe not. Probably not. She hadn't mentioned it last night when Wes called her. Jesus, she probably didn't care at all.

For some weird reason, that didn't make him feel desperate or frustrated or hurt — only strangely wistful.

It was weird. For so long, he'd been carrying this hope that when Lana found out about Wizard's cheating ways she'd leave him and come running into Wes's open arms. He'd had this fantasy that Lana secretly loved him, too, but that she was staying away

158

from him because she was a good, honest woman, honoring her wedding vows.

But she'd known about Wizard for some time now. Wes's fantasy was nothing but a silly, childish fairy tale. *And they lived happily ever after.*

Yeah, sure.

"Look, just come with me," he told Brittany now. "Help me out here. Please?"

"I love a man who cooks dinner, cleans up afterwards and says please." She stood up. "Give me two minutes and I'll be ready to go."

Chapter 9

Sure enough, Amber answered her door wearing clothes that left very little to the imagination. Gauzy white pants that were nearly transparent over red thong panties. A halter top made of red silk that was so sheer, she might as well have come to the door topless.

"Thank God you're here," she said. And then she saw Brittany. "Oh."

"Hi," Britt said.

"Amber, you met Brittany at your party." Wes draped a casual arm around Britt's shoulders.

"Sure," Amber said. "The nurse. Right. Come on in. I certainly didn't mean to drag you all the way out here, Brittany."

But she did mean to drag Wes. And his giant . . . flashlight.

"It's no trouble," Britt lied. "We were just about to go for a walk on the beach, you know, before going to bed." She smiled at Wes as she said that — let Amber think whatever she wanted to think. He grinned back at her, his hand warm at her waist now as they went into Amber's house. "This isn't that much of a detour."

"Well, thanks so much for coming," Amber lied, too.

"You really should think about full-time security," Brittany told her. "I'm sure there are even female bodyguards — if you don't want a bunch of guys with no necks hanging around, watching your every move."

Wes was holding her hand now and playing with her fingers, as if he couldn't bear not to touch her — as if they really were going to go home and go to bed together. As if he couldn't wait.

Brittany had to work hard to keep her pulse from racing. *This wasn't real.*

"Where were you when you first heard the noise?" he asked Amber.

"In my TV room," she said as she led the way to the back of the house, her perfect buttocks glowing like a beacon beneath those sheer pants. Brittany was tempted to take Wes's flashlight and shine it on her buns. It was hard to look anywhere else, but Wes was watching Britt and smiling. Probably at the expression on her face.

"Actually, I offered Wes a job as head of my security," Amber turned slightly to say to Britt. "Maybe you can help talk him into it. I'm sure you'd prefer it if he were in L.A. full-time, instead of down in San Diego."

He'd put his arm around Brittany again, and his fingers slipped up beneath the edge of her T-shirt, warm and slightly rough against her bare skin.

"Oh, I'd never ask him to leave the SEALs," Britt said. Her voice sounded breathless. "Absolutely not."

Wes was doing a really good job of looking at her as if he couldn't think of much else besides getting her home and into bed. He had such heat in his eyes. And his smile had vanished as he continued to stroke the curve of her waist.

Maybe he'd picked up on the hints Britt had dropped at dinner — especially that comment about him having to carry her to bed. She couldn't believe it when that came out of her mouth.

But after a day at the hospital, filled with such suffering and pain, she didn't want to spend the night alone. She wanted comfort. She wanted to lose herself in full-body contact with this man whom she'd come to like so much in such a short amount of time.

And he either wanted that, too, or he was a better actor than Amber Tierney could ever hope to be.

"You can't be a SEAL forever," Amber said. "My sister's married to a SEAL, and she's told me it's just a matter of time before he gets too old to go running around in the jungle or whatever it is that he does, saving the world. She said it's a young man's game."

"She's right," Wes said. "Eventually, I'll get too old to keep up with the new guys, but I'm not there yet."

Brittany gently extracted herself from his grasp. "When Wes retires from the Navy, he's coming back to L.A. He's quite a talented actor."

"What?" Wes said with a laugh.

"You are," Britt told him.

He was looking at her as if she were completely crazy.

"Okay, here's where I was sitting," Amber interrupted them. "Right there on the sofa. And the noise seemed to come from that direction." She pointed toward the patio. "It sounded like, I don't know, like maybe someone was throwing something against the side of the house."

"Or climbing up the outside? Did you get the windows on the third floor hooked into your alarm system yet?" Wes asked.

"No," Amber answered. "That'll happen next Thursday. Do you really think —"

"No," Wes said. "I don't. But to be absolutely safe, you should pack a bag and stay in a hotel tonight. And tomorrow get your manager working on hiring a security team. You know, it's actually pretty amazing that you've gotten by for this long without one."

Amber didn't look happy. "Are you sure I can't talk you into staying here tonight?" She looked at Brittany. "Both of you. I have plenty of room."

"There's no way one person could keep you safe in a house this size," Wes said. "I mean, sure, I could do it if we all camped out in one room, but . . . Britt's son is away for the weekend, and I've got to be honest — we had other plans for tonight."

Amber nodded, definitely subdued. "All right. I'll go get a bag. Make yourself comfortable. There's wine in the kitchen fridge. I'll only be about ten minutes."

"Thanks, but we'll walk you up," Wes told her. "We'll wait just outside your room. This is a big house, and I don't want to scare you unnecessarily, but until you get the third-floor windows wired, you're really not safe here. I'm sorry I didn't make that more clear to you the other day."

Amber really *had* heard a noise outside. She really *was* scared. Because if she wasn't, now was the time when she'd reassure them that she'd be fine and send them on their way. But she turned slightly pale, and her eyes got even bigger.

No, this wasn't just a ploy to get Wes over here. At least not completely.

They followed her upstairs and, after Wes checked out Amber's flowery bedroom to make sure that no one was hiding inside, they waited for her in the hall.

"I think she's finally catching on," Wes said

164

to Britt in a low voice. "Thanks for coming out here with me."

"You're welcome," she said. "Do you really think she's in danger?"

"She's famous. And there are a lot of crazy people out there. Some of them — not all of them, but some — know how to climb and could get into a third-floor window," he said. "Do I think she's in danger tonight? No. But we could sit around and talk about it for a couple of hours. And then she could call again at 0300, after she hears another noise. At which point, I'll come back here and help her get checked into a hotel room. I figured I'd skip the drama and go directly to the thrilling conclusion — one in which it's possible for me to get a good night's sleep. Or at least to have an uninterrupted evening."

Wes was looking at her again with that molten lava look in his eyes. Except this time Amber wasn't around to see it.

He had a wonderful smile, but even when he wasn't grinning his mouth was still beautiful, with lips that were almost delicate and quite gracefully shaped.

Oh, God, Brittany was staring at his mouth, as if she wanted him to kiss her. She looked up into his eyes instead.

Oh, God, she did want him to kiss her.

He smiled very slightly. "You want to help me make sure she never hits on me again?" he murmured.

Now he was the one who was gazing at *her* mouth.

"Okay," Britt told him, hypnotized. "How?"

"Kiss me," he said. "And then when she's packed and ready, she'll come out of her room and find us in a liplock. That should take care of any last lingering doubts."

"She said she'd be at least ten minutes," Brittany said. It was a stupid thing to say, considering how badly she wanted him to kiss her.

Wes smiled. "I can endure it if you can."

She laughed, and he did it.

He kissed her.

Lightly at first. Gently. Sweetly. His lips were so soft and warm as he brushed them across hers.

Britt felt herself sway toward him, and then, God, he was holding her in his arms.

"Oh, man," he breathed, and kissed her again, more completely this time, covering her mouth with his.

And oh. My. God.

She melted.

It was a kiss for the world record books — Most Romantic Kiss of All Time. Or at least it would be if it had been real.

Who would've thought that rough and tough U.S. Navy SEAL Chief Wes Skelly — a man with a reputation for salty language and a total lack of tact, a man who was known for speaking before thinking, for knee-

166

jerk reactions, for bursts of temper and lack of restraint — would be able to kiss so beautifully, so worshipfully, so utterly sensitively, and completely tenderly?

God, if he could kiss like this, making love to him would be . . . it would be too perfect. Her head would explode. Bang. Complete overload of all of her systems. She would simply cease to exist.

Oh, but she wanted to risk it. She wanted to try it and see.

Except, this kiss was just a show for Amber Tierney. And Amber wasn't likely to show up in Brittany's apartment. Although maybe Britt could use that as an excuse. *Hey, Wes, just in case Amber decides to come over, maybe you should sleep in my bed tonight. And just in case she happens to come into the room, we should probably make love, you know, all night long. You know, just in case, and just to make it clear that you're not interested in her.*

Uh, yeah.

"Hi, this is Amber." Wes lifted his head to glance toward the bedroom, but Amber was only talking on the telephone, and he quickly returned his attention to Brittany.

"You're completely killing me," he whispered before he lowered his head and kissed her again.

Was she really? God, she hoped so, because he was killing her, too.

Kissing Wes for these past few minutes had

167

been better than her entire years-long sex life with her ex-husband.

She wrapped her arms around his neck, pulling him closer. She brushed her hips against him, and . . . oh, boy.

He stopped kissing her, pulling back to look at her, and at first she thought she'd gone too far. Yes, he was obviously aroused, but maybe he didn't want her to know that, or to acknowledge it or . . .

But the heat in his eyes nearly incinerated her. He didn't say a word. He just looked at her.

And then he kissed her again.

This time, it was instant combustion. A total meltdown. He was kissing her as if he, too, had been thinking about nothing else but making love to her for the past few days. He was kissing her as if he thought he might be able to touch her very soul if he could get as much of his tongue as possible into her mouth.

Which was really great, because she wanted his tongue there. She wanted his hands on her body, too, sweeping down across her back, across the curve of her derriere, pulling her closer, even closer to him as if he were trying to absorb her completely into him.

"Whoopsie! Sorry!"

Amber.

Wes let go of Brittany so fast, she almost fell over.

"Sorry," he said, too, but it wasn't clear if he was talking to Amber or Britt. But then he definitely turned to Amber. "I just, uh, don't get leave very often and . . ."

"And Brittany's son is out of town," Amber finished for him. "You don't need to drive me to a hotel. I can drive myself. Just . . . if you don't mind, will you walk me down to the garage?"

"Sure," Wes said. He looked at Brittany again. "Sorry. I'm . . . sorry."

Was he apologizing for nearly knocking her over, or that incredible kiss?

"I'm the one who's sorry I interrupted your evening," Amber apologized, too, and it was possible that she actually meant it.

"It's okay," Britt said. She looked at Wes. "It's really okay, you know."

He looked at her, but he didn't say anything. What could he say in front of Amber?

Silently, they trooped down to Amber's garage.

Wes drove with both hands on the steering wheel, aware of Brittany's silence, aware that his immediate apology after Amber had gotten into her car and pulled out of her garage may not have been the right thing to do.

He shouldn't have kissed her, period. He should have kept his hands to himself. He should never have gotten a taste of her sweetness and fire.

But goddamn, she'd kissed him like he'd never been kissed before.

Even now, all these long minutes later, he was still feeling shell-shocked and emotionally dizzy.

And despite his apology, despite his admission that he'd gone too far and that kissing her in the first place had been a mistake, he wanted to kiss her again. He wanted to go even farther. He wanted . . .

He glanced at her.

She was looking out the window, subdued, pensive, tired. Hurt?

He honestly didn't know. She'd had a long, grueling, emotionally draining day at work. She certainly had the right to be tired.

But Jesus, what if she'd actually wanted him to kiss her, and then he'd gone and called it a crazy mistake?

Except, after Amber had come out of her room and interrupted them, Brittany had stood there, looking for all the world as if she were about to cry. He'd apologized — for what he wasn't sure. Maybe for having to stop kissing her.

Maybe for being born.

And she'd said it was okay, but she was so obviously not okay.

And she was still not okay.

And he wasn't either. He felt shaken and desperate and completely turned upside down.

Wes dragged his eyes back to the road. It

was late, but the street was pretty busy. Stores were closed, but some of the restaurants were open. And the bars were still hopping, their neon lights flashing.

Joe's Cantina, dead ahead on the right, with its colorful lights and Mexican decor, looked like the kind of place he and Bobby used to hang, sometimes all the way to last call. They'd drink and drink and drink, and then drink some more.

There was a parking spot open right in front, and he hit his brakes hard, skidding slightly.

The car behind him blew his horn, then went around them with a flurry of obscene gestures and a squeal of tires.

That caught Britt's attention, and she turned to look at him in surprise while he parallel parked.

"What do you say we go get a drink?" he said as he straightened the car out and pulled up the parking brake. "I could use a shot of tequila."

She looked at him, looked at Joe's Cantina, looked back at him. "I don't think that's a good —" She cut herself off. Sat very still for a moment. Took a breath. "Of course, it's up to you if you really want to go in there and —"

"I don't really want a shot of tequila," he told her. "I want, like, ten."

Silence.

Then, "What do you want me to say to that, Wes?" she said quietly. "You tell me you think you're an alcoholic. You tell me you want to stop drinking completely. And now you tell me . . ." She shook her head. "I'm not going to tell you not to drink. If you think you've got a problem, you've got to stop because you want to, not because of anything I say or do."

"I do want to," he said. "I just . . . Right now I really, really want to get trashed." He couldn't look at her, so he looked at his hands, still holding onto the steering wheel as if it were a life preserver. "See, if I get trashed," he struggled to find the right words, "then, you know, I can say all the things I can't possibly say when I'm sober. Like . . ." He forced himself to look at her. "Like, I want you so freaking bad, I don't think I can spend another night on the living room couch without completely losing my mind."

She laughed — it was more of an exhale than a real laugh, but it was enough to take the edge off of the terror that came from having admitted that.

"I think you just managed to say it," she told him.

"Yeah," he agreed. "I did, didn't I?" He looked at her, and she didn't look as if she were about to run screaming from the car. She looked . . . glad?

"Let's skip the getting trashed part, okay?" she said, "and just go home and make love."

Her words were music to his ears. God, she was beautiful. She was only partly lit by the streetlamps, and shadows played across her face, accenting her cheekbones and that luscious mouth. Her eyes were shining, and she gave him such a smile, that for a half a second he was sure he heard a choir of angels singing.

He was either going to cry or laugh, so he laughed and reached for her, and then she was in his arms and kissing him.

And kissing him and kissing him.

He wanted to pull her across his lap, wrestle her out of those shorts and unzip his pants and . . .

He didn't give a damn about the fact that they were on a public thoroughfare. That wasn't what held him back.

It was that she deserved better than some kind of slam-bang joyride in the front seat of his car.

Truth was, she deserved better than him, period.

But, damn, her lips were so sweet, her body so soft. His hand was already up her shirt, his fingers sliding against the smooth perfection of her silky skin, his palm filled with the full weight of her breast.

She opened her mouth wider, inviting him in, and he kissed her more deeply. But still slowly. If she changed her mind, he wanted her to be able to pull back. To stop him at any point.

But she didn't. She made a sexy noise, deep in her throat, as her fingers found the edge of his shirt and she slipped her hand up along the bare skin of his back. Her hand was warm and soft and perfect, just like the rest of her.

"I want you naked," she stopped kissing him to whisper.

Oh, man. He kissed her again, but then had to ask, "Are you sure you really want . . . this? Me and you, like this? Doing this?"

"Yes." She kissed him again, harder, hotter, but then she pulled back. "Are you?"

"What, are you kidding?" he reached for her.

But she kept him at arm's length. "No, I'm not." She gazed at him searchingly, looking for . . . what? Reasons they shouldn't spend the night making love? Man, he hoped she didn't find them in his eyes.

He started the car. "Let's go home, because I really want you naked, too, and that could draw a crowd here."

"Seriously, Wes," she said as he pulled out into the traffic, signaling to get into the left lane. "What about Lana?"

"Lana who?" He didn't know this part of town well, but he was guessing they were about three minutes, tops, from Brittany's apartment. Three minutes to mind-blowing pleasure.

Britt laughed. "Don't be a jerk."

"I'm not," he protested. "I'm just . . . When I'm with you, baby, I don't even think about her."

"Okay," she said. "Be a jerk if you have to, but just don't be a liar. Please?"

"It's the truth."

"Okay, look," she said. "If you want to sleep with me —"

"I do!" *If.* She'd actually "if-ed" him. *If* was such a little word, but it wielded tremendous power. Thirty seconds ago there had been no *if,* but now there was, and his estimate of mind-blowing pleasure in three minutes was suddenly in jeopardy. One little *if* could turn a wait of three minutes into a wait of three weeks. Or three years.

"I really do," he said again. "Honest, Britt."

"Yes!" she said, grabbing his knee and squeezing it. "Honesty — that's what we need. If you want me to sleep with you, you've got to be honest. We both know this isn't going to be long term or permanent or even particularly meaningful. We're just . . . two people who like each other —"

"Really like each other," he added.

"Who find each other attractive —"

"Outrageously, stupendously attractive."

She laughed. "Yeah, but the bottom line is —"

Here it came.

". . . that we're just two people who are tired of being alone. And for tonight and the next few nights — or however long you're going to be in town — we don't have to be."

Thank you, God. Wes pulled into her driveway. "Race you to the door."

Brittany laughed. "Do you promise —"

"Yes."

"Wes, I'm being serious."

"I am, too, babe. I want to take off your clothes with my teeth and lick every inch of your body. Slowly."

Well, that stunned her into silence. He used the opportunity to pull her to him and kiss her, long and hard.

"Please just be honest with me," Brittany said between kisses. "Please? About everything, okay?"

"I will," he said, kissing her mouth, her face, her throat, and her breasts, right through the cotton of her shirt. "I promise."

"That's all I want." She laughed. "Well, besides the licking thing."

"Let's go inside," Wes said.

He kissed Brittany on each of the stairs going up to her apartment.

And he'd unfastened and unzipped her

shorts before she even got her key into the door.

As the screen slammed behind them, Wes kicked the wooden door closed with his foot as he tried to pull her T-shirt up and over her head.

Britt laughed and tried to wriggle out of his grasp, but he was persistent. "Andy?" she called.

That stopped him.

The room was dark, and she turned on the little light near the door.

"I just want to make sure he didn't come home," she told him. "Trips can sometimes get canceled and —"

"Yo, Andy," Wes called. "You here?"

Silence.

Patience not being one of his strong suits, Wes went into the kitchen and down the hall to Andy's room. Brittany followed more slowly, but he was back in a flash.

"He's definitely not here," he said, and kissed her. And this time she helped him get her shirt off, even as she kicked her sandals from her feet.

His shirt followed, although he was far more interested in unfastening her bra.

He swore. "Help me with this, will you? What does it have, a combination lock?"

Brittany laughed, stepping out of his grasp and reaching behind her to unfasten it, but then she held it on, suddenly feeling not quite shy, but not quite as bold as she had earlier, either. "You really want to get naked in my kitchen?"

"Absolutely." He laughed softly. His muscles gleamed in the moonlight coming in through the window, and he looked breathtakingly beautiful, all broad shoulders tapering down to a narrow waist and slim hips. It was amazing that there was actually moonlight to add such atmosphere to this moment. "We've spent a lot of time these past few days sitting in here, talking. I've gotta confess, the entire time, I was dying to see you naked. This is kind of like fantasy fulfillment for me."

"Well, when you put it that way . . ." Britt took off her bra, hanging it over the back of one of the chairs.

"Oh, yeah," he breathed. He didn't reach for her, he just looked, his eyes hot.

She pushed her shorts off as he watched, then slipped her panties down her legs.

"Here I am," she said, loving that look in his eyes, knowing she'd made the right choice tonight. This may not be a forever thing, but it was going to be wonderful. It would be a memory she would cherish for the rest of her life. "Naked in my kitchen. You want some tea?"

"No."

"What? You mean, that's not part of the fantasy?"

He laughed. "Nope."

"How about hot sex on the kitchen table?"

"Yup," he said, slowly reaching out to touch her. Her hair, her cheek, her shoulder. He ran his fingers lightly down her arm, and then over to her breast. The way he was looking at her made her feel impossibly sexy. "But later. First I want to make love to you in your bedroom, in your bed. You know, I've spent a lot of time dreaming about that, too."

Brittany reached for the button that fastened his shorts, touching him the same way he was touching her — lightly, with only the tips of her fingers. The zipper didn't go down easily, and she looked up at him and smiled.

And he kissed her — one of those impossibly tender kisses that he did so well.

She melted, closing the gap between them, and he drew her in, sighing his pleasure at the sensation of her body against his, her breasts against his chest.

There was more urgency to his kisses now, or maybe he was just responding to the way she was kissing him, holding him, touching him.

His hands were everywhere, sweeping her body, touching, exploring, as he kissed her, licked her, tasted her.

More, more, more. She wanted more. She wanted . . .

He knew. And he picked her up, her waist

at his shoulder, his hands on her bare butt as he carried her into her bedroom.

It was so much the opposite of that first sweet kiss they'd shared, that Brittany had to laugh. It was . . . so Neanderthal, and almost shockingly politically incorrect. And yet it was a total turn-on.

Maybe it was because physically, Wes wasn't any kind of a real, hulking caveman, and she wasn't a lightweight in any sense of the word. Yet he carried her so effortlessly.

But the tenderness was back as he carefully lowered her to her bed, which was also a turn-on, especially when he took a moment and let himself look at her, and let her see the desire in his pretty blue eyes.

She was the one who reached for him and finally pulled off his shorts.

He had nothing on underneath.

And so much for that cruel myth about short men . . .

"Gee," she said, "I was so anticipating finding out whether you wore boxers or briefs."

"Laundry crisis," he told her with a grin that made her heart flop around in her chest as he joined her on the bed.

He kissed her and she kissed him, too, reaching for him, wrapping her fingers around him. He was solid and smooth and so incredibly male.

He laughed.

"What?" she asked.

He lifted his head to look down at her. "I'm having one of those 'This can't be real' moments," he said. "You really want honest?"

She nodded, her heart in her throat.

"I feel like I'm getting away with something here. I've talked more with you than any woman I've ever known, and you still want to make love to me. I mean, I didn't have to pretend to be someone I'm not to get you to sleep with me."

His honesty would have been breathtaking even if he'd stopped right there. But he kept going.

"For the first time in my life," he told her, struggling to find the right words, "I don't have to worry about, I don't know, what to say or what not to say. I can say whatever I want, you know? Because I know that you already like me enough not to run away if I say something really stupid or . . . wrong."

Brittany touched his face. "I don't just like you, sweetie. I think you're wonderful."

"I think you're pretty wonderful, too, babe."

And there they were, smiling at each other, like a couple of kids at the ninth grade dance.

Except they were naked and in her bed.

"I want to make you feel good tonight," he told her with a smile that made her heart do another somersault. He lowered his head to kiss her and as his mouth met hers, her heart did an entire circus act.

And oh, no. No, no. She couldn't let herself fall in love with this man. Oh God, wouldn't that be a mistake.

Too bad it was too late.

That was ridiculous. Of course it wasn't too late. She'd barely known the guy — what was it now? Four days?

And yet here she was — in bed with him. After only four days. What did she think that meant?

Nothing. It meant nothing. It meant that she was a woman with a woman's needs and desires and it had been much too long since she'd last had a sexual relationship. It meant that she was human. It meant that she liked Wes.

Liked?

Yes. And, oh man oh man, she certainly liked what he was doing to her. She heard him laugh softly as she moaned. He held her shoulders down, keeping her from pulling him on top of her as he kissed and licked his way from her breasts to her belly button.

"Please!" she gasped. "Do you have a condom?"

"I do," he said. "It's on your bedside table. But I wasn't kidding when I told you I wanted to lick every inch of your body."

"Oh," Brittany said. "God. Can we add that to the 'Later' list, you know, along with the kitchen table? Because I haven't made love since about a year before I adopted Andy, and that was a really awful relationship that lasted only about a week."

And it had only lasted that long because the sex was so great. After divorcing Quentin, she'd needed to know that their relationship hadn't failed because she was lousy in bed. And Kyle Gherard had helped her prove Quentin wrong. Of course, Kyle was also a total idiot who'd made Britt exceedingly reluctant to engage in that kind of a relationship ever again.

Yet, here she was, doing it with Wes.

Who was looking at her as if she'd just announced her plans to launch herself into space and orbit the moon. Confusion, disbelief, shock — it was all over his expressive face. "Are you telling me you haven't had sex in, what? Nine years?"

"No," she said. "God. Not nine years." She had to count on her fingers. "Only eight."

He laughed at that. "Only?" and grabbed for the condom, tearing it open with his teeth.

It took him about two seconds to cover himself and protect them both as he kissed her, as he nudged her legs open wider, and . . .

He stopped. She could feel him against her, but . . . he stopped.

"How slow should I go?" he asked. He was

serious. "I don't want to hurt you, baby. I mean, if it's been eight years . . ."

In less than a heartbeat, she pushed him off of her, rolled him over, onto his back and straddled him, driving him deeply inside of her.

The burst of pleasure was so intense, she heard herself cry out.

"Sorry," she gasped, moving on top of him slowly at first, loving the way he filled her. "Sorry. I didn't mean to . . . I just needed . . ."

He was laughing. "Do you hear me complaining? I don't think so."

"Oh, Wes, this feels so good."

"Yeah," he breathed. "Oh, yeah. I guess it's like riding a bicycle, huh?"

"Believe me, this is better than riding a bicycle."

He laughed. "I meant, it's something that you just don't forget how to do."

"I want to do this all night," Brittany said. "Can we do this all night?"

His smile was so beautiful as he sat up to hold her in his arms, to kiss her breasts, to draw her into his mouth and tease her with his tongue and lips. "I vote for all weekend."

"All month," she gasped.

"All year," he agreed, pulling her head down so he could kiss her mouth.

Seconds, minutes, hours — Brittany had no idea how much time passed as they moved together, touching, kissing, stroking, loving.

Loving.

She pushed his shoulders back against the bed then sat up straight, so he could fill her even more completely.

He held her gaze as she moved, faster now. She could tell from the way he was breathing that he was close to his release.

The phone rang, but neither of them made the slightest move to stop, neither so much as looked away from each other.

In the kitchen the answering machine picked up. "You've reached Britt and Andy. Leave a message at the beep."

"Hey, Britt, it's Mel," her sister's voice came through on the answering machine speaker. "I'm just calling to see how your dinner went — your date with Wes Skelly. Call me back and tell me everything, okay?"

Wes laughed at that, his eyes sparkling. "Not everything, I hope."

Britt laughed, too, and reached behind her to touch him. Oh, he liked that. Very much. Maybe a little too much.

"Whoa," he gasped. "Wait, baby. Brittany. Britt . . ."

She exploded with a cry, and he was right behind her, bucking beneath her as his world crashed into a million tiny pieces, too, as his life surely fragmented, as it flew apart and spun around, before slowly coming back together again, in one piece. Like her, he was irrevocably changed.

Wes pulled her down and held her tightly, her breasts against the solidness of his chest, as he kissed her.

Tenderly.

As if she'd just given him the sweetest gift he'd ever received.

"You're incredible, Britt," he whispered.

She lifted her head to smile at him, loving his eyes, the lean line of his face, even the slight stubble on his chin.

"Okay," she said, "I think I'm ready for the licking thing now. I mean, feel free to take as long a break as you need, of course, but —"

He tickled her.

She shrieked and rolled off of him, but he quickly pinned her to the bed.

Holding her gaze, he lowered his head and licked her. From her breast all the way to her ear.

Brittany shivered and he grinned.

"I don't need a break," he said. "Like I told you, I'm going to make love to you all weekend long." He kissed her mouth so sweetly. She would never get used to that. Not in a weekend, not in a lifetime. How did he manage to be so incredibly gentle? "You just tell me what you want and when you want it," he told her. "Okay?"

She nodded again, her heart going through its gymnastic routine as he gave his full attention to her collarbone.

She was such a fool. Great sex did not equal love. So this guy was good in bed, so what?

He was more than good in bed. He was smart and funny and sweet. But just because she thought that, didn't mean she was in love with him.

Yeah, right.

Hearts could pound and do flips because of attraction and lust.

And yes, she lusted after him. Definitely.

She liked him, too. A lot. An awful lot.

But it wasn't love.

She'd be a fool to fall in love with Wes Skelly, because he loved somebody else.

Chapter 10

The phone rang.

Again.

Wes turned to look at Brittany, who was sleeping amidst the rumpled sheets and blankets, her hair a cloud of gold on the pillow, one gorgeous leg thrown across him.

"You ever going to answer the phone again?" he asked her.

She opened her eyes and looked at him. And smiled. "Hello."

He smiled back at her. "Yeah, that's what you're supposed to say *after* you pick up the phone." He ran his hand from her shoulder to her tush and back up again. And down again. Her skin was so soft and smooth. He could touch her like this for hours and be completely entertained.

The answering machine clicked on, but then clicked off as whoever was calling hung up. He'd picked up the phone a few times when Brittany was sleeping, but whoever it was had hung up as soon as he'd said hello.

"Only person I want to talk to right now is

here, in bed with me," she told him, her smile getting even warmer. She stretched and snuggled closer to him. Man, she killed him. Continuously. "Did you have a nice nap?"

"I didn't nap. I ran to the store — after I finally wore you out."

She laughed. "If you honestly think you've worn me out . . ."

"Yeah?" Wes said. "What? I think you're going to have to prove that I haven't."

"Kind of hard for me to prove it when I've already worn you out," she countered.

Oh, he was up for that challenge. Literally. "Just say the word," he said. "I'm ready when you are." He took her hand and placed it on the fly of his shorts. "See?"

"Well, well," she said. But then she frowned. "Why are you wearing clothes?"

"I told you. I went to the store."

Brittany stopped unzipping his shorts to narrow her eyes at him. "Not to get cigarettes."

Wes snorted. "Yeah, like I'd dare smoke and then climb back into your bed." Man, the way she touched him . . . "I went to the store to deal with my other addiction."

She kissed him and then looked up at him, all big blue eyes and that not-so-innocent smile. "Which is . . . ?"

"You," he somehow managed to say. "I'm completely addicted to you. I got us more condoms."

"Good," she said and kissed him again as he ran his fingers through her hair.

Yes, this was heaven.

The phone rang.

"This is getting annoying," she said. "I know it wasn't Andy calling before, because he would've left a message."

The answering machine picked up. "Hey, you've reached Britt and Andy. Leave a message at the beep."

"Mom, it's Andy."

Brittany sat up.

"Are you there? If you're there, please pick up."

She rolled across the bed, reaching for the telephone extension on the bedside table and clicking it on. "Hey, I'm here, buddy. How are you? How's Phoenix?" She looked at Wes. "Sorry," she mouthed.

He shook his head. This was not a problem. He knew she'd been hoping that Andy would call.

"I'm not in Phoenix." Wes could hear Andy's voice still coming through on the answering machine speaker. "I'm in San Diego."

"What?" Brittany said.

"San Diego," he said again. "At Dani's sister's apartment. Mom, I need you." His voice shook. "Can you come down here?"

She stood up, getting clean underwear from her drawer, and putting it on as Wes

190

refastened his shorts. "What happened?" she said. "Are you all right?"

"Yeah," Andy said. "I'm . . . Mostly all right."

"Mostly? What does mostly mean? What's going on?"

"Do you know if five days is too long to wait after a sexual assault to, you know, to use a rape kit?"

"Oh, my God," Brittany said. "Andy . . ."

"Dani was raped, Mom. She didn't sleep with Dustin Melero voluntarily. I heard him bragging to some of the other guys, talking about Dani and some other girls, telling how he put vodka into water bottles, and . . ." The kid could barely speak. He was crying.

"Oh, Andy . . ." She stood there, her hand over her mouth, looking at Wes, like she wanted him to say or do something, like wake her up from a bad dream.

He crossed the room to her and touched her arm, hoping that might help even just a little.

"*Give 'em enough of that,* he said — I heard him say it," Andy continued, "*and no doesn't really mean no.* He said that. The son of a bitch said that!"

"I'm so sorry," Brittany said. She turned away from Wes. "To be honest, Andy, I don't think a rape kit's going to turn up much evidence at this point. Did she shower? She must've showered, right?"

"Yeah, only about a hundred times."

Wes pulled on his T-shirt as Brittany put on a pair of jeans and a shirt, and brushed her hair, tying it back with a ponytail holder.

He hovered close by, wishing there was something he could do to save the day. But there wasn't. Not in this situation.

"Did he injure her?" Britt asked.

"Obviously."

She shook her head, hand to her forehead. "No, Andy, I know that he . . . I'm asking if . . . God. If he was rough. If he injured her physically, if there are any marks of violence." She looked at Wes, tears in her eyes. "I can't believe I'm having this conversation with my son."

Wes held her gaze, wishing he could track down Dustin Melero and tear his ass to shreds. But he knew that what Brittany needed most right now was for him just to stand here, beside her.

"I don't know," Andy said. "She won't talk to me. She locked herself in the bathroom. Mom, she's so messed up about what happened. She thinks it was her fault. I'm scared to death she's going to hurt herself. Please come down here. If anyone can get through to her, you can."

"I'm on my way, but first give me your phone number," Brittany said. She found a pen but no paper on her dresser, and searched frantically for something to write on.

Finally something he could do. Wes held out his arm. She looked at him and he nodded, and as Andy recited the number, she wrote it. On him.

"That way we won't lose it," he told her. "Let's get the address, while we're at it."

"You're coming with me?" she asked.

"Of course," he said, and her eyes welled with tears again.

But she brusquely wiped them away. "Andy, what's the address?" Britt asked, and as he told her, she wrote that, too, on Wes's arm.

"Let me talk to him," Wes said.

She handed him the phone.

"Hey, Andy, it's Wes Skelly," he said. "Look, your mom and I are going to leave right now, but it's going to take us a couple of hours to get there. We'll call you from the car to touch base, all right?"

"Yeah."

"In the meantime, I'm going to call a friend of mine who's a professional. She's a shrink — a psychologist who's actually had some experience working with rape trauma victims. If I can catch her at home — and I'm betting I can considering what time it is — she should be able to get to you in just a few minutes. Her name is Lana Quinn."

Brittany turned sharply to look at him, but then quickly looked away, as if she didn't want him to see her reaction to that news.

The news that he was going to call Lana.

Lana, whom he'd loved for years.

Lana, whom he hadn't thought about once in the past twenty-four hours.

Lana, whose name made Brittany take notice, and quite possibly feel . . . jealous?

Wow.

Wes had an awful lot to think about, but no time to sort any of it through right now.

"Lana will talk to Dani," he continued. "Right through the bathroom door, if she has to. She's good, Andy. She'll be able to help, okay? So when she comes over, let her in."

"Yeah," Andy said. "Thank you."

"We'll be there as soon as we can." Wes hung up the phone and looked at Britt. "Let's go. I'll call Lana from the car."

It was late, but there was still traffic on the side streets, heading over to the freeway.

Brittany sat in Wes's car, trying not to squirm with frustration. Andy needed her, and she was miles away from him. It was enough to drive her mad.

And even if it weren't enough, Wes was on his cell phone, calling Lana-the-Bitch.

God, she hated Lana more than ever now.

"Hi, it's me," he said, because of course Lana would immediately recognize his voice over the phone, even after midnight on a Saturday night.

Maybe especially after midnight on a Saturday night.

Don't be jealous. Don't be jealous. Don't be —

Well, why the hell not? Minutes ago she'd been on the verge of having more mind-blowingly hot sex with this incredible, wonderful man. And now she had to sit here and listen while his voice got all soft and gooey because he was talking to Lana.

Lana, who was going to get out of bed and rush over to Dani's sister's house, to try to help Andy's girlfriend, who'd fallen victim to date rape.

Oh, God. Poor Dani.

Poor Andy.

Poor jealous Britt.

"Sorry I woke you," Wes said into his cell phone as he signaled to get on the freeway and kicked his car up to eighty. Britt had to hang on to the handle at the top of the window. At least she didn't have to be frustrated because he didn't drive fast enough. "But we've got something of an emergency happening, not too far from where you live."

He quickly told Lana what Andy had told them. About Dustin Melero's bragging. About Dani leaving school, and then locking herself in the bathroom when Andy came to confront her with the truth.

Andy — the son of "Cowboy Jones's sister-in-law, Brittany Evans."

Boy, she didn't even rate as "my friend, Britt."

Brittany listened while Wes read the address off of his arm.

"Thanks," he said. "And we'll be there as soon as we can." He paused, listening as on the other end of the phone Lana — Lana-the-perfect — spoke. Probably in perfect, pearl-like, clear round tones. "Thanks," he said again, his voice especially warm. "I knew you'd come through for me, babe."

Babe.

Wes called Lana *babe,* too?

Oh, God. Jealous, jealous, jealous. There was no doubt about it now. If Lana were in range, Britt would have given her the evil eye. And maybe even an audible snarl.

But she had no right to feel angry or even hurt. She knew this would happen, right from the start. She went into this thing completely aware of Wes's feelings for Lana.

But hoping that after a night or two with her, Wes would forget about Lana completely . . . ?

No. She wasn't that stupid.

Oh, yes, she was.

Well, yeah, maybe. Oh, okay, yes, darnit.

God, she was a fool.

Wes hung up the phone, but then dialed another number.

"Who are you calling now?" Brittany asked. *Your other girlfriend?* Ooh, easy there. Deep breaths. Calm blue ocean.

"Hey, babe," Wes said, and Brittany stared at him in disbelief. "It's Wes. Sorry I'm calling so late. Is your devastatingly handsome husband around?" There was a pause, then, "Hey, Lieutenant, it's Skelly. I'm sorry to bother you. Yeah, I do know what time it is, sir, but I'm here in my car with your gorgeous sister-in-law and we're heading for San Diego at warp speed. Andy's in a jam, I was hoping you could go over to his girlfriend's sister's place ASAP and provide a little extra support until we can arrive."

He was talking to Harlan Jones, the SEAL officer with the ridiculous nickname of "Cowboy" that Britt's sister Melody had married.

It was Melody that he'd *babe*-ed. Apparently *babe* wasn't as intimate a term of endearment as Britt had originally thought. Which made his *babe*-ing of Lana a little bit easier to swallow.

Just a little.

She still felt jealous, but it was accompanied by an overwhelming wave of adoration for this man who was thoughtful enough to call Harlan Jones — a man Andy knew and trusted — to provide the first wave of reinforcements.

She wouldn't have thought to do that.

Wes gave Jones the address and ended the conversation by saying, "See you in a few."

He closed his cell phone with a snap, and

stuck it on the seat in front of him, between his legs.

He glanced at Britt, sending her a smile of encouragement. "Traffic's pretty light now. We'll get there as quickly as we can."

"Thanks for driving," she said. "Thanks for coming with me."

He glanced at her again. "Why is it that bad things happen to good people? Andy sure as hell doesn't deserve this. And I'd bet the bank Dani didn't, either."

"No woman, anywhere, deserves to be raped," Britt told him. "Not ever."

"Yeah, I'm with you on that," he said. "But still. Why did this have to happen to them? I don't get it — you know, the way the universe works."

Brittany watched him drive, knowing he was thinking about his brother Ethan, dead at age sixteen because of a patch of ice on a wintery road.

"I don't know," she said. "Some people flirt with disaster and walk away unscathed. Others just quietly live their lives and end up getting slammed. It's definitely not fair, but face it, life's not fair."

He nodded. "Yeah, I'm well aware of that."

And now he was surely thinking about Lana and her cheating husband Quinn and . . .

But he reached over and took her hand. "It's going to be all right, Britt," he said.

"Andy's a tough kid. He's going to help Dani get through this." Bringing her hand to his lips, he kissed her. "And just in case you were wondering, I'm here for you, too. For as long as you need me."

There was no doubt about it.

Brittany may have been a fool, but Lana Quinn was a total idiot.

"Dani's got to go to the hospital," Lana reported to Wes and Brittany. "The boy was rough with her. I haven't given her any kind of medical examination, but I think she's got a broken rib along with, well, a variety of contusions."

Britt made a soft sound of pain, and Wes took her hand. Her fingers were icy cold.

"I've advised her to have a rape kit done, too. It's important she goes to the hospital, not just for her health, but also to have medical records of her injuries," Lana continued.

"I know," Brittany said. "I've worked as an Emergency Room nurse."

"Yes," Lana said. "Andy told me. He's been wonderful, Brittany. He's incredibly supportive and patient — a real solid rock. He's exactly what Dani needs right now, emotionally. He's going to go with her to the hospital."

"I'll go, too," Britt said. "Of course."

"Well, actually," Lana said.

At that moment, Andy came out of the

back room, closing the door behind him.

Brittany pulled away from Wes and went toward him.

The kid reached for her, his face looking a lot like a two-year-old who was about to cry. As Wes watched, they just held each other tightly.

"She's amazing," Lana said softly. "You know, I could probably count on the fingers of one hand the number of nineteen-year-olds I've met who would call their mother for help. You've got to be a good mother to invoke that kind of trust from your kid. But good grief, she must've had him when she was twelve."

"He's adopted," Wes and Lt. Jones both said in a near unison.

"Ah," Lana said, in that shrink way she had of seeming to comment without really saying anything.

"Dani's getting dressed," Andy said. "She'll be ready to go in a few minutes."

"I'll go with you," Britt told her kid.

But Andy pulled back slightly to look down at her, shaking his head. He had what looked like was going to be one hell of a shiner on his face, along with a swollen lip. "Mom, she's mortified. We're just going to go, the two of us. We'll be okay. I know what needs to be done. Lana went over it with me."

"Sweetie, you're not going to be able to be in the examining room with her," Brittany protested. "Doesn't Dani know I'm a nurse?"

"Yeah," Andy said. "But —"

"I can stay with her while the doctor is —"

"Mom, there'll be a nurse in the E.R. who'll stay with her and, you know, hold her hand. A nurse who's not her boyfriend's mother. A nurse she doesn't have to run into in her boyfriend's kitchen."

Brittany nodded. "I understand. I just . . . Sweetie, who's going to hold your hand?"

"Dani will," he told her quietly.

Britt nodded. She reached up to gently touch his bruised face. "I'm so proud of you."

He touched his own lip and winced. "Yeah, well, that's the other thing we need to talk about. I think I might've lost my scholarship. I'm not sure, but I think there might be a rule or two about scholarship recipients not breaking the starting pitcher's nose."

Brittany laughed. "Thank God," she said. "I was afraid you were going to tell me you killed him."

Andy got grim. "I wanted to."

Her smile faded, too. "I know."

"He was laughing about it," he told her, and his eyes filled with tears.

Wes turned away, his heart breaking for Andy — and for Brittany, too, who would have done anything, he knew, to take away her son's pain.

Cowboy had wandered into the kitchen,

but Lana was watching Wes with her hazel eyes that were so different from her half sister's.

"Love heals all wounds," she said quietly. Her hair was brown with only the slightest red highlights. Her face was more plain than Amber's, too. She wasn't even half as exotically beautiful, but she had a genuine warmth that made her lovelier than Amber would ever be.

Or so he'd always thought. But next to Brittany's fire, Amber seemed plastic and Lana seemed cool and distant and pale.

"I don't know about that," Wes told her. "It seems to me that most of the time love's the thing that makes the deadliest wounds. I mean, if you don't love someone, then they can't hurt you when they, like, die. Or when they screw around with someone else. Right?"

She blinked. Then she smiled, her perpetual calm kicking in. "You've been talking to Amber about Quinn."

Wes didn't say anything. What could he say? *No, actually, I've known Wizard-the-Mighty-Quinn's been stepping out on you for years now.*

"I spoke to her just this morning," Lana told him. "I understand congratulations are in order for your upcoming marriage." She glanced at Brittany. "She seems wonderful."

"She is," he said.

"I'm happy for you, Wes." Her smile seemed a little forced. But maybe that was just his imagination. The tired circles underneath her eyes weren't, though. "You know, it's crazy, and I probably shouldn't be saying this, but . . . I used to think that we would get together someday — you and me. Seeing as how Quinn's such a jerk. . . ."

"Why do you stay with him?" Wes asked. He couldn't believe he was having this conversation with her here and now — a conversation he'd dreamed of having for years.

It was twice as surreal, because even while he was talking to Lana, he found his attention drawn back to Brittany, who, across the room, was still deep in conversation with her son.

"I love Quinn," Lana admitted. "I guess I keep hoping that he'll change. You know, both times it happened, he came to me and confessed and begged me to forgive him. Of course, after the second time, it got a little harder to think that he wouldn't do it ever again, but . . ."

Wes stared at her then, completely unable to respond, totally unable to utter a word.

Both times. *Both times.* She thought Wizard had only cheated on her twice.

Wes could think of seven or eight instances where the Wiz had slept with some random woman he'd scooped up in some hotel lounge. And that was just off the top of his head.

And those were just the women Wes had known about, just the tip of the iceberg, so to speak.

"It's not real," he blurted, because he had to tell her at least part of the truth. "My engagement to Brittany. It was just . . . Your sister was hitting on me, and . . . I mean, she's nice and all, but I wasn't interested in . . . So Brittany agreed to play my fiancée and . . ." He shook his head. "It's not real."

"It isn't?"

"No."

"Your entire relationship with her is complete fiction?"

"The engagement," he clarified. "Yeah."

Lana looked at him, tipping her head slightly sideways. "Do you honestly expect me to believe you're not sleeping with her?"

Wes laughed, embarrassed. "Well, I didn't exactly say that."

"Ah."

"It's, you know, casual. A fling. She was the one who made a point of setting an end date."

"And how do you feel about that?"

He laughed again, but it felt forced. "Don't try to psychoanalyze me, babe. If you must know, I'm fine with it."

"I see."

"And don't *I see* me either. Jesus."

"Dani's almost ready to go," Andy said, interrupting them. "Do you mind if we clear the living room so she doesn't have to walk through a crowd to get to the door?"

"That's a good idea," Lana said. "I think I'll just get going. I have things to do early in the morning, so . . ."

Chapter 11

"I'll walk you out," Wes said to Lana.

Brittany tried to hate her, but she couldn't anymore.

Not after meeting the woman. Not after seeing how genuinely, honestly, freaking nice she was, and how very kind she'd been to both Dani and Andy.

In fact, Lana made a point to take a detour in her direction on her way to the door. And she actually embraced Brittany, surrounding her with a faint cloud of a very subtle yet enticing perfume. She was beautiful, smart, kind and she smelled good, too. Wes sure knew how to pick 'em.

"It was so nice to meet you," Lana told her. "If there's anything you need, don't hesitate to give me a call. Wes has my number."

"Thank you," Brittany said. "And thanks for coming over here so quickly."

Andy had told her that Dani's sister was in Japan on business, and Dani hadn't wanted to call her father, who'd remarried and started a new family after her mother had died. She'd been alone for all those days. Thank God Andy had come looking for her. And thank God both Lana Quinn and Harlan Jones had been able to get over here so quickly.

"I'm available, too, if the police or the D.A. want to talk to me," Lana said. "I would love to help nail the guy who did this."

"That's not going to be easy," Brittany said.

"I know." Lana's gorgeous hazel eyes filled with tears. "I do know. I've seen it so many times before."

This time it was Brittany who hugged Lana.

They both had to wipe their eyes as they pulled apart.

"Don't let him get away," Lana said to Britt in a low voice. "He's a good man."

What? Weren't they still talking about that jerk Dustin Merlero? Or . . . "Excuse me?"

But Lana was already heading for the door.

And Melody's husband, Harlan, aka Cowboy, was at Brittany's elbow.

"Why don't you come on home with me?" he said in his cute little western accent. He'd slapped a baseball cap on over his hair, and he'd slipped his feet into his sneakers without any socks in his haste to get here. Even dressed down the way he was, with bedhead and stubble on his chin, it was easy to see how Melody hadn't been able to resist getting busy with him in an airplane bathroom — an event which had led to her first pregnancy.

Britt watched Wes follow Lana out the door, watched the way his T-shirt fit snugly across the muscles in his back, watched the way he walked, with jaunty self-confidence that was, she knew, part of his whole act. He was taut, he was tense — some might even describe him as being on edge — but she saw him as barely harnessed, limitless energy. A lightning bolt in cargo shorts.

An all-too-human man who needed a little help learning how to relax.

She could help him with that. He'd been real relaxed just a few short hours ago, in her bed.

Oh, God.

"Mel and Tyler would sure love to see you," Harlan was saying. "Of course, they're both asleep right now, but in the morning . . ."

Brittany laughed. "It *is* the morning. Tyler's going to be up and awake in a matter of hours." Her nephew, like most little boys, was an early riser.

"Mel ordered me to bring you home," he persisted, leading her toward the door. "So I'm not going to take no for an answer."

"You're going to have to," she said, turning back to Andy. "Sweetie, are you sure you don't want me to —"

"Mom," Andy said, giving her a hug. "I'm sure. I'll call if I need you." He shook Harlan's hand. "Thanks for coming over, sir."

"Any time you need me, Andy," Harlan said, "all you have to do is call."

"Andy?" Dani called from the bedroom.

"Thank you." And Andy was gone.

"Come on, Britt," Harlan said. "Andy's a big boy now. You've got to let him do this the way he and Dani want to do it. They're going to need some time alone, to talk, after they get back from the hospital."

"I know," she said.

"He told me he was going to try to talk Dani into coming back to L.A. on Monday — get her to go to the school health offices for counseling. And he's going to contact some of the other girls this guy Melero mentioned, see if all together they can't find the strength to press charges. I suspect you'll get a call from him in a few days, asking for help. But right now I'm pretty sure his priority is to make Dani understand that he's not going anywhere."

"I know," Brittany said again. "I do know all that. But thank you for reminding me. And thank you for the offer of a bed, but no thanks. Tell Mel and Tyler I promise I'll come for a visit soon."

He was frowning at her. "You aren't planning to drive back to L.A. tonight, are you?"

"I'm not exactly sure what we're going to

do," she told him, and watched as he processed that *we*.

Harlan laughed and uttered an expression that wasn't repeatable as he looked at Brittany, grinning at her like the devil. "Really? You and Skelly are a *we*?"

"Shh," she said. "Andy doesn't know. He may never know. It's just . . . temporary insanity. You know, a short-term brain disorder. Promise you won't tell Melody, okay?"

Harlan looked pained, and she loved him even more for it. "Don't make me promise that, Britt. I love you like a sister, you know that I do, but don't ask me to keep secrets from Mel."

"It's just that . . . if too many people know about it, it'll end," she told him. "I mean, I know it's going to end before too long anyway, but . . . Between you and me, Jones, I'm having a heck of a lot of fun. I'm not ready for it to be over yet."

"Maybe —"

She cut him off. "Don't say it. It's just a fling. I made that clear to him before it started. I'm not about to change the rules on the man now."

"But what if —"

"No," she said. "See, that's what Melody is going to do if she finds out. Start *what if*-ing the situation to death. And that'll be it. Way to kill it dead. She'll freak me out, and I'll start acting weird and that'll freak Wes out and . . . Give me another week before you tell her. Please?"

He shook his head and sighed. "I don't know . . ."

"Four days. Please?"

"All right. Compromise. I'll tell her, but I won't let her call you or tell anyone else for a whole week."

Yeah, like that was going to work. But it was definitely worth a try. "Fair enough. But get it in writing from her before you tell her. And if she does call, I'm hanging up."

"You know, Britt, if you really like him that much —"

"Stop," she said. "You don't think I've thought about this? Trust me, I have. I don't know how well you know him, but . . . Wes is . . . Well, let's just say that he's emotionally attached to someone else. Someone he can't have."

Someone he was out in the driveway with right now. Someone as wonderful as he was.

Jealous, jealous, jealous.

Harlan got grim. "He's attached, but he's messing around with you? The son of a bitch. I'll kill him."

"Oh, that's exactly what I want." Brittany rolled her eyes. "God save me from testosterone."

"Okay, fine. I'll talk to him."

"And the result of your little chat will be that he'll stop seeing me. Thanks a lot."

"All right, I won't talk to him. For a week."

"You can't glare at him either," she said.

"That's going to be hard."

"No, it's not. He's on leave — you won't see him for another week and a half. Just walk out this door, get in your truck and drive away — go home to your pregnant wife and son."

Harlan let Brittany pull him out the door and into the coolness of the night.

Where, out in the street, Wes was standing over by the driver's side window of Lana's car, leaning down so he could talk to her as she sat inside.

Jealous, jealous, jealous.

"I'll talk to you in a week," Harlan said as he headed straight for his truck, completely ignoring Wes, just as she'd asked.

Except now, standing there, looking at Wes talking to Lana, Brittany was hit with a wave of doubt.

As Harlan pulled off with a wave, she realized that turning down a chance to sleep at her sister's house might've been a big mistake.

It was one thing for Wes and Brittany to be together in the nonreality of Los Angeles, but back here in San Diego where Wes lived . . . Where Lana lived . . .

As Brittany watched, Wes straightened up and stepped back from Lana's car. She pulled away, and as her taillights faded into the night, he rubbed the back of his neck as if it ached.

Heartache and longing could do that to you. Make you hurt all over.

Wes sighed, a big, deep, down-to-the-pit-of-his-soul type sigh, and shook his head in disgust or regret. Brittany wasn't sure exactly which it was, but either way, it wasn't good.

He stood there for such a long time, she was a little afraid that he'd forgotten about her.

She cleared her throat. "So, is there, like, a sofa in your apartment that I could use to catch a little sleep?"

He turned to her then, and the look on his face was one of complete confusion. "I thought . . . You don't want to —" He stopped himself and started over. "I do have a double bed. Is there some reason you suddenly don't want to share it with me?"

"No," she said. "I just thought that you might not want to . . . You know, that seeing Lana might've . . ."

"Might've what?" he asked. "Made me stupid? I don't think so, babe. Come on, let's get out of here so Andy can take Dani to the hospital." He started for his car.

Brittany followed. "I wish they'd let me go with them."

"I know you do," Wes said gently, opening the car door for her. "But you can't. Andy's no fool, Brittany. He's got my cell phone number. If he finds out he's in over his head, he'll call."

She got into the car, and he closed the door behind her.

"Hey, the sun's about to come up," he said as he got behind the wheel. "What do you say we go to the beach and watch it rise?"

"Sure," she told him. "That's a good idea. I probably couldn't sleep now anyway." She was thinking about way too many things. Andy. Dani.

Lana.

He started the car and, as they pulled away, she looked back to see Andy helping Dani out of the house. The girl was moving slowly, gingerly. It was hard to tell if the worst of her injuries were physical or emotional.

Either way, her road to recovery was going to be a rough one. And Andy, God help him and God bless him, would be there, for the entire bumpy ride.

It was all she could do not to cry.

"This is my favorite beach in San Diego," Wes said as he parked, and Brittany burst into tears.

"Whoa," he said. "Hey, it's not that great a beach."

"I'm sorry," she said. "I'm so sorry." She bolted out of the car.

It was a dumb move — his trying to make a joke when she was obviously not in any kind of a joking mood.

He chased after her, dashing pretty far down the beach in the spooky, foggy light of predawn. She was faster than he would have guessed just looking at her and knowing what he knew about aerodynamics, but that was typical of Brittany. She was full of surprises. He had to hustle to catch up. "Hey!"

"Leave me alone, okay?" she said. "Just for a few minutes. I have to cry now, and I don't want to make you uncomfortable."

He laughed. "So what if I'm uncomfortable? Jeez, Britt, don't you ever stop thinking about other people and focus on yourself for a change?"

She sat down in the sand and buried her face in her arms. "Please, just go away."

"No." Wes sat down next to her and pulled her into his arms. "Baby, look, it's okay if you cry. This has been one tough night."

Brittany resisted for about a half a second, and then she clung to him, her arms tight around his neck.

He just held her and stroked her back and her hair as the sky slowly grew lighter. The fog was rolling in with a vengeance now, thick and wet and cold against his face and arms.

Britt didn't seem to notice, and he just let her be — let her grieve.

"God, you must think I'm such a wimp," she finally said, wiping her eyes with the heel of her hand.

He pushed her hair back from her face. "I think you're amazing. I think Andy's the luckiest kid in the world to have you for his mother. You know what would've happened in *my* house if I had a scholarship for college and I stood a chance of losing it because of getting into a fight?"

She shook her head.

"My mother would have gotten really grim, and my father would have barely even looked up from his dinner. He would have said — and God knows I heard this often enough," he imitated his father's voice, *"The only surprise about this, Wesley, is that it took three months to happen instead of two."*

Tears filled her eyes again. "That's a terrible thing to say to your own child."

He kissed her. "Hey. Shhh. I didn't tell you that to make you cry all over again."

"You told me that your father didn't hit you," Brittany said, "but he might as well have. Telling you that he expected you to fail is tantamount to a vicious beating, in my book."

"Yeah, well," he said. "Easy with the accusations there, because, you know, I really was a screwup."

"See?" she said. "You believed him. You still believe him."

He gently changed the subject, still running his fingers through her hair. Somewhere on her dash down the beach, she'd lost her ponytail holder. "What are you going to do if he does lose his scholarship?"

She settled back against him, her head on his shoulder. "Exactly what I told Andy. We'll figure something out."

"Such as you put your nurse practitioner degree on hold?"

Brittany nodded. "I *am* going to school on the money I saved for Andy's education," she told him. "He was planning to go to Amherst — it was a pretty short drive from our house in Appleton, you know, in Massachusetts. He wanted to live at home. In fact, he was adamant about it. I kept trying to talk him into living at college. First-year dorm. Lots of fun. Roommates and parties and all that stuff, but he just laughed and told me he spent years in the foster-care system, living with strangers. Why would he want to go live with strangers again when he was just getting used to having a real home?"

"Smart kid," he said, as aware as hell of her hand on his thigh.

She smiled, playing with the zipper pull on the pocket of his cargo shorts. "Yeah, I guess so. Then when he got the full scholarship at the college in L.A. — a baseball scholarship — God, he wanted to go so badly. But he was going to turn it down. And I suddenly thought, shoot. I've been wanting to go back to school for a long time. Surely I could find a nursing school in L.A. We could move out here together. It's kind of weird, you know, Andy and his mom go to college together. Like some kind of bad teen comedy movie. But it's what he wanted and it seems to be working." She took a deep breath. "It'll work just as well without the scholarship. With the nursing shortage, I could get a full-time job at the hospital in a heartbeat."

"That would be a shame."

"No, it would be life. Life happens, you deal with it. I'll get my degree, it'll just take a little longer than I'd hoped." She noticed the fog for the first time. "Oh, my God, who turned on the dried ice machine?"

It was kind of spooky, as if they were the last two people in the universe. Spooky, but nice. They couldn't see anyone else who might've come to the beach at this early hour, but no one could see them, either. He kissed her.

"California has the weirdest weather," she said.

"I love this kind of fog," he told her. "It's good cover for black ops."

"What are black ops?" she asked, kissing him this time. Oh, yeah. The fog no longer seemed quite so cold. He pulled her back with him, so that they were both lying in the sand.

God, he couldn't remember the last time he'd made out on the beach.

Probably for good reason. Sand and sex really didn't mix too well.

"Black ops are operations — missions — that are ultra top secret," he told her eventually. "They're usually so secret your immediate superiors on your chain of command don't know what you're up to."

She smiled down at him, pressing herself intimately against him. "I bet your immediate superiors don't know what you're up to."

He laughed. "That's for sure."

"You know, if I were wearing a skirt instead of jeans . . ."

"Damn you, Levi Strauss." She laughed, and he reached up to touch her face. "Britt, you know I love it when you laugh, but don't ever think I don't want you to cry in front of me, okay?"

She nodded, her eyes suddenly so soft. "The same goes for me."

He laughed. "Yeah, thanks, but . . ."

"But tough guys don't cry?"

"No," Wes said. "I've seen plenty of tough guys cry. I just . . . I try not to make a habit of it, myself. I'm a little afraid . . ."

She waited.

"That if I start I won't be able to stop," he admitted.

"Oh, Wes," she said softly.

The fog had soaked them both so thoroughly by now, that water beaded and ran down her face. Her T-shirt was practically transparent. Too bad she was wearing a bra.

"You should enter a wet T-shirt contest," he said. It was a stupid thing to say — he would bet big money that Britt disapproved of such blatantly sexist exhibitions. But he was desperate to change the subject.

She looked down at herself and laughed. "Yeah, right."

"I'd vote for you."

"Thanks," she said. "I think. Although I'm not sure I should thank you for suggesting I humiliate myself and all women everywhere by standing on a stage in front of an audience of howling men and being judged for the size and shape of my breasts."

Ding. Correct for ten points.

She narrowed her eyes at him. "How would you like to enter a 'who's got the biggest penis' contest? Okay, boys, drop your drawers and face the crowd!"

"Yeah, okay, at least women get to keep their T-shirts on."

She snorted. "Like that really makes a difference when a T-shirt is wet." She reached up under her shirt and, like a magician, she managed to unfasten her bra and pull it off through the sleeve of her T-shirt. "See?"

Oh, yeah. He saw. She was soaking wet and hot for him. It was unbelievably sexy.

Or maybe she was cold from the fog. He

sat up and kissed her and she shivered. He couldn't quite tell if it was from desire or the fact that she was freezing her butt off.

"Want to go to my place and take a hot shower?" he suggested as he licked her nipple into his mouth and suckled her, right through the cotton of her T-shirt.

She moaned as she rubbed herself against him, through his shorts and her jeans.

And then he could feel her fingers, working to unfasten his shorts. The top button was tricky, but . . . Ah, she got it and the zipper was easy and . . . *yes.*

"Two questions," she said. "Do you have a condom in your pocket, and when the fog's this thick, how long does it usually take to disappear?"

He laughed but it came out sounding more like a groan as she touched him. "Yes," he said, "and it's a crap shoot. When it's like this it usually doesn't burn off til mid-morning or even noon. But I'd be willing to bet the fog'll last at least five more min-utes — which is about four minutes longer than I'll last if you actually do take off your jeans and —"

Brittany let go of him and unzipped her jeans. They were wet and pulling them off was a challenge. She was up for it, though, and by the time she got one leg out, he'd covered himself with the condom he was car-rying.

And then she covered him, too, driving him so deeply inside of her he nearly lost it right then and there.

She moved on top of him, hard and fast, as if her need for him consumed her completely.

Obviously, it did. She wanted him so much she was willing to make love to him on a public beach.

God, what a total turn-on.

"Britt, I was serious," he gasped. "I'm so crazy for you, I'm not going to last."

Her response was her immediate release. Hard and fast and powerful as hell, it shook her and shook her as she cried out his name.

And he was undone. Game over. He couldn't have stopped himself from climaxing if his life had depended on it. He crashed into her with an explosion of pleasure that was so intense his eyes actually watered.

"Thank you," she gasped as she clung to him. "Oh, my God, thank you. You always know exactly what I need."

Wes had to laugh. *She* was thanking *him.* "Right now, I think you need a hot shower. And a cup of tea." Man, did he even have any tea? He hoped so.

If he didn't, he get some from somewhere.

Hell, if she wanted the moon, he'd figure out a way to get that for her, too.

Chapter 12

By Monday morning, Brittany's jeans had finally dried and they could — if they wanted to — go out.

Wes had been a little nervous when they'd first arrived at his apartment early Sunday morning. The place wasn't exactly neat and tidy. And even if it had been pristine, it completely lacked all of the warmth and cheerful personality of her apartment back in L.A.

He'd gathered up his laundry and quickly washed the dirty dishes and emptied the ashtrays while she was in the shower. He uncovered two packs of cigarettes and tossed them into the sink, getting them good and soggy before he put them in the trash.

The thought of smoking one while she was in the bathroom didn't cross his mind. At least not for longer than two or three seconds. Which was pretty damn amazing.

He'd looked around instead, wondering what to do to make the place more acceptable in Brittany's eyes. God, his apartment was ugly. And there was nothing he really could do about the science fiction movie posters taped to the walls without frames, or the worn and faded secondhand furniture — including a purple-and-green plaid chair that now seemed to scream that not only did its owner have no taste, but he had no life as well. Because, really, no one could spend any significant amount of time in that room with that chair without going insane. It announced that this apartment was really just a place Wes came to sleep now and then. It wasn't his home.

But his worries hadn't been real. They'd spent all of Sunday in his bedroom.

In his bed.

Brittany had called both work and a colleague from school to tell them what had happened with Andy, and that she wouldn't be back in L.A. for several days. So there was nothing to do but wait for Andy to give them an update.

The kid had called several times on Wes's cell phone, the latest just this morning. Dani had an appointment with her family doctor in San Diego, late this afternoon. On Tuesday, they were returning to L.A. The district attorney there wanted to meet with Dani and discuss the possibility of her pressing charges. They currently had another complaint against Dustin Melero, and Dani's testimony would make that case more solid.

Of course it was always a crapshoot in the

instance of sexual assault. It tended to come down to a "he said, she said" battle. Dani's reputation and sexual history — in fact, her entire personal life — would be scrutinized by people attempting to show that she willingly consented to having sex with Melero.

Sure. She willingly consented to getting her rib broken. She must've liked that a whole lot.

The good news was that Dani didn't have any skeletons in her closet. She was, as Wes had pointed out days earlier, a "public virgin." She'd been quite vocal in her decision to wait to have a sexual relationship. And she hadn't just discussed that with other kids. She'd talked to her doctors and her college mentor about it, as well.

Because she was a "good girl," there was a chance that her testimony would help convict Dustin Melero.

Brittany, however, was pretty steamed. After she got off the phone with Andy, she vented. "So I could go back to L.A., and in a week, when your leave is over and you're gone, say I'm walking home from the hospital late one night, and I'm attacked. Say I'm pulled into an alley, and I'm raped."

Wes winced, sitting down next to her on the bed. "I don't want to say that. Why don't we say instead that you don't ever walk home alone at night?"

She sighed in exasperation. "I'm just using

myself as an example, but no, you're right, it's not going to happen, because I'm careful. I get a cab if it's too late to call Andy for a ride."

"That's good to know."

"Okay, say instead that I finally agree to have dinner with Henry Jurrik — he's a pulmonary specialist at the hospital. He asks me out about once a month." She laughed. "He must put it into his calendar or something. It's like clockwork."

"He's a doctor?" Wes asked, trying not to sound jealous, and failing miserably.

Brittany kissed him. "I have a *no doctors* rule," she told him. "But just for the sake of argument, let's say I lose my mind and agree to have dinner with him. We go out, he drives me home, walks me to my door. You know. Wants to come inside, but I won't ask him, of course, because it's only a first date. He's about as perceptive as a two-by-four, and he tries to kiss me, so I turn my head — you know, I'm completely giving him all the *no sex tonight, you idiot* signals. But he persists, and I finally have to tell him flat out, no. But Andy's not home, so he pushes me inside where he forces himself on me."

"This is a really unpleasant conversation," Wes said.

"Yeah, well, it happens to women all the time," Britt told him with that stern look he'd come to recognize and love. She wanted to talk about this, so they were going to talk about it. It was hard to imagine anyone forcing anything on her when she got like this, but Wes knew too well that despite her tough attitude, he himself could overpower her with one hand tied behind his back.

"It happened to Dani," she continued. "She said no, and Melero said tough luck. She fought him hard enough to get a broken rib. It happens, Wes."

"It better never happen to you."

She kissed him again. "Don't worry. I'm careful. If I ever did go out to dinner with someone, I'd either drive myself, or I'd make sure Andy was home."

"You weren't that careful with me," he countered. "You just invited me into your house."

"Don't change the subject. My point in this is that afterwards? I could go to the police and press charges, but the D.A. might not take the case, because the doctor's scumbag defense attorney would dig up all kinds of dirt on me — including the fact that I haven't exactly lived like a nun these past few years — in particular these past few days. I slept with you willingly. And you weren't the only man I had a short-term relationship with after my divorce. They'd find out about Kyle, too. And, oh yeah, before I got married, back when I was in college, I had two different relationships. They were more intense — a few months each, but they make the list even longer. So they would try to prove that I was some kind of loose woman, sleeping around. Surely, I'd wanted Dr. Jurrik, too."

"It sucks," he agreed. "But I think the jury would look at you and see —"

"So what you're saying is that if I didn't look quite so wholesome, I'd be out of luck? That's not fair."

"You're right, it's not."

"Even if I'd had sex with every man I'd ever met," Brittany said, "even if I were a prostitute, no means no."

"You're absolutely right." He cleared his throat. "You actually had relationships in college that were more intense than, uh, what we've got going here?"

She smiled at him. "I meant in terms of length," she said. "I don't know about you, but this you and me thing is pretty different from anything I've ever done. I mean, I think in the past three days I've had more sex than I had during all the years I was married."

Wes laughed, relieved. "Good. I was a little nervous for a minute. Like I wasn't doing a good enough job or something."

"You're doing a marvelous job," she told him with a grin. "And how'm I doing, sugar pie? Am I managing to keep you from constantly thinking about how much you want a cigarette?"

"Definitely." He kissed her, and there it was again. Desire. Damn, he just could not get enough of her.

Maybe it was knowing that there was an end date to their affair, that he only had her until the end of his leave.

God, he didn't want his leave to ever end.

"Let's go out," she said. "The paper said there was some kind of celebration at something called Old Town San Diego this evening. Let's go and dance and get really hot for each other and then come back and make love on that hideous purple chair in your living room."

Wes laughed. "What? Why?"

"You need a good reason to keep it in your living room," she told him, laughing as she danced beyond his reach. "You need to have an incredibly steamy memory associated with it, so that when people come in here and see it, you can say, 'I keep that chair for a reason.' And when they look at you, you can just smile and say 'Mmmm, yeah. I know it's something of a visual assault upon the senses, but, you know, I really like that old chair.' "

The phone rang, and Britt scooped it up. "Wes Skelly's house of ugly furniture. How may we help you?" There was a pause. "Hello?" she said. She held out the phone to Wes. "I think I scared them away."

"Skelly," he said into the phone, but there

was a click as whoever was on the other end hung up.

"Sorry."

"Nah," he said. "Don't worry about it. I think there's something wrong with the phone company. I was getting a lot of hang-ups at your place, too. If it was someone from the Team, they would've left a message. And Andy would've called on my cell. Besides, he would've recognized your voice." He kissed her. "So you want to go out?"

"Do you?"

"Yeah," he said. "Old Town San Diego isn't too far. We could take my bike."

Brittany's eyes widened. "Your motorcycle? Really?" She'd been intrigued when she saw it parked in his carport. "Do you have an extra helmet?"

"Of course." Wes found his boots in the closet and put them on.

"Do you promise to go really slowly?"

He smiled at her. "Your wish is my command."

Wes Skelly was not the world's best dancer. But what he lacked in style and creativity, he made up for in enthusiasm. Besides, some men who should forever remain nameless — Quentin — flatly refused even to try to dance.

And frankly, it didn't matter that Wes didn't have the smoothest moves on the dance floor when he smiled at her the way he was smiling right now.

He leaned closer, so he could speak directly into Brittany's ear, so she could hear him over the sound of the salsa band. "Do you want to get something to drink? Or — I know. There's a place around the corner that sells ice-cream cones."

She let him pull her from the dance floor.

The place was mobbed. Even off the dance floor, the crowd was thick. But everyone was smiling and having a good time.

As they finally moved beyond the band's loudspeakers, she said, "You know your way around here pretty well."

He glanced at her. "Yeah. I've been down here . . . a few times."

"Old Town San Diego?" She lifted an eyebrow. "Somehow I wouldn't have guessed that a historic museum village was quite your speed."

"Yeah, well . . ." Was he actually blushing? "I'm interested. You know. In history. I like going to places like this."

"Really?" She stopped walking, and someone bumped into her. "Sorry." She pulled Wes out of the stream of traffic.

"It's stupid, I know," he said.

"No, it's not," she countered.

"Yeah, no," he said. "I know it's not stupid to come here. I meant, it's stupid to keep it a secret. It's just . . . I have a reputation in the teams, you know? Tattoo. Motorcycle. Profanity. I've been trying really hard to keep it clean around you, you know."

"And I appreciate that," she said. "But I don't understand. You don't think you're allowed to be smart? To go places besides pool halls and bars that have wet T-shirt contests?"

He laughed. "It's not that." He searched for the right words. "Most guys who become SEALs are wicked ass smart. Like, you know, Harvard, he actually went to Harvard, right? I'm telling you, some of these guys are fuh— are brilliant. Even Bobby — he reads a lot. He's always giving me book recommendations, but . . . . See, I read really slowly. I mean, he gets through a book in like a week, and it'll take me two months. Maybe. So I'm carrying it around for all that time, and I start to feel . . . I don't know."

"What?" she asked. "You start to feel what?"

He gazed at her, and she knew he was deciding how much he actually trusted her.

"Stupid," he finally admitted, and her heart went into her throat. His telling her that was almost better than his saying that he loved her. Almost. "I had to work my ass off to become a chief, Britt. Bobby, he did it without blinking. All that reading and the written crap — excuse me — it was hard for me."

"Are you dyslexic?" she asked.

"Nah," he said. He forced a smile. "I wish I had that excuse. I'm just . . . slow."

"Maybe when it comes to reading," she said. "But the rest of time . . . I don't think so, Wes. I've never met anyone who's as quick witted as you are — and that translates to smart in my book. So, it's not easy for you to read. So what? That doesn't make you stupid. You just have to learn things other ways. Like by coming to a place like this and taking a guided tour. That way you can hear the history instead of having to plow through some dusty old book."

His smile was more genuine now. "Yeah, I know. I watch a lot of the History Channel. And I sometimes listen to books on tape, too."

God, he was surely telling her things he never told anyone. Probably not even his best friend, Bobby.

Now her heart wasn't just in her throat, it was expanding and cutting off her ability to speak.

Good thing, because if she wasn't careful, she might go ahead and tell him that she was in love with him, and falling harder every minute that they spent together.

Instead, she kissed him. She tried to kiss him even half as sweetly as he'd kissed her that first time in Amber Tierney's house.

"I can tell you anything, and you'll still like me, huh?" he said softly.

"Yeah," Brittany said. "You can tell me anything, and it won't go any farther, either."

His eyes were so blue. "It feels good," he said. "That kind of trust. And it goes both ways, you know."

She nodded. "I do know." She smiled. "But I don't have any secrets."

"Honest?"

No. She was in love with him. But that was one hell of a big secret that she wasn't about to share with anyone. Still . . .

"Okay," she said. "You really want to hear . . . ?"

"Only if you trust me."

She did, without hesitation. "If I won the lottery, I'd have a baby. I'd go to a sperm bank and, you know, make a withdrawal."

He smiled. "That doesn't shock or even surprise me, you know."

"Well, gee, sorry for being so transparent."

"That's not what I meant," he countered. "It's just . . . maybe I've gotten to know you so well these past few days . . . But it's kind of obvious to me that if you won the lottery you wouldn't spend it on sports cars — except maybe the ones that you'd buy for me and your sister."

She laughed.

"So, you'd really do it, huh? If you had the cash," he said. "You'd willingly be a single mother?"

"Yes. Adopting Andy made me realize how

precious children are — and how much I really would've liked to have had the experience of raising one right from the moment they were born," she said. "And as for being a single mom — I've been doing it for almost seven years now. I think I'm doing okay. I mean, it seems pretty unlikely that Prince Charming's going to come along at this point in my life, so . . ."

Wes looked out at the crowd and nodded. "Yeah, I guess not."

Darn.

That was where he was supposed to push her hair back from her face and kiss her and tell her that he was her Prince Charming, and he was here to stay.

God, she was still hoping for the fairy tale happy ending.

And they lived happily ever after.

Fool.

"Kids scare me to death," he admitted. "I helped take care of Liz and Shaun when they were born. I'm not afraid of changing diapers — that's not what I meant. It's just . . . you love them so much, and . . ."

"And they sometimes die on you," Brittany said. "Like Ethan, right?"

"Yeah," he said. "Just like Ethan. You know, I joined the Big Brothers program a few years ago."

She laughed. "Okay, sweetie, ten minutes ago, that would have surprised me, but it doesn't anymore. I guess we're even now. What made you join?"

"It was Ethan's birthday," he told her, "and I was feeling like crap, so . . . I just went in and signed up. They accepted me, and matched me with this kid — Cody Anderson. I used to bring him here, and we'd always get ice cream afterwards. It was . . . He was a great kid. I really liked him — he was a real troublemaker — I could really relate to that. We got pretty tight pretty fast. He liked coming here. He had to pretend that the big draw was the fudge ripple, you know? But that was okay. Then his mom got remarried and they moved up to Seattle, and . . . I was supposed to call the office and get reassigned, but I never did. It was too . . ." He shook his head. "It felt a little too much like going to get a new puppy after your old puppy, you know, ran away or something."

She hugged him. "I'm sorry."

"Yeah, I'm sorry, too. I didn't mean to go all pathetic on you. I just . . ." He sighed. "I don't know, Britt. I don't think I'm cut out to have kids."

"Well, you have plenty of time."

Unlike a woman, whose clock ticked louder when she was approaching forty, like Brittany.

"I don't know," Wes said again. "I was thinking about getting a vasectomy. You know, make sure it never happens."

Whoa. "That's pretty drastic. Maybe you should check with Lana before you do that."

He held her gaze silently for several long seconds. And then he looked away and laughed. "You're like, the only person in the world who would dare to talk about that — about her, you know — to just say something right in my face like that."

"She seems really special," Brittany said quietly.

Wes nodded. "Yeah. But she's never going to leave Quinn, so . . ."

"You don't know that."

"Yeah, I do," he said. "She actually thinks he's only cheated on her two times." He swore softly. "Try two hundred and two. We talked about it a little the other night, but I couldn't tell her the truth. I just . . . She seemed so . . . I don't know, hopeful, I guess, that he was going to change."

"Maybe I should tell her," Brittany suggested.

What was she, stupid? Did she actually want Wes and Lana to live happily ever after?

Yes. Someone might as well. And she loved Wes enough to want him to be happy.

"I'll tell her," Britt said. "I'll talk to Harlan first, see if he knows Quinn —"

"He does," Wes said. "But —"

"I'll tell Lana that Harlan told me — that way she doesn't somehow blame you. You know, death to the messenger and all that. I don't mind if she gets mad at me and hates me forever."

He was shaking his head. "No. Britt, I don't want you to, okay?"

"Why not?"

He just kept on shaking his head. "Look, are we going to get ice cream, or what?"

"Think about it, sweetie," Brittany said. "Maybe you could actually get what you want."

"Right now I want ice cream — and a cigarette," he told her, tugging her back into the crowd of humanity pushing its way along the sidewalk.

Chapter 13

Trouble erupted pretty much out of nowhere.

Wes was leading the way to the ice-cream shop, thinking about how much he'd really like to take a pint home. Cones were nice to eat with eleven-year-olds. But Brittany . . . What he really wanted was to lick a few scoops off of her gorgeous body.

Okay, down boy. She might not be in the biggest hurry to rush back to his place — not after having that heavy duty conversation about Lana.

God, he didn't know what to think. And then he stopped thinking as two high school kids faced off right in the middle of the crowd, directly behind them.

"You looking at my girlfriend? Who told you you could look at my girlfriend?"

Idiot One pushed Idiot Two hard in the chest, and just like that sides were drawn. Every kid wearing colors in the crowd appeared out of nowhere. Real violence hadn't exploded yet, but it was just a matter of time before it did.

Wes let go of Brittany's hand. "Go down these stairs, cross the street and take the first right. I'll meet you over there. Move as fast as you can, all right?"

"Be careful," she said.

"Yeah." He started for the pair of idiots. "Hey!" But it was already too late.

Idiot One launched himself at Idiot Two.

And just like that, they were in the middle of a fricking brawl.

Crap.

He shouldn't have left Brittany to try to play hero. He pushed his way through the crowd, trying to get back to her as quickly as he could.

And saw her lose her footing and tumble down the stairs.

"Brittany!"

There were people in front of her, so she couldn't have fallen all the way, but he saw her go down. And she didn't get up again.

It took him twenty seconds longer than he wanted to get to her. Twenty terrifying seconds of icy fear.

Was she getting trampled by this crowd? Had she hit her head when she fell? Where the hell was she?

Twenty year-long seconds later, when he finally reached the stairs, she was sitting up, thank you Lord God Jesus. Someone — God bless them — had helped her move to the side of the stairs. Although, she was holding her head with one hand.

"God, baby, are you okay?"

"Yeah," she told him as someone hurrying down the stairs past them smacked her in the back of her head with their backpack.

"Watch it!" Wes growled, turning quickly back to Britt, protecting her with his body. He wasn't big enough to block her completely from the crowd though, and he silently cursed his mother's side of the family for giving him the five foot eight gene instead of the one from his father that would've made him six-four.

"I hit my head on something," Brittany told him, "but it's really my ankle that's . . ."

Someone else knocked into him in their haste to get down the stairs, and Wes scooped Brittany up and swiftly carried her away from the crowd, away from the fighting idiots.

His heart was still racing and adrenaline was still surging through his system, and if he'd needed to, he could have carried her all the way back to L.A. without slowing down.

"I'm okay," she said as they rounded a corner. "My ankle's just . . . It's just a slight sprain. I'm sure —"

"There's a first aid station not far from here," he told her shortly. "I'm taking you over there."

"Oh, Wes, please, I just want to go home. I know what they're going to tell me. Ice and

241

elevation. I'm going to be fine."

"Humor me," he said.

Two police cars, sirens wailing and lights spinning, passed them, heading toward the fight.

"Ouch," Brittany said. "Ow, ow, ow! Put me down, put me down!"

Hastily, he lowered her to the ground, the fear returning instantly. She'd injured her neck. She had internal bleeding. The possibilities were endless. "What hurts?" he asked, slipping even further into Navy SEAL Chief mode. "Where? Show me." Fear was always pushed aside in favor of action and efficiency.

"Nothing," she said. "Nowhere. I just wanted you to put me down."

He shouldn't have opened his mouth, because when he did, some words came out that he'd promised himself he wouldn't ever use in front of her. But instead of recoiling in horror, she put her arms around him.

"Oh, honey, I'm okay," she said into his ear as she held him tightly. "I'm a little shaken and I'm going to have some bruises, but I'm really okay."

He held her just as close. "I saw you fall. And all I could think of were those stories about people who get trampled to death at rock concerts."

"I'm okay," she said again and kissed him.

Relief plus adrenaline plus a kiss like the

one she gave him equaled a physical reaction that she couldn't miss.

"Oh, baby," she said, pulling back to look at him, amusement in her eyes. "You really do want to rescue me, don't you?"

He laughed, too. It was freaking weird. Just a few minutes ago, he couldn't have imagined laughing again — not in the near future. "Yeah," he said. "But only *after* I take you to the first aid station and have them look you over."

Brittany was shaking her head. "That place is going to be jammed," she said. "Let's just go home."

"What if you have a concussion?" he asked.

She smiled. "Maybe — as a precaution — you should make sure I don't sleep at all tonight."

Her smile and that suggestive comment went a long way to convincing him that she really was okay — along with the fact that she was experimenting by gingerly putting her weight on her right foot.

"I think I mostly hit the funny bone," she told him, showing him that she could, indeed, walk unassisted. Like she'd said, she was merely shaken and bruised.

But head injuries could be tricky. He definitely was going to watch her like a hawk for the next day or so. There were things she shouldn't do — such as ride home behind him on his motorcycle.

He could see the ice-cream shop down the street. It was doing a brisk business despite the mayhem that had broken out just a few blocks away. There were umbrella-covered tables out in front, right on the sidewalk.

"Let me get you an ice cream," he told her. "You can sit here and eat it while I take the Harley home. I'll get the car, come back and pick you up."

"But I liked being your motorcycle chick," she said. "Shades of Gidget, you know?"

"Sorry, but I'm not taking any chances," he said.

She knew he was talking about her head. "It's just a little bump."

"Give up," he told her. "You're not going to win this one. I'll be back in . . ." He looked at his watch. "Twenty-eight minutes."

Brittany laughed. "Twenty-eight? Exactly? I had no idea I was having a fling with Mr. Spock."

"Very funny. I know how long it takes me to get home from here — thirteen minutes. Add a few for going inside to get the keys to the car . . ." He opened the door for her. "Careful, there's a step up — don't trip again."

"I didn't trip down those stairs," she told him as they went into the shop. "I was pushed. Hard."

Jesus. Probably by some six foot tall coward rushing to save his own sorry ass.

"Damn it." He turned back the way they'd come, and she tugged him inside.

"Whoever it was, he or she is definitely not still there," she said. "Your thirst for revenge will have to be sated by chocolate ice cream."

"I'm a vanilla man, myself," he told her. "But I'm going to pass right now. Ice-cream cones and bikes don't mix." He slapped a five-dollar bill onto the counter and gave her a quick kiss. "I'll be back."

Brittany sat outside, in the warmth of the afternoon sun, eating ice cream and watching people pass by on the sidewalk.

Her ankle was sore, and her head had a tender spot where she'd connected with the stairs, but other than that, she was absolutely fine.

She sighed. She'd been looking forward to riding home with her arms wrapped around Wes's waist. She'd been looking forward to dancing with him some more, too.

Now he was going to watch her all night.

Well, okay. Good. He could look all he wanted. And Brittany, well, she'd give him something to watch.

She realized she'd been ignoring her cone, and she had to lick all the way around it to keep the ice cream from dripping onto her hand. When she looked up, there was a man standing slightly off to the side, watching her.

At first glance, he seemed to be a nice

enough looking guy. He was hair challenged, but that didn't take away from the handsome bone structure of his face.

But then he moved closer and she saw his eyes.

After working in countless emergency rooms on both the east and west coast, Brittany recognized mental illness when she saw it. And this guy, although he dressed nicely and even normally — no mismatched plaids and stripes, no superhero cape, no protective headgear to ward off killer bee attacks — had something in his eyes that set off all of her alarms.

Not that he necessarily was dangerous. Just that he was different.

He was holding a set of car keys, so obviously he was highly functional. But he was definitely challenged.

He couldn't hold her gaze. But he spoke to her. "You made her cry."

It was pretty remarkable, actually. They always approached her. All the certifiable ones did. There could be seven nurses working the shift, and sure enough, the patients who were mentally ill would sidle their way over to Brittany.

Andy said it was because she spoke to them as if they were real people.

Britt had laughed at that. "But they are real people," she'd argued.

"My point exactly," the kid had told her.

She looked at the Hairclub for Men candidate and tried to make both her face and her voice neutral. She didn't want him coming over and sitting down next to her, but she didn't want to ignore him, either. On closer inspection, he had the look of a man who'd gone off his medication. "I'm sorry. Have we met?"

"You made her cry," he said again, and both the tone of his voice and the look in his eyes made her stand up and start backing away.

Okay, Wes, any time now. She glanced at her watch and saw that it was at least ten minutes before his estimated return.

"I'm sorry," she said, "but I really don't know what you're talking about."

"She cried," he said. "Her heart is broken."

"I'm sorry about that," she said again.

"No you're not."

The man slowly shuffled closer, and Britt kept on backing away, just as one of the employees came out of the ice-cream shop — a kid with a rag in his hand to wipe off the outside tables.

"Is there a pay phone inside?" she asked him.

"Nope. Sorry. Nearest one is down the street. Kelley's."

"Thank you." Brittany looked the direction he pointed, and could see the shamrock green sign for Kelley's bar. Her heart sank. It was way down at the very end of the street. Her ankle wasn't seriously injured, but it would take a lot longer to heal completely if she hiked on it.

"Move along, mister," the kid said to the bald man. "Don't hassle the paying customers."

"Can't I order an ice-cream cone?" He aimed his anger at the kid as he sat down at the same table Britt had been sitting at moments earlier. He carefully took out his wallet and extracted several dollar bills. "Chocolate chip."

"You have to order from the counter," the kid said, and as they went inside, Brittany took the opportunity to slip away.

Wes made it back to the ice-cream shop in record time, only to find that Brittany was gone.

The only people sitting out front were a mother and her four young children.

Maybe Britt was inside, and he just couldn't see her through the glare on the plate glass.

Wes tried to push away thoughts of Britt having suffered from a worse head injury than he'd imagined, falling unconscious, or becoming disoriented and wandering off. . . .

He shouldn't have left her here. He should have stayed with her and taken a cab home. Or to the hospital. But when he left her, she seemed fine. She *was* fine. He just had to take a deep breath and calm down. She was inside. She didn't see him pull up. This was not a big deal.

He pulled into a no standing zone, and jumped out of his car, leaving his flashers on.

But as he got closer to the shop, he quickly saw that she wasn't there and the fear returned.

He opened the door and called to one of the kids behind the counter. "Hey. Do you have a ladies' room?"

"No, sir," she told him, eyeing him oddly.

"There wasn't just an ambulance here, was there?" Wes asked, his heart actually in his throat. Please say no . . .

"No, sir," she told him.

Thank God. But where the hell was Brittany? "Do you remember seeing a blond woman, about my height? Mid-thirties? Pretty . . . ?" Jesus, he could be describing anyone. "Kind of pointy nose. She was wearing a blue shirt . . . ?"

"No, sir."

"I saw her." A kid who was wiping tables straightened up. "She asked if we had a pay phone, and I sent her down to Kelley's." He gestured down the street with his head.

"Thanks." Wes was back in his car in a flash. Why did Britt need to make a call? Was she feeling worse? Had she called a cab to take her to the hospital? Why hadn't she called him?

He broke about four traffic laws getting over to Kelley's as quickly as he could, and parked — again — in a tow zone.

Kelley's was a bar about the size of his living room. One glance around told him she wasn't there. Of course not — there was a big sign on the pay phone: Out of Order.

Jesus, where was she?

Everyone had looked up when he came in, and Wes used the opportunity to call to the bartender, "Hey, pal, did a pretty blonde come in here asking —"

His cell phone rang. He had it out and open in record time. Please, God . . . "Britt?"

"Oh, no," she sounded dismayed. "You got to the ice-cream place and I wasn't there."

The relief that flooded him at the sound of her voice nearly knocked him on his ass. "Are you all right? Where are you?" His voice actually cracked. "Jesus, Britt, you scared the crap out of me."

"I'm sorry — I'm fine. Some weird guy was hassling me outside of the ice-cream shop. So I went down the street and . . . I'm around the corner at a restaurant called The Toucan. I thought I'd be able to get to a phone and call you before you got back."

"I made good time," he told her, waving to the bartender as he went back out onto the sidewalk. "Who the fuh— who was hassling you?" He'd find him and break his knees.

"Just some guy who was angry at the entire world. He was hassling everyone, not just me. But he was a little scary so —"

Some angry guy scared her. God. "I shouldn't have left you alone," Wes said. "Are you really okay?"

"Please deposit thirty-five cents for another three minutes," a computer voice cut in to their call.

"I'm out of change," Brittany told him.

"I'm on my way." Wes hung up the phone and nearly ran into a man who was standing by his car, right by the front bumper. "Sorry, I didn't see you there."

"You're not supposed to park here," the man said. Something about him was slightly off-kilter, like he wasn't playing with a full deck of cards.

"It was an emergency," Wes told him. He opened the door to his car. "Better get back on the sidewalk, buddy — I'm going to pull out, okay?"

The man shuffled over to the curb. "I'm not your buddy," he said. "You made her cry."

Oo-kay.

"You should probably stay out of the street," Wes told him before he got into his car and pulled away.

Chapter 14

Wes was silent on the ride home — except when he asked a half a dozen different times if Brittany really was all right.

She finally turned to him. "Wesley. I'm fine. My ankle's a little sore and I bumped my head. What do I have to say to get you to believe me?"

The muscles jumped in his jaw. "Sorry."

He pulled into his driveway and got out of the car. He came around and closed her door for her after she got out, and then followed her to his kitchen door. He unlocked it and pushed it open for her, all without saying another word.

He was tightly wound, every muscle tense.

Brittany waited until he closed the door behind them. "Are you angry with me?"

"No."

"You're acting as if you are," she pointed out.

He closed his eyes for a moment. "Okay," he said. "Maybe I am. Maybe I'm . . . God, I don't know what I am, Britt. When I couldn't find you, I thought . . ." He shook his head. "I was scared to death. And I don't like being scared."

She nodded. "I can relate. I don't like it, either. I'm sorry I didn't call you sooner, but —"

"Can we not talk right now?" he asked. "I just . . . I don't want to talk, okay?"

"Maybe now's the best time to talk," she countered. "If you're really that upset, you should get it out instead of internalizing it."

"Thanks but no thanks." He took a glass from the cabinet and got himself some water, his movements tight, almost jerky. "You know, we talk too much. I thought this relationship was supposed to be based on sex. On . . ." He used a verb that should have made her take a step back. A verb that was meant to make her take a step back.

But Brittany knew exactly what he was doing.

Or rather, trying to do.

And she didn't even flinch. It was going to take more than a few bad words for him to push her away just because his feelings for her scared him.

"You care about me too much," she guessed — correctly from his reaction. "And realizing just how much you care has really freaked you out, hasn't it?"

He made a sound that might have been laughter, might have been pain. "I don't have room for you," he said and winced, swearing softly. "That sounds awful and I'm sorry, babe, but I —"

"No," she said. "No, Wes, I know what you mean. I know why you said it." And she did. She knew, without a doubt, that he was thinking about Ethan. He was thinking about loss, and about how he wouldn't feel the pain of loss if he had nothing to lose. "I'm not going to die, honey. I'm not Ethan."

"Oh, perfect," he said, famous Skelly temper flaring. "Bring Ethan into it. Why the hell not? Let's make this a complete misery-fest."

"I think that everything you do comes back to Ethan's death," Brittany told him quietly. "Everything. Your love affair with Lana — the wife of a close friend. Unrequited love — how perfect is that for you? You can't lose her because she's not yours to lose. Except you can't win, either. You can never win, never be happy as long as you —"

"Look," he said. "I'm really not interested in this. I'm going to go take a nap. You want to come lie down with me, fine. You don't, that's fine, too."

But she blocked the door that led to his bedroom. "You said you were scared today. What were you afraid of, Wes?"

He didn't answer.

He didn't need to — she knew. "You were afraid I was hurt worse that I let on," she said. "You were afraid I was badly injured. And what if I had been?"

Wes shook his head. "Brittany, don't. I already spent too much time there. It was not fun."

"If I had been badly hurt," she asked instead, "whose fault would it have been?"

He said one choice word on an exhale of air.

"Mine," she answered for him. "It would have been my fault, not yours. I'm the one who tripped down those stairs —"

"You said you were pushed."

"Yeah," she said. "Okay. I was pushed. So it wasn't completely my fault, but that doesn't make it yours either."

"If I had been with you, no one would've gotten close enough to push you — you better believe that."

"Right," she said. "And if you had been with me the summer I turned twenty-two, I never would've gone out to the movies with my ex-husband that first time. So does that make my entire fiasco of a rotten marriage your fault, too?"

He grimly shook his head. "That's not the same thing."

"You weren't there when those creeps took a potshot at the president last year," she said. "So is it your fault that that Secret Service agent died?"

"No."

"So why, then, is it your fault that Ethan died?"

He was silent, just glaring at her. "You just don't know when to stop, do you?" he finally said.

"Wes, why is it your fault that Ethan died?" she asked again.

"Goddamn it. It's not. That's what you want me to say, right?"

"No," she said. "It's what I want you to believe."

"Well, I do believe it," he said harshly. "I couldn't have saved him even if I were in the car with him. I'm not a superhero — I have no delusions about myself. None at all. Some of the guys in Alpha Squad think they're one step short of immortal. They think they're goddamn invincible. But hey — remember me? I'm the family screwup. I have a long history of annoying the crap out of everyone I ever meet —"

"Not me," she said.

"Yeah," Wes said, his voice breaking. "Jesus, I can't figure that one out. You're, like, one of the nicest women I've ever met and no matter what I do or say, you still like me. I don't get it."

He actually had tears in his eyes. Brittany took a step toward him, reaching for him, but he backed away.

"Sweetie, it's because I see the real you," she told him, refusing to be daunted. "I see a wonderful, kind, compassionate, very strong and very intelligent man who is so much fun to be around, who gives so much of himself so generously. I see someone special —"

"That was Ethan." His voice got louder as he used anger to keep himself from crying. "Not me. He was the special one. I was the one who always pushed the boundaries, the annoying kid who tested everyone's patience day in and day out. I'm the troublemaker, the roof-walker, the risk-taker, the tormentor. I'm the one who should have died. If one of us had to go, it goddamn should have been me!"

Silence.

Brittany suspected Wes had surprised himself with that statement more than he'd surprised her.

"It should have been me," he whispered as he used the heels of his hands to wipe his eyes before any tears could escape. God forbid he actually cry. "It's been years and years and I'm still angry as hell that it wasn't me in that car instead of Ethan."

"Oh, honey," Brittany told him. "I for one am so glad it wasn't you. And, for what it's worth, sweet kids are nice, but I've always preferred the annoying ones. They grow up to be the most fascinating men."

Wes reached for her then. He practically lunged for her, pulling her close and kissing her almost painfully hard.

She kissed him back just as fiercely, knowing that he needed this, that even though he wasn't going to let himself cry, that right now he could use sex as an emotional outlet.

He wasn't the only one.

God, she loved him. But she didn't dare tell him, afraid he would take her words as another burden, another worry, another problem to have to deal with.

So she just kissed him.

Wes had stopped thinking.

Thinking hurt too much, and if he didn't think, then all he did was feel, and right now he was feeling Brittany.

Brittany, who thought he was a fascinating man. Brittany who just kept on liking him, who wouldn't let him scare her away.

He felt Britt's mouth on his mouth, her breasts pressed tightly to his chest, her legs locked around his waist as he buried himself inside of her again and again and again.

She was hot and slick and he couldn't remember the last time anything — anything — had felt this incredible.

"Condom," she gasped. "Wes, we need —"

A condom. He wasn't wearing a condom.

Now there was a thought that was able to cut through the haze of all that intense pleasure, and Wes froze.

He opened his eyes and realized that not

only was he inside of her without protection, but he was nailing her with no finesse, his pants around his thighs, no consideration for her comfort, her back pressed hard against the living room wall.

But even though he'd stopped, she was still moving as if she liked it. No, forget liked — as if she loved what he was doing to her — as if she wanted and needed him as much as he needed her.

"Please," she said. "We need to get a condom. But I can't seem to stop. This feels too good. . . ."

God, she was beyond sexy and he kissed her as he reached for the wallet in the back pocket of his pants.

"Please," she begged, between kissing him again. "Please, Wes —"

Oh, yeah, the sexiest woman he'd ever had the pleasure of making it with was now begging him. But for what? To pull out, or —

She gripped him with her legs, pushing him deeply inside of her, and she made a noise that was almost enough to make him drop his wallet.

He'd put a condom in there in the event that they didn't make it home from Old Town San Diego before needing to make love again.

Because that's what being with Brittany was like — it wasn't so much that he wanted her, as a "yeah that would be nice" kind of thing, but rather that he needed her, like "if you don't make love to me right now I'm going to die." God, he needed her so badly, all the time.

Maybe he should get her pregnant and marry her.

God, okay, now he went from not thinking at all, to thinking crazy thoughts. Except merely being inside her like this, with no protection, was enough to knock her up. Enough damage had already been done.

Surely she knew that. She was a nurse.

And he wanted — needed . . .

Brittany. In his life.

For more than just the next week.

Oh, God, what she was doing to him, despite knowing that he wasn't wearing protection.

Maybe she wanted him to get her pregnant. Maybe she wanted him to marry her, to start a family. He knew she still wanted to have a baby. How incredibly terrifying. What would he do with a baby? And yet the idea of coming home to Brittany every night was a damn appealing one.

"I want to come inside of you," he gasped, unable to form the words to really tell her all that he was feeling. Surely she would understand what he meant by that. "Britt . . ."

She didn't say no, but she didn't say yes, either. She just exploded around him, and just like that, it was over for him, too. He pulled out, but it was, of course, too late.

Brittany kissed him. "Tell me," she said, before he'd even had a chance to catch his breath. "Right now, right this very moment, aren't you even just a little bit glad that you weren't the one who died?"

Wes laughed and kissed her. "Yes," he said. "Whenever I'm with you, baby, definitely yes."

The phone rang just after 4:00 a.m., waking Brittany from a restless sleep.

Wes cursed like the sailor that he was as he reached across her for the cordless phone sitting in the recharger on his bedside table. "If this is another hang-up, I'm turning off the ringer."

"What if it's Andy?" Britt asked, reaching to turn on the light.

"Skelly." Wes's scowl softened when he caught sight of her face. No doubt she looked as anxious as she felt. "It's not Andy," he mouthed silently. But then whoever was on the other end of the phone had his full attention. "What?" He swore. "When?" Another pause. Whoever he was talking to, it was extremely serious. "Are they sure?" He swore again, then took a deep breath and blew it out hard.

His hand was shaking as he ran it down his face, as he swore again. "No," he said into the phone. "I know. I never thought . . .

I mean, if anyone was indestructible . . . Oh, God. And they're sure it's not a mistake?"

Oh, God — indeed. Someone had died. Someone Wes cared about.

As Britt watched, he threw back the covers and got out of bed.

"Yeah," he said into the phone, pulling clean underwear and socks from his dresser, and a T-shirt from another drawer. "I'll call Bobby. He's on his honeymoon, but he'll definitely want to know. Jesus." He rubbed the back of his neck as if it ached. "Yeah. Thank you, Senior Chief. I appreciate the call, and . . ." Pause. "Yeah, I'll see you over there."

He hung up the phone and stood there for a moment, with his back to Brittany, taking another deep breath and exhaling hard.

"Wes," she said softly. "What happened?"

He turned toward her, his face stony in its grimness. "Matt Quinn's dead."

Matt . . . ? For a second, Brittany didn't recognize the name. But then she did. She just hadn't heard his given name all that often. But Matt Quinn was the Mighty Quinn. Wizard the Mighty Quinn.

Lana Quinn's husband. And Wes's good friend.

And he was . . . dead?

"Oh, my God," she breathed. "How?"

"Helicopter crash. His SeaHawk went down over the ocean, on the way back in from an op. Jesus, I have to take a shower."

Brittany followed him into the bathroom. "Was everyone on board lost?"

"No," Wes told her, turning on the water and waiting for it to heat. "The rest of his squad was pulled out of the water, but Quinn and two members of the helo crew were killed on impact. The PJ's didn't get them out before it went under, though. Apparently there's some kind of storm cooking in that area right now — it's going to be a few days before they get divers in to recover the bodies — if they manage to do it at all. Which is going to make it that much harder for Lana." He looked at her, as if seeing her for the first time since he got off the phone with the senior chief. "Will you do me a favor?"

"Of course."

"I have to call Bobby. Somewhere on the desk in the kitchen is a piece of paper with the phone number of the resort where he and Colleen are staying."

"I'll find it," she told him.

"Thanks." He stepped into the shower.

"Wes." Britt stopped him from closing the shower curtain. "It's okay if you cry when you find out that a friend is dead."

But he had that stoneman look on his face again. "Just find me that number, please."

Brittany went into the kitchen via the bedroom, where she pulled on a T-shirt and a pair of Wes's boxers.

Maybe he'd just never cry. Maybe he'd go through life using high-intensity, mindless sex as his way of expressing his emotions.

Mindless to the point of ignoring all birth control and safe sex precautions.

A chilling jolt of disbelief went through her. God, what had they done?

Having unprotected sex was stupid. There was no good reason to do it, no acceptable excuse.

And the really stupid thing was, they hadn't even talked about it yet. After, Wes had dragged her into the shower and washed them both clean. One thing had led to another and they'd ended up in his bed, communicating once again through touch.

They'd spent the whole night sleeping and waking up to make love — with proper protection each time.

All night long, every time she'd thought about getting up the nerve to say, "So. Wesley. Sex without a condom. What were we thinking?" he'd kissed her.

And lordy, lordy, how that man could kiss!

He'd sucked all the unspoken words right out of her mouth, and managed to empty her brain of all thoughts besides those of immediate gratification.

Up to a few minutes ago, when that phone call came, Brittany had played out the "what if she were pregnant" scenario right to a fairy-tale happy ending. She'd get the baby she'd always wanted, and a husband she loved — who loved her, too. Because Wes did love her. She knew that without a doubt.

The trouble was, he loved her second best.

But now, suddenly, with Quinn's untimely death, Britt was the potential obstacle that would keep Wes from finally finding true happiness with Lana.

And wouldn't that be just his luck? Lana was finally free, although not in a way that anyone had hoped for, except, whoops, Wes might well have just gotten his girlfriend — no, make that his casual sex partner — pregnant.

Oh, God.

After Wes got out of the shower, he was going to get dressed and go over to Lana's house. *I'll see you over there.* They'd all go over to Lana's house — all of Wizard's friends and teammates, and their wives and girlfriends as well. They'd sit shiva, so to speak.

Melody had once told Brittany how tight-knit the SEAL community was. Wes and his friends would take care of Lana. They'd comfort her.

Yeah, Wes was pretty good at comfort.

In the kitchen, Britt sifted through torn slips of paper that had Wes's odd, almost spidery handwriting on them. ABC Cab, here in San Diego. His brother Frank's new phone number in Oklahoma City. Aunt Maureen and Uncle George in Sarasota, Florida. The phone number of a comic book store in Escondido. The 800 number for Alamo car rental at the airport.

Gee, that might come in handy.

Aha. Bobby and Colleen. They had an entire full, untorn sheet devoted to them.

Wes had written down their new address and phone number, as well as the dates of their honeymoon — which ended last night. Yes, according to their flight information, they'd arrived in San Diego shortly after 8:00 p.m. last night.

The shower had shut off, and by the time Brittany went back into the bedroom, Wes was already dry and getting dressed.

"I want to get over there quickly," he said to her, "so if you want to shower —"

"I'm not going," she said. "You know. To Lana's. The last thing she needs is a stranger hanging around right now."

He stepped into his pants. "It's just . . . I'm not sure how long I'm going to be."

"That's okay," Brittany said. "Of course you'll stay as long as she wants you to stay. I know that. Don't worry about me. I'm going to call a cab. I'll rent a car and head back to L.A. Andy's doing fine — he and Dani seem to have things under control. You don't need me hanging around here, so . . . I'll call work, see if they need me to do a shift tonight. It's a good thing for me to do — I'll win brownie points with my supervisor."

He nodded, clearly distracted. "I wonder if anyone called Amber."

He picked up the phone and dialed.

Brittany sat on the bed and watched as he made sure the word about Matt Quinn had made it to Lana's sister in L.A. It had. Amber was already in San Diego, with Lana.

She watched as he finished dressing in a tan uniform — a chief's uniform. It was less formal than the one he'd worn to the party, yet it still managed to accentuate his broad shoulders and trim hips.

He took his cell phone from the charger and slipped it into his pocket, found his hat. . . .

"You can stay as long as you like," he told Britt. "Go back to sleep if you can."

She shook her head. "I can't." She handed him the piece of paper with Bobby's phone number on it. "Don't forget to call Bobby. He and Colleen got home last night."

"Thanks. I was going to call him from the car," he said, folding up the paper and putting it in his shirt pocket. "How're your head and ankle this morning?"

"They're fine," she told him. And they were. It was her heart that was breaking.

He kissed her — briefly — on the mouth. For the last time? Maybe. Probably. Oh,

God.

"I'll talk to you later," he said. "I've got to go."

Of course he did. Lana needed him.

The stupid thing was, it was Wes's love for Lana that had truly made Brittany fall for him. He was an amazing man. He'd cared about Lana so deeply for so long. And yet, he'd always done what was best for Lana, regardless of his own wants and needs — even when it would have been easier to do otherwise.

And wasn't that the exact opposite of That-Jerk-Quentin, Britt's ex, who wanted everything in life to be easy, who wasn't willing to work to make their relationship last even a few short years.

God, what she wouldn't give to spend the rest of her life with Wesley Skelly.

Brittany figured that her best chance was to be patient and steadfast and become the woman he would settle for. And yeah, loser that she was, she was willing to be his second choice. He was that great, and she loved him that much.

But now she wasn't even going to have that opportunity. Because Lana was suddenly no longer unattainable.

Britt heard the door close as he left the apartment, heard his car start as he drove away.

Out of her life.

Please God, don't let me be pregnant.

It was one thing to be his second choice when his first choice wasn't an option. It was another entirely to be his burden.

No matter what happened, she wouldn't do that.

Chapter 15

Wes had to park six houses down — there were that many cars in the street outside of the little bungalow Lana had shared with Matt "Wizard" Quinn.

Bobby and Colleen were pulling up just as he was getting out of his car, and he waited for them.

Jesus, his sister was young. Every time he saw her, he couldn't believe that she was married. God, before he knew it, she was going to tell him that she and Bobby were going to have a baby. And wasn't that going to be freakin' weird.

Bobby looked . . . like Bobby. Like a guy who was as big and as mean as a football linebacker, like a guy who could chew you to pieces if he got mad enough. With his long black hair tied in a braid down his back, and his Native American heritage showing in his cheekbones and coloring, people stopped and stared when he walked down the street.

Wes knew they were something of a visual joke when they were together. Bobby and

Wes, the inseparable team of chiefs from SEAL Team Ten. Wes and Bobby. Mutt and Jeff. Ren and Stimpy. Fleaman and Gigantor.

Wes's lack of height and girth was accentuated when he stood next to Bobby, but the truth was that there was nowhere he'd rather stand. And Bobby, God bless him, never made Wes feel lacking in any way, shape or form.

He may have looked like a bruiser, but Bobby Taylor was one of the nicest, kindest, gentlest guys Wes had ever met, a guy with a goofy smile and dark brown eyes that could see inside of Wes's head in a single glance.

Wes held out his hand for Bobby to shake, but Bobby pushed it aside and hugged him. He and Colleen were both crying. She'd never met Quinn, but that didn't matter.

He could tell just from looking that his sister was scared to death. This was her first taste of loss of life in the teams.

Well, welcome to the harsh reality of being married to a Navy SEAL during wartime, babe. She'd been so keen to marry Bobby. Now she had to face the risks and dangers, up close and personal.

"I can't believe he's gone," Bobby said.

"Have you been inside?" Colleen asked. "How's Lana?"

"I just got here myself," Wes admitted. "So

I don't know. I'm sure she's emotionally wrecked."

"Last time I talked to Quinn was, man, it must have been four months ago," Bobby said.

"I got an e-mail from him right after you guys got married. He wanted me to tell you that he wished he could've been there." Wes had to clear his throat. He swore.

Bobby hugged him again, and then Wes found himself looking into the eyes of the man who was his best friend in the whole flipping world — and wanting to tell him about Brittany. But it didn't quite line up with all this pain about Wizard.

His news was going to have to wait. Until he figured out exactly what kind of news it was.

"You okay?" Bobby asked him.

"Yeah," Wes said. "No," he added. "I'm like you — It's so fricking hard to believe. I mean, the senior chief called to tell me, and I kept asking was he sure, you know, that it was Quinn who was dead. How could he be dead?"

Bobby sighed as he shook his head. "I don't know. We should go inside though. You're probably in a rush to see Lana."

"Yeah," Wes said, although it wasn't true. He was dragging his feet, and wasn't that strange?

He followed Bobby and Colleen up the

path to where Lana's front door was wide open. They all just walked in.

The little house was crowded. Most of Team Ten was there, pulled straight out of bed upon receiving the news. Crash Hawken and Blue McCoy and even the CO, Joe Catalanotto were near the fireplace. Lucky, Frisco, and the senior chief, Harvard Becker stood by the window. Harlan "Cowboy" Jones — Britt's brother-in-law — was right by the front door, talking to Mitch Shaw.

They'd all worked with Wizard at one time or another.

"Excuse me, sir. Where's Lana?" Bobby asked Lt. Jones.

"She's taking a walk on the beach with Veronica Catalanotto," he told them, his eyes narrowing slightly at he looked at Wes.

Jesus, that kind of look meant . . . Did Jones know about Wes and Britt? Oh, man, look at him — he did. What had Britt told him the other night, at Dani's sister's apartment?

Knowing Britt, she'd told Jones the truth.

Oh, boy. Wes was so dead.

"There's coffee in the kitchen," Lt. Shaw told them.

Wes escaped, certain that Jones would somehow be able to tell from looking at him that Wes had quite possibly gotten Jones's sister-in-law pregnant just last night.

He poured himself a mug of coffee and

took a bracing sip. It was hot as hell and burned all the way down, but that was just as good. It distracted him sufficiently. This wasn't the time or place to be thinking about what he and Britt had done last night.

Oh, but holy God, he hadn't been able to stop thinking about it, all night long. He'd even dreamed about it, while he'd slept.

If she was pregnant, he'd marry her. He didn't have to think twice about it — but that wasn't what was on his mind.

No, what he couldn't stop thinking about was how badly he wanted to make love to her like that again. With nothing between them. If she were pregnant, then hell, he couldn't exactly get her pregnant again, now could he? So they could throw away their condoms and . . .

And spend the rest of their lives laughing and talking and making love the way they had this past incredible week.

Yeah, some time between last night and this morning, Wes had started praying to God that Brittany was pregnant.

And wasn't that the weirdest flipping thing?

No. Actually, it wasn't so weird. It made sense in an odd sort of way. If Britt was pregnant, Wes would have no choice.

Those things she'd said to him last night had struck home. Some truths had come out — including the fact that for all these years, Wes had felt as if he should have died instead of Ethan. It was crazy. It didn't make sense — he wasn't even in the car — but that didn't matter. He was the loser in the family, so he should have been the one who died.

He'd thought about it some last night — when he wasn't losing himself in Brittany's sweet love.

This was why he didn't go home to visit. Because he couldn't face his parents and his brothers and sisters. Because surely they looked at him and shook their heads, and wondered why God had taken Ethan and left screwup Wes on earth, instead.

So yeah. Brittany had been right about a lot of things. His loving Lana. Yes, it was true that people couldn't help falling in love. But they didn't have to spend over five years pining away, for God's sake.

Unless maybe they were punishing themselves.

Losers like Wes didn't deserve to live happily ever after. They didn't deserve a beautiful, warm, caring woman who loved them fiercely and passionately.

They could, however, get a woman pregnant and have that happy ever after forced upon them.

Jesus. He clearly needed some serious therapy.

Or a whole pack of cigarettes.

Or maybe he just needed Brittany.

The back door opened, and the CO's wife, Ronnie, came into the kitchen with Amber and . . .

Lana.

Wes's heart twisted when he saw her, but it was a different kind of twisting than it had been in the past.

She looked exhausted, with dark circles beneath haunted eyes, and a face that was pale and pinched with grief.

It was more than obvious that all three of the women had been crying.

Lana slipped past Wes without saying anything, with only the briefest touch of her hand on his arm. He watched her head down the hall to her bedroom, feeling helpless and useless.

He wasn't what Lana needed or wanted right now.

She wanted Quinn to come through the front door, laughing and telling them all that he wasn't dead, that it had been some kind of crazy mistake.

But Wes knew that wasn't true. The senior chief had told him that Lt. Jim Slade — the SEAL known as Spaceman — had been on that op, and had seen Quinn's body.

Ronnie followed Lana, sending Wes a look filled with sympathy and compassion, but Amber stayed behind, in the kitchen.

"They won't tell her anything about the mission he was on," she said to him, her voice tight. Amber was amazing. She even managed to look beautiful right after she'd cried.

Or maybe she was just plastic.

"Yeah," Wes said. "That's the way it works. The Navy can't give out details, and for a good reason. It puts other SEALs and other ops in jeopardy. But I think Lana probably knows in her heart what Matt and his team were doing out there. It wasn't just some pleasure cruise."

The SEALs had been making the world just a little bit safer, even if it was just by eliminating one terrorist at a time.

"That doesn't make it any easier for her," Amber said.

"No," he agreed. "It doesn't."

Amber sighed. "I know it was probably hard to tell, but . . . Lana's glad you're here, Wes. She's told me a lot about you, just over the past couple of days — we'd been talking a lot, on the phone, before this happened. It's crazy. I just had this conversation with her where I actually asked her if Quinn died, would she hook up with you."

Wes took a step back, not sure he wanted to hear what Lana's answer had been.

But Amber didn't seem to notice his reluctance to continue this conversation. She just kept on talking. "She said she didn't really know if that was something you wanted any-more — you know, a relationship with her. I pushed her, asking what she wanted, and she finally said maybe she would, and God help me, because I like you so much better than Quinn, I said, well, then I hope he dies."

Her face crumpled like a little girl's as she started to cry again, and Wes put his arms around her.

"Come on, Amber," he said. Like Lana, she was much shorter and slighter than Britt, and it felt odd — almost as if he were embracing a child rather than a woman, as if he had to be careful, to treat her as if she were fragile and might break if he held her too tightly. "You know saying that didn't make it happen."

"He was a complete scumball," she sobbed into his shoulder, "but Lana loved him. I didn't really want him to die."

"I know that," Wes said. "And I'm sure Lana does, too."

"I just thought she deserved better."

"She deserves someone who loves her enough to be faithful," Wes said. "Everyone does."

"I'm supposed to be asking everyone to leave." Amber looked up at him through her tears. "Lana said she was going to take one of the sleeping pills the doctor gave her, and . . . But maybe you should stay."

"I don't think —"

"Maybe you could make her feel better, make her start thinking about the future. Maybe —"

The future? "That's not such a good idea."

Amber pulled back slightly. "Why not?"

He sighed. "Well, for one thing, Lana doesn't need to think about the future today. She needs to grieve. And that's not about look- ing ahead. It's about reflecting and, well, being. En- during these next few days and weeks."

"She needs someone to hold her," Amber countered, wiping her face with her hands and stepping more fully out of his embrace. "She needs someone who loves her."

"That's why you're here," Wes said gently. "Right?"

Amber nodded. "But —"

"I'll stay if she asks me to," Wes said. "I'd do almost anything for her — I think she knows that. But she's not going to ask." She'd barely even looked at him when she walked past him. It was beyond obvious that she didn't need him. And funny, but that re- alization didn't upset him the way that it would have just a few weeks ago.

A few weeks ago, he would have followed Lana out of the kitchen — no, he would have gone out onto the beach, looking for her when he first arrived. He would have fought through a crowd to get to her side to comfort her — whether she'd wanted him to or not.

"She needs you and Ronnie to stay right now," Wes continued.

Amber wouldn't let him escape out the

back door. "Lana told me that she kissed you once."

Oh, man. "Yeah," Wes said. "And the key word there is once. It shouldn't have happened, and it didn't happen ever again."

"She said you were the most honorable man she's ever met."

"Yeah, I'm not so sure about that." Time to change the subject. "How's it going with the new security team?"

Amber shrugged. "Fine. My manager found a security company that specializes in guards who fade into the background. It's working well. The weird phone calls have completely stopped."

"That's good to hear."

"Yeah, maybe he's given up and is stalking Sarah Michelle Gellar instead."

Wes glanced over at the door leading to the living room, checking out an alternate escape route, only to find Lt. Jones leaning in the doorway, listening. How long had he been standing there? He turned back to Amber. "Maybe you better go let people know Lana would like us all to leave."

She nodded, giving Jones a somewhat blatant once-over before leaving the two of them alone.

Jones — tall and lean with a face like a movie star and sunbleached hair — didn't so much as glance at Amber twice. "Where's Brittany?" he asked.

"She's heading back to L.A.," Wes said. "She's renting a car — she didn't want to stick around. She said she didn't want to get in Lana's way."

Jones didn't look happy. "So you just . . . what? Put her on a bus to the car rental place?"

"No, sir. She said she was calling a cab. I tried to give her money, but, you know, she's a big girl, Lieutenant. I can't force her to do anything she doesn't want to do."

"She's in love with you," Jones told him.

Wes laughed — mostly because he was so surprised. It was either that or faint. "Whoa," he said. "Wait. She actually told you that?"

With Brittany, anything was possible.

"Not in so many words, no," Jones said and the accompanying disappointment that hit Wes at that news surprised him even more. God, maybe it shouldn't have, considering what he'd been thinking these past few hours. "I know her pretty well, Skelly. She's not the type of woman to have casual sex."

"She's not some kind of nun, either," Wes told him. "She's incredibly hot and —"

Jones closed his eyes and made a face. "Yeah, don't go into any details. That's already more than I want to know."

"She's great," Wes said simply.

"Yes," Jones said. "She is. So don't mess with her. I don't know what you've got going here with Lana —"

"Nothing," Wes said. And damn if it wasn't the truth in every single way. He still loved Lana — on some levels he would always love her, but it was a pale emotion compared to his crazy feelings for Brittany. Brittany — who was so much more to him than a distant and unattainable goddess. She was his friend, his lover, his partner.

His heart.

Wes took out his cell phone. "Excuse me, sir, but I have to call Brittany. There's something I forgot to ask her before she left."

Brittany parked the rental car in her driveway in Wes's spot.

Wes's spot. Listen to her. The man had only been around for about a week, and somehow this particular patch of the driveway had become his?

Yes, he'd parked there, but big deal. It was where Melody parked when she and Tyler came to visit, too.

God, she was exhausted. And yes, let's be honest. She was sad. Very, very sad.

She was in love with Wes Skelly.

Who, right now, was probably sitting with his arms around Lana Quinn, comforting her while she cried over her scumbag of a dead husband.

Britt dragged herself up the stairs to her door, unlocked it and stepped into the past. Inside her apartment it was still three days ago. Everything was carefully preserved as if it belonged in a museum devoted to late last Saturday night.

The dishes they'd used for dinner were still in the sink. The newspaper was open on the table, to the entertainment section. Yeah, like they were actually going to go out to see a movie. They'd considered it for all of four minutes before falling back into bed.

They'd left in a hurry, though, when Andy had called.

The garbage was ripe — man, it smelled awful in there. And the dishes in the sink didn't help.

She carried the garbage pail through the living room and set it down on the porch, outside the front door.

The dishes were handled quickly, too, but the room obviously needed a good airing out. Brittany pushed the air conditioning to a colder setting, and then there was no reason to procrastinate further.

She picked up the kitchen phone and dialed Wes's cell. She already knew the number by heart.

Please God, don't let him be there. Let her leave a message. It would be much easier that way. And God knows this was going to be hard enough.

She'd come up with a plan during the drive home from San Diego, and although it involved fighting for Wes, trying to make him see just how good they fit together, it had to start with her setting him free.

Completely. Like that stupid, sappy saying about the butterfly or the bird or whatever it was that she'd always rolled her eyes over in the past. Or . . .

If you love someone, set them free. . . .

She had to do this.

"You have reached the voice mail for . . ."

"Skelly," growled a recording of Wes's voice.

"Leave a message at the beep or press one for other options."

Britt took a deep breath as the phone beeped. "Wes. Hi. It's Brittany. I'm back in L.A. — I made it here, no problem. I just wanted to . . ." She had to clear her throat before she said it. "I wanted to tell you that I truly enjoyed the time we spent together these past few days. I wanted to thank you for that, with all my heart." She said the words in a rush. "But I really think it would be smart if we didn't see each other again. At least not, you know, romantically." God, now she was even starting to sound like him when she talked. "And not at all for at least a few months."

She cleared her throat again. "I'm going to pack up your things — your clothes and toothbrush and whatever else . . . I'll send them back to you. I'll overnight the package so you'll have it right away.

"I hope you aren't too upset with me, but I really do think it's best that we make a clean break, and that we do it now. I know your leave's not up yet, but I've got school and Andy and his scholarship to handle, and this thing with Dani to help with. I don't need any distractions right now, and let's face it, you're pretty distracting. And you . . . well, you've got a . . . well, a rather full plate right now, too."

Here came the really hard part. The flat-out lie. "I know you're probably freaking out about last night, thinking that I might have gotten pregnant, but you don't have to worry about that. Everything's fine. I got my period this morning.

"So," she said, trying her best to sound breezy and upbeat. "Okay. Thank you again. It was . . . fun."

Hang up the phone, fool, before you say something you regret.

"Good luck, Wes," she said. "Take care of yourself."

She cut the connection.

Don't cry, don't cry, don't cry.

Have a cup of tea instead.

Brittany emptied the kettle and filled it with fresh water, then turned on the stove. Her eyes were watering merely because it still smelled so bad in here.

She rummaged under the kitchen sink for the Lysol, and sprayed the room. Too bad she couldn't erase her feelings for Wes as easily.

But okay. She'd done it. She'd survived step one.

Step two was going to be hard, too. If he called, she'd have to refuse to talk at any length, to be polite but firm. No, she didn't think it would be smart to see him again. No, it was no problem, in fact, she already sent his stuff. Yes, she definitely wasn't pregnant.

Liar.

She hated liars. She'd worked long and hard to teach Andy that no matter what the situation, telling the truth was the only real option.

Although, at the time, she hadn't encountered the situation in which her lover might have knocked her up on the night before finding out that the husband of the woman he truly loved had been killed.

God.

With luck, she wouldn't be a liar for long. She should be getting her period in a matter of days. And if she didn't . . .

She didn't want to think about that. If it happened, she'd cope.

Step three in her plan was waiting. One month definitely. Probably more like two. Matt Quinn's body had to be recovered — if possible. There would be a funeral, or at least a memorial service. And then time had to pass. Weeks. Maybe months.

Enough time for Lana to begin to stop grieving.

Enough time for Wes to feel comfortable about courting Matt Quinn's widow — if that really was what he wanted to do.

Of course, this plan could backfire. Wes and Lana could very well leap into a relationship right away. And then Brittany would lose.

But if that happened, so be it. It would mean that Wes would never have been happy with Britt. It would mean that Brittany *would* have been his second choice. And, after a great deal of thought and reflection, she had come to the realization that being someone's second choice would never really be enough to make her truly happy.

But, in a few months, if she hadn't heard about Wes's pending engagement to Lana through reports from Melody and Jones, Brittany would plan a trip to San Diego. And while she was there, she'd make sure she bumped into Wes. Heck, she'd knock on his door if she had to.

And, at that point, after giving him plenty of time to think and recover from the shock of Quinn's death, Brittany would do her darndest to make Wes see that he belonged with her. She would fight for him. She would convince him that this thing that they'd found together — friendship, passion, compatibility, laughter, love — was worth keeping. She would convince him that she was not just his best choice, but his only choice.

But first she had to wait until the confusion and grief and emotion surrounding Matt Quinn's unfortunate death began to fade.

The phone rang, and she braced herself before she picked it up. It would be just like Wes to call immediately upon receiving her message.

"Hello?"

Silence. Then, click.

Annoyed, Brittany hung up. The phone company definitely had to troubleshoot their system. This was getting ridiculous.

Brittany took a mug and a tea bag from the cabinet, aware of how quiet it was in this apartment without Andy.

Without Wes.

The answering machine light was flashing — there were three messages — and she pushed the play button as she unwrapped the tea bag and waited for the water to finish boiling. God, it still really smelled bad in here.

The first message was from her sister, and it had come in on Sunday morning. It was uncharacteristically terse. "Britt, it's Mel. Call me the minute you get home."

Oh, perfect. So much for her brother-in-law's promise that Melody wouldn't call her until Wes's leave was up.

At least Mel hadn't called while she was at Wes's.

The second message had come in just an hour ago, while she was still on the road.

"Britt, it's Wes. We need to talk. Call me back, baby, as soon as you can, okay?"

Oh, shoot. He sounded so serious, as if he needed to break some bad news.

Like, "Gee, Britt, we had fun together, but now that Quinn's dead, I'm moving in with Lana."

She made herself breathe slowly and evenly, calmly, as she poured her cup of tea. If Wes and Lana were meant to be together, so be it. If it meant that Wes would finally be happy, she could live with it.

She could learn to live with it.

The third message had been recorded just minutes before she got home. Maybe her luck would change and it would be George Clooney. Maybe he'd gotten her number from Amber, and . . .

A stream of shocking obscenities came out of her innocent little answering machine.

Who the heck . . . ?

The voice was male, but it sure wasn't Andy or Wes or any other man she knew. The words were slurred together, but they ended with two that were quite clear. "Die, bitch."

Dear God, was it . . . ?

She pushed the repeat button and the words washed over her again. God, she'd need a shower after this. She listened hard, but the voice definitely wasn't Andy's sworn enemy, Dustin Melero, either.

And she couldn't think of anyone else in the entire world who would record any kind of a threat on her answering machine.

It was probably a wrong number.

Still it was creepy enough to make her want to call Wes.

Of course, anything that happened was going to make her want to call Wes. She was going to have to stay strong, be tough, and keep her hands off her telephone.

First thing she had to do was pack up his stuff and take it to the post office, so that when he called she could tell him that it was already taken care of. There was no reason for him to drive up to L.A. None at all.

She went down the hall. Her bedroom door was closed. And it must have been her imagination, but it sure seemed as if that funky spoiled garbage smell was getting worse.

She pushed open her bedroom door — and dropped her mug of tea.

Someone or something had been slaughtered in her bed. The stench was hideous and she gagged, but — even though it seemed impossible that whatever was in there could still be alive — her nurse's training kept her from backing away.

But no, a closer look revealed that there was no body anywhere in the room — no animal carcass even. Just blood, everywhere. Some of it dark and drying, some of it still quite garishly red. It was on the sheets, on the floor, on the walls. And entrails — the kind you might buy from a butcher shop for your pet alligator — were part of the gory mess.

It only *looked* as if someone had been murdered in her bed.

But, God, this meant that someone had been in her apartment. Someone who might still be here.

Someone who'd recorded a message on her answering machine that said, "Die, bitch."

Brittany bolted. Out of her bedroom, down the hall. She scooped up her purse and her car keys from the kitchen table and raced through the living room.

She threw open the door and —

There, standing on the other side of the screen, was the hulking shape of a man. He was smaller and wider than Andy, but bigger than Wes.

She tried to slam the door shut, but he was too quick. He opened the screen and got a foot inside the door, pushing it open with his shoulder. The force threw her back, down onto the floor.

Telephone.

She scrambled for the kitchen, screaming at

the top of her lungs. But her downstairs neighbors weren't home. They were never home during the day.

And what were the chances of anyone else hearing? All her windows were closed — the AC was on.

This guy could slice her into tiny pieces while she screamed her throat raw, and no one would hear a sound.

She grabbed the phone from the kitchen table, but he was right behind her and he hit her on the back of the head with something solid, something that made her ears ring.

She dropped the telephone as she hit the kitchen floor. It skittered across the linoleum, out of reach.

God, this couldn't be happening. But it was. Oh, Wes . . .

Die, bitch.

Not if she could help it. Wes wouldn't just lie back and wait for some psycho to snuff out his life. He'd fight like hell.

Britt tried to clear her head as she braced herself for the next attack, turning and scrambling to face her attacker. Her wrist was on fire, but she ignored it as the least of her worries.

She'd taken self-defense training as part of a program the hospital provided for nurses who worked the late shift, and she struggled to remember something — anything — that she'd learned in the course.

Use words to defuse a situation.

"Look, I don't know what you want or why you're here, but —"

"Shut up!"

She found herself staring up — oh, God — at the barrel of a gun.

But that wasn't the only bad surprise. The man holding the gun was the same man she'd seen just yesterday, in San Diego. At the ice-cream parlor. The angry man. The mentally ill man who'd clearly gone off his meds.

"You!" she said. My God, had he followed her here?

But no. That mess in her bedroom had been there for a while.

Unless he'd followed her to San Diego on Saturday night . . .

He put the gun down on the counter, then picked up the telephone from the floor and held it out to Brittany. "Call him."

His words didn't make any sense. Although once she got her hands on that phone, she was dialing 9-1-1. *Be agreeable and compliant. Go down to zero. Don't be aggressive. Wait for an opening. . . .*

"Call who?" She pushed herself up into a sitting position and reached for the phone.

But, oh, God, he pulled it back, out of her grasp, as if he knew what she was intending to do. "I'll dial. Tell me the number."

"Whose number?" She tried to keep her

voice even and calm, tried not to look at the gun on the counter even though internally she was trying to estimate how many seconds it would take her to reach it if she suddenly sprang to her feet. But her right wrist was definitely badly injured from her fall, possibly even broken. That put her at a serious disadvantage.

"Amber's boyfriend's," he told her.

What?

Amber. Holy God. This was about Amber Tierney. This guy was . . .

Amber's stalker. The meek little guy who — according to Amber — would never hurt anyone.

"I only met Amber twice," she said, her mind racing, trying to make sense of this. Why would Amber's stalker start stalking her? "I don't know Amber's boyfriend."

"You were just with him in San Diego. You were . . ." He used some incredibly foul language that wasn't quite technically accurate.

But what he was saying didn't matter, because she knew who he was talking about. He was talking about Wes. Dear God. He thought Wes was . . .

"Why do you want to talk to him?" she asked, trying not to sound hostile or aggressive, but rather simply curious.

"I'm not going to," he told her. "You are." He called her a name that left no doubt about it. He'd left that foul message on her answering machine.

"Why?" she persisted. "What do you want me to tell him? I don't understand."

"Tell him to come here. Now."

Fear made her hands and feet tingle and she couldn't keep herself from glancing at that gun on the counter.

"Why?" she asked again with far more bravado than she felt. No way was she calling Wes and telling him to come here just so this crazy son of a bitch could shoot him. "What do you want with him?"

"Just tell him to come. What's his number?"

"I don't remember," she lied.

He picked up the gun and pointed it at her. "What's his number?"

Chapter 16

Brittany didn't want to see him again.

Wes listened to the message she'd left on his voice mail for a third time, even though he'd understood every word she'd said quite clearly the first time around.

It was over.

Just like that.

She was done with him.

It was fun.

No way. No freaking way.

It just didn't sit right with everything he knew about this woman.

Of course, maybe he didn't know her that well.

Bullshit. Even though it had only been a handful of days, Wes knew Brittany Evans better than he knew any other woman on earth. He knew her inside and out.

She flipping loved him. He would bet his life's savings on that.

Well, okay, so his life savings weren't all that much, making that a statement that didn't hold all too much weight.

But he would bet his pride on it.

In fact, that's what he was doing right now by driving up to Los Angeles, by forcing her to say that final-sounding goodbye to him again, face-to-face this time.

It was going to be another half hour before he arrived, despite the fact that he was breaking the speed limit.

But she sounded just a little too cheerful, a little too okay with the idea of never seeing him again.

What if he was wrong? What if these past few days had been nothing more than a fling for her? Some laughs, some high intensity sex, some fun.

Brittany was still looking for Mr. Right, for her personal Prince Charming. Sure, she wasn't actively looking, but he knew that deep down, she still wanted the whole fairy tale package. A husband who loved her. A family. A baby.

And they lived happily ever after.

She'd told him that she wasn't pregnant. That was too bad, but so what? He could get her pregnant easily enough.

Wes smiled tightly. Sure, he would step up to that task with absolutely no arm twisting needed.

Except he was no Prince Charming. He wasn't even close.

He was a guy who was fun to have around for a few days, sure, but he wouldn't blame

Britt one bit if she didn't want him hanging out in her kitchen for an entire lifetime.

Crap, now he was good and scared.

And this flipping half hour before he got a chance to talk to her was lasting too freaking long.

He dialed her number on his cell phone.

It rang once. Twice.

Come on, Britt. Be home.

"Hello?"

Okay, dumbass. Say something brilliant. "Hey, Britt. It's me. Wes."

"I'm sorry," she said. "Andy's not home."

Huh?

"Yeah," he said. "I know. He's not going to be back until tomorrow —"

"Oh, hi, Mrs. Beatrice," she cut him off. "I didn't recognize your voice. Do you have a cold? No, he went to Nevada with the baseball team."

What? Andy's trip was to Phoenix, but that was besides the point since he was in San Diego right now with Dani. And who the hell was Mrs. Beatrice? "Brittany, what's —"

"I'll tell him you called," she said. Her voice sounded strained and odd. "And that his library book came in. What was that title? *From Flintlocks to Uzis: A History of Modern Warfare*? Yes, I'm writing it down."

"Brittany, Jesus, what is going on? Is there someone in your house with you?"

"Yes," she said.

Of course. He was an idiot. "Is there someone there with you?" Someone she couldn't speak openly in front of.

"Yes," she said.

From Flintlocks to . . . "Someone with a weapon?" he asked, dreading her answer.

"Yes."

Oh, Christ. Wes slammed his foot to the floor. This car could do 120 mph without hesitation and neither he nor the car were hesitating now.

"Oh, there's another book, too?" she said.

"How many? Who are they?"

"Just one. Okay. *Gemstones of North America.* Yes, I've got it. Thank you, Mrs. Beatrice."

Jesus, she was trying to tell him something with that second title, but what?

"Brittany, I don't get it. What are you telling me? Gemstones . . . ?"

"Yes, that's right. Andy was particularly interested in the stones which actually have prehistoric insects trapped inside of the rock. What is it called . . . ?"

"That's amber," he told her, then realized what he'd said. "Damn! This has to do with Amber Tierney?"

"Yes."

"Is she there, too?"

"No, he's been a rock collecting fan for a long time."

Fan. Amber's stalker. Jesus God.

"Has he hurt you?" he asked.

"Not really — Oh, I'm sorry, Mrs. Beatrice," she said. "I have to go. Someone's at the . . . at the door."

"I'm on my way, baby," Wes said. "I'm already about thirty minutes from you."

"No," she said, talking fast. "I'm . . . I'm glad to hear Andy's been using your reference desk at the library. I've often encouraged him to *get help*."

"I will," he said. "And I'll be there as soon as I can. God, baby, I love you. Be careful."

But she'd already cut the connection.

As he damn near flew down the freeway, Wes dialed 9-1-1.

Brittany's wrist was on fire, and it hurt even more as the phone was wrenched out of her hands.

Wes was on his way.

Damn it, she didn't want him to be on his way. She wanted him to call the police from San Diego, where he was safe and well out of range of the crazy man's deadly looking little handgun.

"You talked for too long." His eyes were flat, almost dead looking. How on earth could Amber have thought this guy was harmless with eyes like that?

"It was Mrs. Beatrice from the library," she told him. "She likes to talk to me — we're friends. If I'd just hung up on her, she would've thought it was weird, and might've even stopped by after work."

It was Tuesday afternoon and the tiny local library was closed. She prayed Crazy Man was just crazy enough not to be familiar with the schedule for the local public library — and to know that a Mrs. Beatrice didn't work there.

He pointed his nasty little gun at her again. "What's his phone number?"

He was talking about Wes again.

She had to stall for time, because — please God — Wes was on the phone right now with the L.A. emergency operator.

"I honestly don't know it by heart," she told him. "I have it written down. It's in my purse." She pointed to her bag, over on one of the kitchen chairs.

He was over there in two strides, dumping the contents out onto the table.

He hadn't walked like that in San Diego. Apparently, the shuffling gait was just an act. Part of his harmless weirdo impersonation, no doubt.

It was all starting to make sense. The repeated hang-up phone calls at both her apartment and Wes's — Amber had gotten similar calls.

The accusation at the ice-cream parlor. *You made her cry.*

He'd been talking about Amber.

"When did I make Amber cry?" she asked him now as he stepped back and gestured for her to approach the kitchen table.

Darnit, this wrist made it hard even to pull herself to her feet.

"She called her boyfriend, and he brought you with him," he informed her. "She went to stay at that hotel, but after she drove out of her garage, she pulled over to the side of the road and cried."

And Mr. Crazy here thought that had something to do with Wes and Brittany. He'd created some kind of twisted love triangle between the three of them.

"Didn't it occur to you that she might've been crying because she was scared?" she asked him. "Of you?"

Oh, so not the right thing to say. He was not a happy camper hearing that.

"I'm sorry," she said quickly. "Of course not."

"Find his number," he said.

"I'm looking," she told him, sifting through all the little bits of candy wrappers and other papers that she'd jammed into her purse over the past few months. "Give me a minute."

Or thirty . . .

Please God, don't let Wes come charging in here all by himself.

"I'm unarmed," Wes reported to Bobby, who was already on board the helicopter. "I've got dive gear — a knife — and a combat vest in the trunk. But as far as weapons go, I've got nothing on me except my hands and feet." Which, with the diving knife would be enough, provided he could get into the house and close enough to the guy. His hands and feet and that knife could do some serious damage.

Even though the son of a bitch had a gun.

"Mike Lee located a field a block and a half from the address you gave us for Brittany's house," Bobby reported. "We'll be there about five minutes behind your ETA."

The L.A. emergency operator had actually put Wes on hold. So he'd called Lt. Jones at the naval base. Luck was with him, because part of Alpha Squad was already in the air, heading out via helo to the firing range to get in a little practice with some nontraditional weaponry.

Jones had patched Wes through to Bobby in the helo, and put through an order directing them to head to the Los Angeles area — to practice a different type of maneuver.

Wes's call-waiting beeped and he glanced at his cell phone. "I've got a call coming in," he told Bobby. "It's Brittany. I'll get back to you ASAP."

He clicked over. "Hello?"

"Yes, hi, Wes? It's Brittany."

Crap, she still sounded like someone had a gun pointed at her head.

"You okay?" he asked. It was a stupid

question. Of course she wasn't okay.

"I'm fine," she said though, obviously trying to make the conversation sound normal from the stalker's perspective. "How are you?"

"I've just about gone completely crazy, worrying about you, baby," he said. "And I think I must be blessed, because I haven't been stopped by the highway patrol, and I'm going faster than I've ever gone on this road. I'm still about seven minutes from your exit. I've tried calling 9-1-1 a couple of times, but I'm not getting through. I turned on the radio, and apparently there's trouble, some kind of demonstration gone out of control, happening downtown. They've got the riot squads out and everything. But that's okay, I'll be at your place soon."

"No," she said hotly, but then broke off.

"Don't worry," he told her. "I'm not going to come charging in there like some kind of hotshot wild man. I've got backup. Bobby and some of the guys from Alpha Squad are meeting me just a few blocks from your apartment. This is one guy with one gun, right?"

"Yes," she said. "But Wesley —"

"No one's going to get hurt," he told her. "I promise."

"I miss you," she said in a very small voice.

Was that something she'd been told to say,

or the truth? Damn, hearing her say that made his chest feel tight.

"Will you come up to L.A.?" she asked because, obviously, that was what the stalker wanted her to ask. Wasn't *that* interesting? "Today? Please?"

"We're going to do surveillance before we come in," he told her. "You're not going to hear us, we're just going to be there in about fifteen minutes. As soon as you hear anything at all, any noise of our entry, drop to the ground, okay? Or better yet . . . I know — in fifteen minutes exactly, tell him you have to go to the bathroom. Get inside and lock the door and stay there. Get into the tub, babe. Lie down in it, okay? I know it sounds stupid as hell, but it'll give you some protection if he starts shooting."

"Do you think you can get here tonight?" she asked, for the gunman's benefit. "By six?"

"Good," he said. "Let him think it's going to be hours before I can get there. That's smart."

"Be careful driving," she said.

"You be careful, too."

"I'll see you at six, then."

"You'll see me soon, Britt. Remember, in fifteen minutes, go into the bathroom. And don't come out until I tell you to, okay?"

"Okay," she said. "Goodbye, Wes."

The connection was cut.

Jesus, that was a final sounding goodbye. What did she know that she wasn't able to tell him?

Wes drove even faster.

Fourteen minutes.

Wes was going to be here in fourteen minutes now.

But, God, from the look in Crazy Man's eyes, Brittany was going to be dead in about two.

"He'll be here at six o'clock," she told him as he put the telephone back into its cradle, and then started opening the kitchen drawers, looking for — of course — the knife drawer.

He found it and took out her turkey carving knife, setting it on the counter next to the sink.

"Whoa," she said. "That's a big knife. Careful you don't cut yourself, there."

"I've never had to cut off someone's head before," he told her, turning to look at her with those scary, crazy eyes.

"Had to?" she said. "I don't think that's something that anyone ever really *has* to do."

"But it's what happens next," he informed her.

My God, was he following some kind of sick script? This was like something out of a bad horror movie with the blood in her bedroom and . . . So okay, okay. Get him talking. Thirteen and a half minutes. She could do this.

"So . . . I come home and find all that blood on my sheets," she said. "What happens next?"

"Your lover comes home and finds you," he told her. "Dead."

"Oh, dear," she said faintly. But it wasn't anything she hadn't expected. "How, exactly, was I killed?"

This was, without a doubt, the weirdest conversation of her life.

But this man, this crazy-assed sicko, was some mother's son. Someone loved him, despite his mental illness. Somewhere inside of him was a human soul. Maybe if they talked long enough, she could connect with him.

"You've been shot in the neck," he reported, "and your head's in the kitchen sink."

Oh, dear God. "That's not very nice," she said.

"What you did wasn't very nice, either," he countered angrily. "Stealing Amber's boyfriend and breaking Amber's heart. She cried and cried."

"Was Amber in this movie?" she asked. This terrible scenario had to be out of a movie. She'd read — somewhere — that Amber had made several truly awful B pictures before hitting it big with her TV series. This had to be one of them.

"Til Death Do Us Part," he said. "It was great. Amber's boyfriend runs off with this other woman, and she cries and cries, because she doesn't know she's got a secret admirer, who punishes them — and everyone else who ever makes her cry."

"What happens to Amber's boyfriend?" Britt asked. She had to keep him talking. Eleven minutes now before Wes got here.

"He's shot," Crazy told her. "Right in the heart. And Amber marries her secret admirer and they live happily ever after."

Oh God. Was that really what he thought was going to happen? "There was no police investigation?" she asked. "He wasn't arrested for murder?"

He looked at her blankly. "Why would he be? No one knew that he knew them."

"What about his fingerprints," she said, "all over the apartment?"

He frowned. "That wasn't in the movie."

"That's what makes it a movie, and not real life. In real life, the police find fingerprints. You don't really want to do this, do you?"

He picked up his gun. "I don't have time to waste. I don't know how long this is going to take."

Ten minutes. "I have to go to the bathroom," Brittany said quickly. It was too early, but God, it was worth a try.

"You won't have to in a minute," he said,

and aimed his gun at her.

Wes called Bobby from the park near Britt's apartment.

"I'm here," he said, as he opened the trunk of his car and put on his vest. "Where are you guys?"

"We're right on schedule," Bobby said. "Five minutes from you."

"I can't wait," Wes said. "I'm going up to her apartment, take a look around."

The sound of a gunshot rang out, loud as hell in this quiet residential neighborhood, followed by another and another.

Wes swore, and ran for Brittany's.

Brittany slammed and locked the bathroom door behind her.

Thank you God for the quality construction of the 1890s, because the solid wood door didn't even quiver upon impact.

Thank you, too, for keeping Crazy away from the local firing ranges, where he might've actually learned to aim that gun, had he bothered to take a lesson or two.

Of course, a person's neck was a pretty small target. Shooting someone in the heart would be a whole heck of a lot easier to do.

Out in the hall, Crazy threw himself at the door again. "Open up!"

Yeah, right, just open the door and let him shoot her in the neck and . . . God!

The bathroom window was painted shut. It was too small for Brittany to squeeze out of even if it could be opened, but she didn't care. She had to break it, so she could warn Wes.

He was going to be here any minute, and Amber's psycho stalker was going to try to shoot him in the heart.

She was not — was not — going to let that happen.

Sobbing, she grabbed the lid off the toilet tank and swung it with all her strength at the window.

It hit with a dull sounding thud and bounced back, hitting her broken wrist.

Wes made himself slow down. If he just went charging in through the front door, the man with the gun would have a definite advantage.

He needed to take just a few moments and do this right.

He had to climb up to the second floor and look in through the windows.

Find out where the gunman was, find out where Britt was.

Please, God, let her still be alive.

Pain.

Brittany's world had tunneled down to pain. Pain and bitter disappointment.

Her wrist hurt so much she was retching,

but the disappointment managed to cut through.

Plexiglas.

Of course.

Andy had told her that their landlord had replaced the broken bathroom window with unbreakable Plexiglas.

She wouldn't be able to break it, and she couldn't get it open.

She had no way to warn Wes.

Wes climbed as swiftly as he could, wishing with all his heart that he was armed with something other than a diving knife.

He could hear the helicopter carrying the SEALs making its approach to the field. He heard the sound of distant sirens, too. Someone had heard the gunshots and had had better luck calling 9-1-1 than he'd had.

The blinds were mostly shut in Britt's room. That was good. They would do a good job concealing him from view while making it possible for him to look into the room between the slats and —

Jesus!

He nearly lost his handholds on the side of the house, and he had to force himself to look again.

It was a bloodbath in there. He was too late. Brittany was dead. She had to be.

No one could bleed that much and still be alive.

Even as part of Wes died, the rest of him clicked into combat mode. Brittany's murderer was there, in the room, by the bathroom door.

The bastard was going to die.

Wes drew his knife and, grabbing hold of the edge of the roof above him, he swung himself up and out and went through the window, feetfirst.

Broken wrist or not, Brittany was ready.

She heard the crash of broken glass, and yanked the bathroom door open.

Just as she'd expected, Crazy's back was to her, and she slammed the toilet tank lid hard onto him. It only grazed his head, but it hit his shoulder, knocking him forward and down.

It wasn't enough to keep him from firing two shots.

They were deafeningly loud, two sharp explosions propelling two deadly bullets that hit Wes square in the chest, driving him back, pushing him onto the ground.

But like some kind of superhuman machine, he was back on his feet in less than a heartbeat, coming at Crazy with a savage look in his eyes.

Brittany.

She was standing there, alive and whole, next to the gunman, without any gaping wounds.

Wes's chest had to hurt like hell, but he didn't care about that. He felt nothing but euphoria.

He knew what Lazarus's mother had experienced on the day her son returned from the dead.

"Get down!" he tried to shout as he kicked the handgun from the son of a bitch's hand, but it only came out a whisper.

Of course, Britt didn't move to safety. She raised what looked to be the lid of a toilet tank over her head, and knocked the gunman unconscious with one beautiful shot.

Wes dropped to his knees, and fell forward onto his hands.

"Get the gun," he tried to tell Britt, but again she didn't listen.

She helped him lie back. God, it was hard to breathe. And the pain . . .

Now he felt it.

It was okay that she didn't go after the gun, because Bobby and the other guys were there, making sure the gunman wasn't going to hurt anyone else today.

"Man, what a stench," Rio Rosetti said.

"Don't die," Britt ordered him as she tried to unfasten his vest. "Don't you dare die!"

He wasn't going to die. He tried to tell her that, but he couldn't suck enough air into his lungs to make any kind of recognizable sound.

Bobby leaned over him, putting his fingers

into the two holes the bullets had made in his vest. "Ouch," he said. "That's gotta hurt."

"God, Skelly," Lucky O'Donlon complained. "Why ask for support only to go through the window before we even get here?"

"Yeah, but look at what he saw," Bobby pointed out. "If this had been Colleen's apartment, and I was out there, looking in at that bed, I'd've gone through the window, too."

"Isn't somebody going to call an ambulance?" Brittany demanded.

She couldn't believe it.

Everyone was standing around, chatting, while Wes was bleeding to death.

With one hand that wasn't working right, Brittany couldn't get his vest unfastened, she couldn't even tell how badly he was wounded underneath the cumbersome thing.

"He's wearing a vest," Rio, one of the newest members of the team, informed her.

"I can see he's wearing a vest," Brittany said. "Can someone help me get it off of him?"

"Bulletproof vest," Bobby explained, and her heart started beating again.

"Oh, thank God."

"But look where he got hit." Bobby pointed to the two holes. "Possible broken rib, probable broken collarbone. Man, that's got to hurt."

"I'm okay," Wes whispered. He reached up to touch Britt's cheek. "In fact, I can't remember the last time I felt better."

"Police are here," Rio announced.

And indeed they were. Paramedics had arrived, too, and they swarmed around Wes, taking his blood pressure and listening to his lungs.

A broken rib could puncture a lung, but his were okay. He'd just had the wind knocked out of him in a very major way.

A temporary splint was put on Britt's wrist, and the Crazy Guy was treated, too. He was carried out on a stretcher as Brittany gave a statement to the police detectives.

It was over — but now her apartment was a crime scene. A messy, foul-smelling crime scene.

Brittany was allowed back inside to pack a bag so she could stay at a hotel until the police photographers had finished taking pictures of her bedroom. Until she got that mess cleaned up.

She gathered up all of Wes's things, too, stuffing them into his duffel and awkwardly carrying it outside, both bags in her good hand.

Wes sat on the steps leading up to Brittany's apartment, with both his side and shoulder on fire. The paramedics had tried to take him to the hospital for X rays, but there was no screaming rush. His collarbone was definitely broken — he knew because he'd broken it before — and there was really nothing they could do for him. It wasn't the kind of break that got put into a cast.

It just hurt like hell for a few weeks. And then it hurt like heck for a few weeks more.

He needed to get the X ray, but he wasn't going to the hospital without Brittany.

She came down the stairs and . . .

"What happened to your wrist?" he asked.

"He hit me and I fell on it the wrong way."

Goddamn it. "I should have killed him when I had the chance. I heard most of your statement to the police. Brittany, God, this is all my fault. If I hadn't come to L.A. —"

She wasn't going to let him take the blame. "Then maybe he would've gone after Amber. Or others of her friends who wouldn't have been able to keep him from hurting them."

"He hurt you badly enough." Just the thought of him hitting her was enough to make Wes feel faint. He didn't want to think about all that Amber's stalker — his name, apparently, was John Cagle — had had in mind for Brittany.

She looked down at the splint on her wrist. "Believe me, it could have been worse."

"I know. Britt, I really am sorry."

"I'm sorry, too." She set something down next to him, and he realized that it was his bag. She'd packed his stuff, just as she'd told him she would in that message she'd left on his voice mail.

What if she had been serious? Jesus, was this really it?

"I'm sorry I had to drag you away from one crisis to a completely different crisis," she said. "How's Lana doing?"

"I don't know," he said. "I didn't stay at her place too long. Ronnie Catalanotto and Amber were going to stay with her while she tried to get some sleep."

"Oh," Brittany said.

What the hell did that oh mean?

"Britt, do you like me?" he asked.

She didn't hesitate. "Of course."

He laughed because her response was so typical Brittany, so definite with a hint of challenge to it. Of course she liked him. Why wouldn't she like him? But laughing made his side and shoulder hurt like hell, so he swore. "Sorry."

"That must really hurt," she said, now all sympathy and warm concern.

And Wes couldn't take it a second longer. "Will you marry me?" he asked.

Well, okay, he'd surprised the hell out of her.

"Please?" he added. Although it was a little late to try to win points for being polite.

She sat down on the steps, next to him. "Are you serious?"

"Yes, I am. Very."

"You did get my message, right?" she asked, looking at him searchingly. "About me not being pregnant?"

"I know," he said. "I don't want to marry you because I think you're pregnant. Although that would be okay with me, too, you know. It's not about that, though. I want to marry you because, well . . ." Just say it. "Because I'm in love with you."

She made a sound that was half-exhale, half-laughter. Was that a good sign or a bad sign? He didn't know. All he could do was try to explain the way he felt when he was with her.

"You were right about me," he told her. "Ever since Ethan died, I've been, I don't know, punishing myself, I guess, just for being alive. I could never let myself enjoy anything too much, I couldn't let myself get too happy. And you were right — I found one hell of a way to make myself properly miserable by falling in love with someone that I couldn't ever have."

The stupid thing was, he didn't realize he was doing that until he met Brittany. Brittany, who liked him.

"And you know, as time went on, I think I probably stopped loving Lana and started loving the idea of Lana. You know, the fact that she was unattainable made her even more attractive, since my goal, you know, was

318

to be miserable. There was one time — I was really drunk, and I think she probably was, too — I kissed her. It scared the crap out of me. I think I was more in love with not being able to have Lana, than I was with Lana.

"And as for Lana, well, what she really wanted was for Quinn to have my kind of, I don't know, devotion, I guess. She didn't ever want me."

He looked at Brittany. "But you do. You want me." He laughed, and it hurt and he swore. "I don't get it, but you seem to like me — you know, even the dark, scary parts of me that I'm afraid to let most people see. There's no part of me that I'm afraid to show you, Britt. There's no part of me that's too intense, too extreme for you. You're just . . . you're okay with it. You're okay with me.

"When I'm with you, baby, even just sitting here like this, there's absolutely no doubt about it — I'm very glad to be alive. And when I'm with you, you know, I'm not so angry at the world, and I'm not so angry at myself anymore, either. When I'm with you, I actually kind of like myself, too. And if that's not freaking amazing . . ."

Brittany, sweet Brittany, had tears in her eyes.

"I want to be that guy," he told her, "the one that I like, the one I see reflected in your eyes — for the rest of my life. So marry me, all right? Put me out of my misery and tell me you love me, too."

"I love you, too," she said. "Oh, Wes, I'd love to marry you."

And it was everything he'd hoped for, this knowing she'd be at his side until the end of time.

But God, the best part of her answer was the warmth of Brittany's smile, the love in Brittany's eyes.

If he'd been the kind of guy who cried, he would have been sobbing right now. As it was, his eyes were feeling dangerously moist.

Wes kissed her.

"You know," Brittany said after she'd kissed him again — carefully so as not to jar his shoulder. "My sister and Jones are never going to let us forget they were the ones who set us up on a blind date."

"That's okay, baby," Wes said, kissing her again. "Because I'm never going to stop thanking them."

Epiloque

"What would you say if I told you I was thinking about taking a year off from school?" Brittany asked.

Wes looked up from his computer, spinning in his chair to face her.

She was standing in the bedroom doorway, leaning against the jamb.

He measured his words before answering her. "I guess I'd ask you why you're thinking about doing that. And I'd tell you I hope it's not on my account."

"It's not," she said.

"Honest?" he asked. It hadn't been easy — living and working in two different cities, but it wasn't awful. "If I've complained too much lately just tell me to zip it, babe. It's not going to be forever, and besides, we have Andy to think about."

Andy needed Britt around more than ever now. Dani was back in school, but Dustin Melero's trial date was approaching. There were no guarantees, rape trials always came down to "he said, she said," but four other girls had come forward, with stories identical to Dani's. Together, they were working to lock that bastard up.

Yeah, maybe Dustin could share a jail cell with John Cagle, Amber's crazy-assed stalker.

Amber had beefed up her security, and Wes and Britt had put an alarm system in both of their apartments, too.

Not that they were worried about him getting out of jail any time in the near future. But the security system made Wes breathe a little easier when he and Britt were apart.

"That was Andy on the phone just now," Britt told him.

"How'd the team do?" They were in Sacramento this weekend.

Andy hadn't lost his scholarship, and with the new baseball season starting, there was already talk that he was going to be the college team's MVP. The scouts were swarming. It was just a matter of time before the kid went pro.

"He called to say he's made up his mind. He's signing with the Dodgers, can you believe it? He'll start playing on their Triple A team in May."

Wes searched her face. "You okay with that?"

"Very much so." Brittany smiled. "Of course, I made him promise that someday he'd go back and finish getting his degree. Even if he plays baseball until he's forty-five.

to school."

Wes reached for her, and she came and sat on his lap. "Wow. So what are you thinking? With Andy playing pro, out on the road, traveling all the time, you're going to come live with me in San Diego?" He tried not to sound too hopeful and failed.

"Yeah," she said. "You got a problem with that?"

"Not even close." He kissed her, but then stopped her from kissing him again. "I do have a problem with this leaving nursing school thing. Becoming a nurse practitioner has been your dream for a long time. I don't like the idea of you giving it up just to be with me more days a week. I'm out of town a lot, too, Britt."

"I know. I thought I could look into transferring to a school in San Diego," she told him. "But not for a few years." She smiled at him. It was the kind of smile he'd learned to watch out for. The kind that said, *Duck and cover! Incoming!* "Not until after the baby turns two or three."

Wes heard the words, but they didn't make sense. And then they made a crapload of sense. He laughed his shock and surprise. "Are you telling me . . . ?"

"Remember about two weeks ago when we weren't really careful?" she asked.

He laughed again. "Uh, yeah, but I seem

to remember a lot of times since we've been married, Mrs. Skelly, that we haven't been particularly careful." And he'd loved every minute of it. But a baby. Jesus.

"Well, I just did a test, and . . . It's definite." She laughed. "Sweetie, you look scared to death."

"I am scared to death. I'm thrilled, of course, you know I am but . . . I'm also scared to death. A baby. Holy Mother of God."

Brittany was glowing. He'd heard that word used to describe pregnant women, but he'd never believed anyone could actually glow. But Brittany sure as hell was doing it.

And he knew why putting her career aspirations on hold wasn't such a big deal for her.

Because even though getting this degree had been a dream of hers for a long time, she'd had another dream, too.

To have a baby.

And even though it had happened accidentally, Wes had helped make that particular dream come true.

"I love you," he told her. "More than you'll ever know."

Her eyes shone with unshed tears. "Oh, but I do know," she whispered. She kissed him.

Good thing he wasn't the crying kind, because if he were, he'd be in a puddle on the floor.

About the Author

Suzanne Brockmann lives just west of Boston in a house always filled with her friends — actors and musicians and storytellers and artists and teachers. When not writing award-winning romances about U.S. Navy SEALs, among others, she sings in an a capella group called *Serious Fun*, manages the professional acting careers of her two children, volunteers at the Appalachian Benefit Coffeehouse and always answers letters from readers. Send her a SASE along with your letter to P.O. Box 5092, Wayland, MA 01778.